Erasto Khalfani, a twenty-nine-year-old Somali ex-fisherman, was now plying the more lucrative trade of piracy. As his small craft approached the freighter, Erasto surveyed the deck with his binoculars. There was the usual skeleton crew wandering about the deck, paying little attention to the waters below. He paused when he came upon some vehicles sitting on the deck: a powerful-looking black pickup truck and what looked like some kind of ambulance. Odd for them to be in the open air rather than in the hold, but that was irrelevant.

The boarding was accomplished seamlessly. Eighteen men, armed with assault rifles and small arms, scrambled up the side of the hulking vessel and were quickly on board. In general, this was when panic ensued. Instead the crew were completely relaxed as they quietly raised their hands and placed them on the backs of their heads. The looks on their faces betrayed neither fear nor anger, but almost a bemused aspect that one might have after hearing something only mildly amusing. Still, they were coopera-tive, and Erasto watched as his men went through what now was an almost routine process, asking the captives for their belongings, and if necessary patting them down to find the "forgotten" valu-ables.

"Where are the keys to these vehicles?" asked Erasto.

"You don't want to mess with those," said the black man. "Pretty on the outside, junk under the hood. That thing is danger-ous. You get my meaning?"

"I think I will be the judge of that, thank you," replied Erasto. He reached for the door of the pickup and began to open it. The door was wrenched from his hand and slammed shut again. Erasto took a step back, his weapon now up and ready to fire. "Whoever is in there, come out immediately or I will fire!"

"With pleasure," responded a voice from within.

The truck began to move. Not forward or reverse like a truck should, but rather every aspect of it was in motion. Parts folded and flipped in upon themselves, creating a completely new image in front of his eyes. Within seconds a towering figure loomed over Erasto. It rose up on two legs, one arm pointing directly at him, no more than a foot from his face. Erasto had stared into the barrel of various weapons during his li[...] rently looking directly into the m[...] ever seen. His AK-47 dropped h[...] in sheer terror at the being in fro[...]

And then it spoke.

TRANSFORMERS™
THE VEILED THREAT

ALAN DEAN FOSTER

BALLANTINE BOOKS • NEW YORK

A Del Rey Mass Market Original

Published in the United States by Del Rey, an imprint of The Random House Publishing Group, a division of Random House, Inc., New York.

ISBN 978-0-345-51592-6

Printed in the United States of America

www.delreybooks.com
www.hasbro.com

9 8 7 6 5 4 3 2 1

For Don Szekely,
From all creatures great and small and Prescott
With thanks and appreciation

(and for Kyle and Rachel, too)

PROLOGUE

The most inhospitable place on Earth is not the middle of the Sahara, with its searing heat and parched landscape. Nor is it the top of Everest, with its lack of oxygen and freezing, howling winds. That title is reserved for the Abyssopelagic Zone of the world's oceans, eighteen thousand feet below the surface of the sea. Here, in the impenetrable dark, frigid waters, the pressure exceeds five tons per square inch. The sun has never brought its cheerful glow to these valleys, and what few creatures live here look like monsters from a child's nightmare.

One of these deep-sea horrors crept along the floor of the Laurentian Abyss, an albino sea spider with legs nearly a foot long. It was on the hunt, using senses barely comprehensible to science to find its prey. Even if it had eyes, it would not have been able to see anything in the perfect dark. But its other senses were suddenly on alert, the fight-or-flee instinct growing rapidly within it. Something was ahead in the dark, something not of this Earth. Flee won the day, and the sea spider backed away, content to resume its hunt in a safer area of its midnight world.

Had it continued, it would have come to a zone from which most life had deliberately fled. Less than a hundred yards ahead, a hulking mass lay on the ocean floor. This colossus had fallen from the surface above, dumped by the surface dwellers who wanted no part of it. Dropped in the hopes that with its sinking, a great fear and danger would be eradicated from the universe. Nonetheless, an invisible web of submarines and underwater surveillance devices kept constant vigil. The colossus, after all, had allies.

Four miles above his resting place, the waves of the North Atlantic rolled peacefully over the ruin of Megatron.

1

The *Pearl of India* freighter, over a thousand feet long and displacing thirteen thousand tons, had an official top speed of twelve knots. But with a following sea and clear weather, she was currently making better than twelve and a half through the Gulf of Aden. Even so, she would be no match for Erasto Khalfani's small fleet of twenty-two-foot powerboats. Each carried a crew of nine and could make twenty-five knots with ease. Erasto lowered his binoculars and gave the order; he found that early-morning attacks were always the most successful.

Erasto Khalfani, a twenty-nine-year-old Somali ex-fisherman, was now plying the more lucrative trade of piracy. It was riskier than fishing, to be sure, but then the rewards were greater than he could realize in a lifetime of hauling nets. He had made himself and his men wealthy, and they trusted his leadership.

Hijacking a freighter under full steam on the open sea was no mean feat. The main deck of the *Pearl of India* rose thirty-five feet off the surface of the water. To board from a small craft like theirs, the pirates would literally have to scale the side of the moving vessel with grappling hooks and sheer skill. Not a task for the faint of heart. And yet this very band had been successful several times in commandeering vessels of similar size, and under even worse conditions. No, the *Pearl of India* was ripe for the picking; the prize was his.

As his small craft approached the freighter, Erasto surveyed the deck with his binoculars. There was the usual skeleton crew wandering about the deck, paying little attention to the waters below. Erasto knew that the continuous throb of the ship's great engines would mask his outboard motors until they were quite close. By then it would be too late for the freighter to take any countermeasures.

In his heart Erasto was a peaceful man. Unlike the pirates of the Straits of Malacca, he had no interest in violence. He found that the show of force was generally more than sufficient to cow the crew of most commercial vessels. Certainly from time to time one found a would-be hero who had to be dealt with, but even then a well-placed blow from the butt of his AK-47 was more than sufficient to remind the gallant man that he was not made of steel.

Erasto took one last sweep of the deck with the glasses; they'd be throwing the boarding lines within the next few minutes. He paused when he came upon some vehicles sitting on the deck: a powerful-looking black pickup truck and what looked like some kind of ambulance. Odd for them to be in the open air rather than in the hold, but that was irrelevant. The ambulance would no doubt provide valuable medical supplies for his village, and the truck, well, that was the perfect ride for the leader of a pirate band. Erasto would ensure that both vehicles were part of his take when they negotiated with the owners for the release of the *Pearl* and her crew.

The boarding was accomplished seamlessly. Erasto, as usual, was proud of his men. Three remained on board each of the small craft, to pilot around the freighter and, if necessary, provide backup fire. Eighteen men, armed with assault rifles and small arms, scrambled up the side of the hulking vessel and were quickly on board.

In general, this was when panic ensued. The crew, realizing they'd been boarded, ran to fight, or hide, or beg for mercy. The first ten minutes were the most dangerous to pirate and crew alike. If a "hero" was going to emerge and start trouble, this was the time. But this crew did not behave this way, and years later Erasto would look back and realize that this was his first warning.

Instead the crew were completely relaxed as they quietly raised their hands and placed them on the backs of their heads. The looks on their faces betrayed neither fear nor anger, but almost a bemused aspect that one might have after hearing something only mildly amusing. Still, they were cooperative, and Erasto ordered his men to begin the process of evaluating the total take. This started with stripping the crew of their personal valuables, and moved on from there to the cargo.

"Gentlemen," began Erasto, "there is an easy way and a hard way to do this. My men and I prefer the easy way. Think of us as simple entrepreneurs, and you will be our guests for the next several days. The wealthy owners of this vessel will parlay for your lives, and you will go home none the worse for wear.

Resist, and things may not go so smoothly for you. My men will now come among you and relieve you of your wallets and other personal effects. Your cooperation is most appreciated."

Erasto watched as his men went through what now was an almost routine process, asking the captives for their belongings, and if necessary patting them down to find the "forgotten" valuables.

He himself walked over to the black pickup. It was impossible not to admire the design. It was, very simply, one badass truck. Two of the captives stood together near the vehicles on deck; the pirates' arrival had clearly disrupted their card game. Both looked like they could take care of themselves, and Erasto decided to take no chances. Placing his AK at chest level, he addressed the man of color first.

"Your valuables, sir, please surrender them."

"Back pocket." The man was incredibly relaxed given that an assault rifle was pointed a few inches from his heart.

"Which pocket?" Erasto continued.

"Left cheek." The man sighed.

At this point the other man, Western European, or maybe even American, entered the conversation. "You and your 'left cheek.' Man, when are you going to learn that sitting on that thing is going to give you back problems later in life?"

"Given our jobs, I try not to think too much about 'later in life.' Besides, we don't get much chance to sit down anyway."

"I hear that. Still, I don't know why you carry that thing around anyway. Not much use for a wallet in the places we end up."

Erasto was not pleased with this at all. He understood fear: he used it to keep things peaceful. This casual banter was entirely out of place in the situation. Given the accents, he now knew both of these men were Americans. What were they doing here?

He addressed the white guy. "You do not carry a wallet? This is unfortunate. However, that ring on your left hand is no doubt of some value. You will give it to me."

"This ring does not, I repeat, *does not* come off."

"If need be, your finger certainly *will* come off. Must we go that route? So messy. Let us come back to it. Where are the keys to these vehicles?"

"You don't want to mess with those," said the black man. "Pretty on the outside, junk under the hood. That thing is dangerous. You get my meaning?"

"I think I will be the judge of that, thank you," replied Erasto. He was impatient with this conversation now. He was certain he would have to pummel one of these two before it was over. He reached for the door of the pickup and began to open it. The door was wrenched from his hand and slammed shut again. Erasto took a step back, his weapon now up and ready to fire. "Whoever is in there, come out immediately or I will fire!"

"With pleasure," responded a voice from within.

"Damn, man, I warned you. You're in for it now, Captain Hook." The two men had backed away from both Erasto and the truck.

Erasto Khalfani had seen much in his twenty-nine years, and he felt he was prepared for virtually all of life's surprises. But his world of experiences could not have prepared him for what was occurring before his eyes at this moment.

The truck began to move. Not forward or reverse like a truck should, but rather every aspect of it was in motion. Parts folded and flipped in upon themselves, creating a completely new image in front of his eyes. Within seconds a towering figure loomed over Erasto. It rose up on two legs, one arm pointing directly at him, no more than a foot from his face. Erasto had stared into the barrel of various weapons during his life, and he knew that he was currently looking directly into the maw of the largest cannon he had ever seen. His AK-47 dropped harmlessly to his feet as he gawked in sheer terror at the being in front of him.

And then it spoke.

"I believe it is time for you to, how do you say? 'Walk the plank.' "

Erasto took two steps backward, stumbled, turned, and ran. His men had followed a similar course when they saw the beast rise from the decks, and several had preceded him into the water below. Erasto knew it would hurt a bit from that height, but anything to get away from this nightmare. He jumped, and was quickly picked up by his crew. In moments they were speeding away: fleeing for their lives.

Epps turned from the view and looked up at Ironhide, a broad smile on his face. " 'Walk the plank'? Where'd you pick that one up from?"

"I have been perusing your military literature at some length, looking for insights into your history of combat. It is a phrase that seemed appropriate to the moment."

"Appropriate to the moment. Right. You loved every minute of it."

"I must admit," replied Ironhide, "the look on his face was indeed a great pleasure to me."

"What do you think, Captain? Think those guys will be pirating again anytime soon?" asked Epps.

"I have a feeling they may be in for a change of career," laughed Lennox. "We've got enough NEST personnel on board to have mopped the decks with those jokers, but what would have been the fun in that?"

"Let's get back to our game," said Epps. "Still thirty hours until we reach Diego Garcia. Ironhide, Ratchet, you guys want in?"

Captain Lennox was in fact correct: Erasto Khalfani never plied the waves in search of booty again. Eventually, when the shock had worn off, he went back to fishing. He already had enough money to live comfortably, and if things got tight he figured he could always write a book. Had to be easier than piracy. To the end of his days, though, his friends noticed his strange habit of crossing the street every time he saw a pickup truck.

2

Kaminari Ishihara loved the sea. Although the lagoon itself could be murky in places, the waters surrounding the Indian Ocean islands of Diego Garcia where NEST had its headquarters were virtually transparent: even clearer than those cold Pacific swirls that lapped the shore near her hometown north of Tokyo. They were also much warmer. Back home she would never have gone into the ocean wearing only the bikini that presently covered only a small portion of her curvaceous yet well-toned form.

"A healthy mind in a healthy body," her grandmother had always told her, "so you can tell those grabby guys on the train what you think of them even as you kick their butts."

But here in the relative privacy of the atoll, she did not have to worry much about prying eyes. And her dossier, she knew, afforded her a level of respect among the base personnel that transcended the normal interaction between men and women. Over years of study, both scholarly and martial, she had turned her mind and body not only into a machine but into a weapon as well. She walked with the confidence of a person who knows where she belongs, and she belonged right here, right now.

An expert in robotics specializing in cybernetic motivation, Kami was well aware of the role for which she had been chosen. People in high places whose task it was to evaluate such things had read and admired her precocious doctoral dissertation, "Subatomic Transitions in Cybernetic Mnemonics," and had quietly recruited her. It was the chance to work directly with the famous but still mysterious mechanical alien lifeforms that had brought her from northeast coastal Honshu to the tropics. She knew that working within the secretive NEST would give her ample opportunity to utilize her specialized knowledge. She had also been warned there could be occasions when she might be asked to fight.

Her own experimental weapon lay back in her room. There was no need to have it close by as she swam in the warm, shallow water. Only small, harmless sharks like whitetips ventured into the lagoon. In any case, Longarm could all by himself have made sushi out of anything up to and including a great white.

The Autobot relished the chance to spend time in his normal, natural shape outside the subterranean confines of NEST. Though everyone at the secret operations center was familiar with and quite comfortable when working in the presence of primary Autobot configurations, it had been decided that for security reasons it was better if they spent the majority of their time while outdoors in the individual guises they had chosen to enable them to blend in among less knowing humans. It was also, a serious Optimus Prime had pointed out to his cohorts, good practice. Known among his companions as an especially hard worker,

Longarm had chosen to move about in the guise of a tow truck.

Now he stood in the shallow water in his bipedal form and watched with interest as the human female paddled lazy circles around his pillar-like legs. She moved through the water by utilizing an outwardly inefficient un-Autobot-like scissoring of her hind limbs. As he attempted to calculate the energy efficacy of the odd motion, she paused in her swimming and went vertical in the water, pushing her face mask up onto her forehead. These organics, he knew, required a continuous intake of the local atmospheric gas in order to internally fuel their bodies. A most peculiar system. Reaching down, he gently placed a gleaming wet hand beneath her and lifted her out of the water. Droplets flung from her long black hair caught the tropical sunlight as she shook her head.

"I much prefer your appearance with the artificial lens in place over the forepart of your upper skull," he intoned solemnly. "It gives your face a more mechanical façade."

Kami grinned. "Your tastes differ from those of the males of my species."

"Forgive my ignorance. I am still comparatively new to this world and have much to learn about your kind. In his spare time, Ratchet has been mentoring me."

She looked up at the long, low sound of a ship's horn. Longarm put her down, and she walked through the shallows to the beach. The sun glinting off her dripping body would have given any man, and even most women, pause, but Kaminari's thoughts were rarely self-reflexive. The ship had arrived without incident, unless one counted the amusing diversion in the Gulf of Aden, and these days that meant a lot. For once, she wanted to greet this ship at the docks. Wrapping herself in a towel, Kaminari walked toward the barracks. She'd be showered, changed, and on the docks in fifteen minutes.

Gazing at the long, slender island that occupied the side of Diego Garcia's lagoon southeast of the heavy bomber airstrip, a visitor would be hard-pressed to believe that it concealed anything more powerful than the kick of the semi-wild donkeys that roamed its emerald-green interior. Save for an unusual profusion of satellite antennas artfully scattered among the palms and casuarinas there was nothing to indicate that buried deep in the limestone and bedrock, the hastily constructed center that had been established to coordinate Autobot and human responses to Decepticon incursions pushed out in all directions. NEST was continuing to expand, its reinforced tunnels honeycombing not only the island itself but also the solid rock that underlay the atoll.

The *Pearl of India* came to rest beside the massive pylons that supported the pier. This was the only location on the atoll that allowed large ships to berth, and it was used infrequently. Given the circumstances, much of the strength of NEST lay in its secrecy, and the atoll did little to give away its true purpose.

Lennox and Epps, along with a third man, walked down the gangplank of the *Pearl of India* onto the one main loading dock on Diego Garcia. Ironhide and Ratchet disembarked from the side loading bay farther aft. Waiting for them on the wharf was Kaminari Ishihari.

"Dr. Ishihari." The greeting came from Lennox. "I heard you had arrived. Good to have you on board." Epps just stared, trying to keep his mouth closed and his eyes front. Front and elevated, that is.

"Please, call me Kami. We'll be working together closely, and anyway, titles make me uncomfortable. I don't need people to call me 'doctor' all day just to pad my self-esteem." This was said in an open and self-deprecating way that disarmed the two soldiers. They warmed to her immediately.

"In that case, call me Lennox. This is Master Sergeant Epps, but I'm sure he won't mind you calling him Epps. We tend to be pretty informal ourselves." Epps just nodded in agreement; still temporarily speechless, an unnatural state for him.

Standing next to him was a man who looked to be in his late thirties, pink cheeks, blue eyes, close-cropped blond hair, similar to his companions in build, but with the restless eyes of an inquisitive soul.

Lennox continued, "Allow me to also introduce Mr. Petr Andronov, one of the world's leading experts in artificial and machine intelligence. We met him and his equipment in Sevastopol, where we all boarded the *Pearl*. Given what we're up against, we're expecting both of you to become invaluable members of the NEST team."

Kaminari eyed the Russian coolly, temporarily allowing the litany of past grievances between their two countries to interfere with her professionalism. But she shook it off: there was a common threat to all humanity, and old feuds must be put aside. Petr Andronov was a colleague now, and they would need to trust each other.

"That's what we're here for, and now that you've arrived, we can get started," replied Kami. "A pleasure to meet you, Petr. We need all three of you, and your Autobot comrades, in the briefing room right away. Everyone else is already assembled and waiting."

"What's going on?" asked Epps, finally able to find his tongue.

"Trouble. Maybe real trouble," Kami replied, the urgency now coming through in her voice. "We may have a sighting."

"Decepticons?" asked Lennox. "Well, we knew this was coming. I suppose it was too much to ask for them to give us the courtesy of being prepared before they made a move."

"Give us five minutes to stow our gear. We'll be right behind you."

Kami turned and walked down the pier, followed by the eyes of every living male creature in the vicinity.

"Damn, that ain't right," sighed Epps. "You can't be putting us in a room with her, not after all this time away from home."

"Easy there, chief," replied Lennox, "she'll kick your ass with one hand while solving Einstein's theory of relativity with the other. Didn't you read her file?"

"No, you're the leader of this team. That means you get to do all the reading."

"Well, if you had, you'd know that she graduated MIT with a PhD in both physics *and* engineering at age twenty-two. She's all kinds of wonky on robots and cybernetics. On top of that, she's got black belts in four different martial arts and spent three years working for Naicho, the Japanese intelligence agency. Something about doing her patriotic duty, rather than cashing in on all that talent with a private robotics firm."

"Damn," replied Epps, "definitely not just a pretty face."

"Oh, and Andronov?" continued Lennox. "Formerly of Russia's Spetsnaz. We aren't dealing with geeks and nerds here."

"Yeah, yeah we are," countered Epps, "we're just dealing with geeks and nerds who are trained to kill. Like I said, 'damn!'"

Lennox leaned forward toward the retinal analyzer that protruded from the wall of the door in front of them. The security device read his retinal pattern, checked it against the records in its data bank, and beeped once. Drawn by an unseen motor, a heavy metal door slid aside to admit them to another hallway. Beyond the security portal they encountered far fewer personnel than previously.

Conversation ceased when Epps and Lennox entered the conference room.

"Glad to have you back, gentlemen." The greeting came from the colonel, who struggled ineffectively to hide his impatience. "Everyone is in now, so we can begin."

Epps took the empty seat on the other side of

Lennox, across from Kaminari. Lennox and Epps represented the very few at this table, talented though the others might be, who'd had multiple encounters with the enemy. They were among the few soldiers, not to mention technical experts, who were personally familiar with both Autobots and Decepticons. As such, they were more or less immune from the petty annoyances of military protocol. The special patch he and Lennox and the rest of the NEST team wore on their uniforms or civilian attire conferred the kind of immunity even agents from the old, disbanded Sector Seven could not have imagined.

As Lennox shifted sideways in his seat the tall white-haired woman Epps knew only as Ariella rose from hers and walked to the far end of the room. The creases in her dark blue business suit were as sharp and set as those in her face. In her younger years she had been a classic beauty, and even at an advanced age she retained an unshakable attractiveness.

The flat surface she waved at promptly lit from within to become a wall-sized screen. The ambient light in the conference room dimmed accordingly. Expecting a different kind of image, Epps was surprised to see a map appear, and not one of the Diego Garcia region. A glance around the room indicated that everyone else seated at the conference table was similarly engrossed in the presentation, from the attentive Kaminari and Lennox to the rest of the military–civilian cadre.

Except for one.

Exasperation plain in her voice, Ariella was forced to pause before she had even begun. "Mr. Andronov, this is important. Could we have your attention, please?"

A voice that was almost deep enough to issue from an Autobot boomed from the far end of the table. "You always have my attention, *miloshka*."

"And don't be snide. This is serious business."

"So is this." He held up a cupped hand.

Petr Andronov's fascination with the small and seemingly insignificant stood in stark contrast with his bulk. The delicacy with which his huge hands could manipulate a butterfly without harming it, or nudge a nudibranch from a coral in order to better position it for study, or peel an onion for one of his famous Siberian soups, was something to behold.

Ariella rolled her eyes. While her attitude might verge on the schoolmarmish, there was nothing but steel in her voice. Lennox had heard rumors about her even before she had assumed command of NEST field operations. Stories that she would not confirm or deny, on which she steadfastly refused to elaborate. That she had risen to the rank of colonel in Israel's Mossad. That in her younger days she had once taken out an entire terrorist cell in the Beyoglu section of Istanbul all by herself and immediately afterward stopped for baklava and tea at a nearby restaurant. That she could disarm or place a bomb with equal skill. And that at any distance over ten thousand meters she could still outrun or outswim almost anyone else on the base's amateur track-and-field team.

She could even get Petr Andronov to pay attention.

With obvious reluctance, the AI specialist bent over and placed his cupped right hand on the darkened floor. Lennox could not see what tiny lifeform scuttled free from the Russian's fingers. Presumably it posed no danger to anyone in the room. With the exception of a small scorpion that could deliver little more injury than a bee sting, Diego Garcia's limited landmass had no room for toxic predators. On the other hand, Petr's quarters on the *Pearl* were known to house dozens of small cages and terrariums, and doubtless those now were shelved in his small dormitory. Lennox forced himself to concentrate on the illuminated wall, the glint-eyed woman standing to its right, and the map that had appeared on screen. Like Epps, he was surprised at the image.

Ever since their defeat at Mission City there had been no sign of, nor trouble from the Decepticons. It was known that Starscream had escaped, but not to where. With the aid of the humans, Optimus Prime and his friends had been hunting him ever since, as yet to no avail. In the interim other Autobots had detected Optimus's signal and had arrived on Earth to join their brethren. Whether any Decepticons had similarly responded, no one could tell. The Autobots as well as their new friends hoped such was not the case, but it was this very eventuality that NEST had been created to deal with.

Like his colleagues, Lennox assumed that any new attack would focus on an important nexus of human civilization, the better to draw the Autobots into battle. London, perhaps, or Tokyo (in such circumstances he always thought of Tokyo).

So he was as surprised as anyone else in the conference room to see that the map that had appeared on the wall was not of North America, or East Asia, or even Europe, but of the southern half of Africa.

Africa. Lennox stared at the map as Ariella's right hand moved over the proximate controls that had appeared on that side of the wall screen. The view narrowed somewhat, but remained wide enough to encompass multiple countries and an enormous amount of territory.

A now wholly serious Epps leaned toward Lennox and nodded in the direction of the screen. "Long way from where we finished up that last work."

The captain gestured toward the left side of the screen. "Maybe they're going to send us to Namibia. You'll like it there. It's *all* desert, you know."

Epps moaned softly.

As it turned out they were not going to Namibia, but that did not make what Ariella had to say any less absorbing. As she gestured with the index finger of her left hand, a glowing pointer appeared on the wall. When she moved her hand in an arc, the pointer circled the southern portion of one particular country.

"I am going to take a wild guess and assume that none of you in this room has ever spent any time in Zambia." In response to the silence that greeted her observation, she nodded understandingly. Her pointer moved again, this time to take in a much wider area.

"Two months ago an F-22 Raptor was observed flying over this portion of the continent. Positive identification was finally made with the aid of a satellite-recorded heat signature, the F-22's being different from that of any other known military aircraft. Apparently, the Decepticon skill at mimicry extends even to the smallest detail. Optimus Prime has confirmed that this ability comes naturally to his kind. When they choose an alternative mode, they duplicate it exactly."

A hand went up from one of the civilian NEST members near the back. "It's clear to everyone in this room where you're going with this, Ariella, but how do we know for certain that it *is* Starscream?"

Instead of replying, Ariella let one of the senior military officers supply the answer.

"We've checked and rechecked flight paths from every base with access to that part of the continent." The man in air force blue spoke assuredly. "Even equipped with extra wing tanks, there are no F-22s capable of overflying the indicated region from any base that we know of. In fact, the nearest F-22 squadron is based right here on Diego Garcia." He smiled thinly. "To the best of my knowledge, Starscream is not among them."

Nobody laughed. Claiming "to the best of one's knowledge" where Transformers were concerned was insufficient assurance. On several occasions while visiting the installations on the atoll's main island, Lennox had found himself looking at passing vehicles or parked aircraft. Even up close, it was often impossible to tell a Transformer from a human-made machine.

Thus far NEST's isolation had protected it, and secondary security was as tight as humans and Autobots working together could make it—but it was not perfect. It was on the morning Lennox had found himself eyeing an obstinate coffeemaker and reaching hesitantly for his sidearm that he had decided to seek therapy. It had been a great help.

But he still found himself looking at every vehicle and every machine he encountered, military or civilian, with a jaundiced eye.

Kaminari spoke up. "This is, however, still a guess, albeit an educated one. While I admit that the indicated speed at which the suspect craft was traveling precludes its being a civilian aircraft, there are many countries that operate illegal overflights of combat jets in that part of the continent." She indicated the man who had voiced the initial uncertainty. "We cannot be sure."

Ariella nodded. "Agreed. Additional verification is required. NEST is taking no chances with this." Her gaze, which was anything but grandmotherly, roamed the room. "Accordingly, all three of the Autobots who survived the clash in America will accompany Captain Lennox, Sergeant Epps, and operatives Andronov and Ishihara on a mission designed to establish the validity of this report. You will be joined by two of our recent arrivals, Autobots Salvage and Beachbreak. Since all Autobots will be traveling in their transformed terrestrial mode, Salvage will transport Beachbreak in his Jet Ski mode."

"Seems like quite an expedition to confirm or deny a rumor," one of the other officers commented.

Even before he had finished, the wall behind him dropped into the floor. Revealed on the other side was a much larger room equipped with a bigger wall screen. It displayed the same map of Africa. Heads and bodies shifted and turned to regard the single occupant of the adjoining conference room.

"We will not be journeying merely to substantiate

an observation." Optimus Prime's head and upper body filled much of the available viewing space while the rest of his enormous form remained out of sight below floor level. "We intend not merely to locate Starscream, but to eliminate the threat he poses to this world." Appreciative murmurs greeted this announcement.

Another of the civilians spoke up. "Governments in that region tend to complain when their territorial integrity is violated, even if done with the intent of defending their citizens."

"Hence the need to travel with the secrecy we have all learned to observe." Ariella's gaze went immediately to a certain officer. "Captain Lennox, do you think you and Sergeant Epps can manage to be credible noncombatants?"

The two men exchanged a glance. "If Optimus can mimic a Detroit diesel," Lennox told her, "Epps and I can transform into civilians."

She looked over at the leader of the Autobots. "As with all NEST combat operations, command will be shared between Captain Lennox and Optimus Prime."

The massive Autobot nodded. "With all due respect to the captain, I hope he will understand that should we actually make contact with Starscream it must be my fellow Cybertronians and myself who will determine combat strategy." All eyes in the room turned to Lennox.

"With all due respect to Optimus Prime, I hope he will understand that should we actually make contact with Starscream, my human associates and I will be more than happy to let the Autobots take the lead in any fighting."

Even Ariella cracked a smile at the captain's response. "Very well, then. Your cover identities have been prepared. A C-17 is standing by to convey all of you to Lusaka. From there you'll be able to access local as well as satellite communications. If fortune smiles on us, by the end of the month maybe the wreck of Megatron will have some company." Murmurs of approval greeted this observation.

"While operating among the civilian populace," she continued, "I'm sure I don't need to remind the Autobots of the need to maintain their terrestrial disguises whenever possible."

"We are aware of the effect our natural appearance has on humans," Optimus assured her. "We have no desire to cause a panic. Besides, exposing our actual selves would only serve to alert Starscream that we are closing in on him."

"Cannot he detect your Sparks?" Petr wondered aloud.

"Much depends on distance, which internal perceptors are active at the time of seeking, and other factors," the leader of the Autobots explained. "To a certain degree our bodies also mask the Spark within. Can you hear the heartbeat of your neighbor?"

"Only when I place certain specimens of arachnid in their hands to be admired," the AI expert replied.

"Everyone understands the mission, then, and what is expected of them." With a wave of her hand Ariella deactivated the screen. "You leave at oh six hundred tomorrow. Gentlemen, ladies . . ." She hesitated. "Autobot."

"I am happy to respond to 'gentleman,'" Optimus informed her.

She smiled. "I'll remember for next time. Better to be overly careful than to give offense."

"It is difficult for humans to offend us," the leader of the Autobots explained. "Though not impossible. I am put in mind of a certain member of your now disbanded Sector Seven organization who—but that is in the past." His electronic gaze focused on Lennox. "Until tomorrow morning, then, Captain."

Pushing back his chair, Lennox nodded. "Get some sleep until—oh, right. I forget. You guys don't sleep."

"No, we do not. But we rest and power down certain heat-sensitive circuitry, and I will surely do that."

Outside the conference room, Kaminari found herself walking alongside Epps. "I've been wanting to ask you, Sergeant Epps, out of everyone here, you and Captain Lennox have the most experience in fighting the Decepticons. Are they really so difficult to destroy? I have read all the reports, of course, but that is not the same as actually engaging in battle."

"Until we figured out to use sabot rounds we didn't have anything that would do more than knock one of 'em back a couple of steps." Epps's tone was somber. "Even utilizing sabots, you have to hit a vulnerable spot between their heavy armor exactly when it flexes in order to have any effect at all. These guys have been fighting one another for thousands of years. They've gotten real good at it." His tone darkened further. "Real good."

They turned a corner, and Epps continued. "Take a modern marine armored division. Now remove all the humans. Give all the weapons intelligence of their own. Combine them into a single entity. That's a Decepticon. Or, thank God, an Autobot." Breaking away from her, he headed in the direction of his own quarters. "Just be glad of one thing."

"What's that?" she called after him.

"That we've got Optimus Prime and the other Autobots on our side. Otherwise we'd end up fighting Starscream with the equivalent of sticks and stones. I understand you've got a new weapon to be field-tested, though?"

"Yes, though I'd have a bit more confidence if I could have tested it first in a controlled environment," she replied. "But I don't think that any of the Autobots, even Ratchet, is willing to act the guinea pig for this."

"How does—or should I say how do you hope it will work?" asked Epps.

Kaminari hesitated only a moment before replying, "It is a portable, directional EMP weapon. Using internal focal points and Gamma reflectors, I've managed to build a prototype that fires an electromagnetic pulse in a single direction, instead of a burst that radiates out three hundred sixty degrees from the origin point. In theory it should work to temporarily destabilize a Transformer's Energon imprint, rendering him impaired, if only slightly.

"The only problem that I have not been able to overcome is the relatively short range of the device. I'd have to be quite close, and that's not generally ideal when it comes to twenty-foot-high killing machines. I understand Petr has his own specialized toy; I'm curious to hear his proposed solution to the human–Decepticon imbalance."

"All due respect, but I'll keep the sabot rounds," said Epps, turning in to his quarters. "In other words, better you than me."

Feeling that the underground air-conditioning was beginning to give her a chill, she broke into a jog as she headed for her own room.

There were preparations to be made.

3

"One pastrami on rye, mayo instead of mustard."

Mayo instead of mustard? *Mayo instead of mustard?* The flint-eyed gaze of Seymour Simmons, former chief agent extraordinaire for Sector Seven, narrowed as he focused on the customer standing at the order counter in Tova Simmons's Manhattan delicatessen. His tone was as rigid as it had been when he had been in charge of dozens of black-suited operatives, and he spoke with great deliberation.

"You—cannot—have—pastrami—on—rye—with—mayonnaise."

In the middle of a typically rushed Manhattan lunch break, the customer blinked at the lanky, white-aproned attendant behind the counter. "Aw, c'mon, man—I haven't got time for this! That's how I like my pastrami." To the amusement of those waiting in line behind him he managed a credible imitation of Simmons's incongruously apocalyptic tenor. "On—rye—with—mayo."

"You can't." The change in Simmons's expression from severe to smiling was so abrupt that the customer was visibly startled. "It isn't good deli. It isn't New York. It isn't—American."

The customer sighed. "All right, then. Have it your way. No pastrami with mayo."

"Good." Simmons's fingers hovered over the automated input that would send the order to the kitchen. "What *can* I get for you?"

"I'll have a hot corned beef on rye." The customer paused for effect, until he could no longer repress the grin that was bubbling up inside him. "With mayo."

Simmons froze. His smile returned, harder than ever. As the man was about to high-five the customer behind him, the former agent reached across, grabbed the man by his shirt collar, and yanked him bodily halfway across the counter. Their faces were now inches apart. Simmons's eyes found those of the startled customer and locked in.

"This is my mother's deli. We do pastrami here. We do corned beef. We do brisket and sturgeon and gefilte fish. We don't do comedy. Comedy clubs you will find in the Village." His fingers tightened on the man's collar. By now the customer's self-satisfied smirk had vanished completely, to be replaced by an expression of an entirely different kind. "Would you like me to recommend something?"

The man's hands fumbled at the iron grip holding him by the throat. "Hey, leggo of me! Are you out of your . . . ?"

A strong feminine voice interrupted. "So, Seymour, what's this? Is there a problem?"

Still maintaining his agent's grip on the customer's neck, Simmons looked over and down at the compact diesel of a woman who had come up beside him. "This guy's a wiseass. Ordered pastrami with mayo.

When I called him on it, he switched it to hot corned beef with mayo."

The dark-haired woman made a face at her son. "When you 'called him on it'? Listen to me, boychick: this isn't Washington. It isn't even Virginia. You're in charge of the register now, not national security." She turned her attention to the struggling customer, whose face had begun to turn red. "You want pastrami with mayo?" The man hesitated, eyed the resolute Simmons, then nodded. "You're an idiot," Mrs. Simmons told him flatly. She turned back to her son. "You also are an idiot, Seymour. *Nu?* Idiot number one, give idiot number two what he wants." So saying, she turned and headed back to the kitchen and the never-ending battle to make sure that part-time employees were not pocketing her sugar and other condiments.

Simmons did as he was told. In his years as a senior Sector Seven operative he had grown used to giving orders. Well, he could take them as well as dish them out. Straightening his shirt, the customer looked quietly triumphant. Simmons ignored him. What did the fool know? As he rang up the order he let his gaze rove over the busy restaurant. What did any of them know? A few images from nearly a year ago, splashed across the media. Brief images of rampaging robotic lifeforms meting out a limited amount of urban destruction. Then—nothing. Secrecy had descended around the entire incident, just as the world's political and military establishment had closed ranks around hard knowledge of what had really happened.

Alien machines had come to Earth. There had been a couple of incidents. That was in the past and they were being intensively studied by the world's best engineers and scientists.

Not a word about the fact that the alien machines were also studying Earth. Or that some of those machines' intentions were less than altruistic.

Stories selectively planted with the pulp news magazines, gossip sheets, and rumor-bloggers on the Net gave the impression that the whole business was nothing more than another political cover-up for another military foul-up. A few reports insisted that all the widely seen images of explosions and damaged buildings were publicity for upcoming films about giant alien robots invading Earth. When he came across a cover story in *The National Enquirer* insisting that Elvis's robot alien offspring were behind the whole thing, Simmons had thrown the scavenged newspaper against the wall of the building he'd been passing. That had resulted in an on-the-spot fifty-dollar littering fine written out by an alert New York cop. The incident had done little to improve the ex-agent's mood.

Ex-agent. Of all the iniquities that had been visited upon him since the existence of the Autobots had been revealed, from being deliberately oiled by one of the mechanical monstrosities to being slapped by a delinquent of a teenage temptress, losing his job and its perks had been the hardest blow of all. Despite his earnest entreaties he had not been recruited to join NEST, Sector Seven's replacement. He had accumulated "too much baggage," they had politely informed him.

"Baggage." How could any undefined "baggage" outweigh his intimate and personal knowledge of the

Autobots and their enemies the Decepticons? He knew the real reason he had been dismissed from service, albeit with his pension intact. It was that kid, that smart-ass Witwicky. The aliens' friend, their good buddy. Him and that—girl. Okay, so maybe he could have been a little nicer to them. Considering events in hindsight, he might have used a little more tact in the course of their initial confrontation. But national security had been at stake. National security! If he hadn't come down hard on them when they'd first been picked up, someone else in the service would have been sure to question his methods.

How could the government dismiss him and not want to make use of what he knew? Because of "baggage"? Because there were whispers that he was "unstable"? It was crazy! Madness! Seymour Simmons, unstable. When had he ever given the slightest indication of being even a little bit offline, unbalanced, over the edge, or slipping on the floor of his attic? As he walked back to his apartment he kicked angrily at every piece of newspaper the wind blew his way. Occasional passersby glanced in his direction—which in Manhattan was saying something. Maybe their reactions had something to do with the fact that he kept shaking his head while muttering to himself.

He didn't really need the job in his mother's deli. His severance package combined with his pension took care of his basic needs. But the food at the deli was the best, and anyway he needed something to do. Something to get him out among people. Because if all he had to do was sit in his apartment and stare at the TV or the computer or work on his project while completely out of touch with the rest of mankind, why, even someone as inherently stable as himself might go a little—mad.

So when his mother, seeing her son adrift, had offered him the job in the deli, he had taken it. Daily contact with others, even thin-tie-wearing twits who were willing to loudly and in public desecrate a pastrami sandwich, helped him to maintain stability. And focus. He needed to focus. As he let the comforting thought wash over him, a knowing and slightly disturbed grin spread across his face. At the sight of it, one couple coming toward him on the windswept sidewalk hurriedly changed course to cross the street.

If he failed to focus, he would never be able to complete his project.

Go ahead and dissolve Sector Seven. Hire a bunch of egghead scientists at inflated salaries to feather their own NEST. Ignore the continuing threat from beyond the solar system. *He,* Seymour Simmons, knew what was going on. He, Seymour Simmons, would take it upon himself to save the world from what he knew was under way.

Invasion.

There was no use trying to pretty it up, no point in searching for a less alarming euphemism. Even as he strode purposefully down the side streets of Manhattan, the Earth was suffering an invasion and humanity's fate hung in the balance. If "they" would not let him participate in its unified defense, then he would do so on his own. One day they would realize what they had sacrificed by not employing him. One day they would know. He would save mankind in spite of itself.

He would do it from his basement.

The lower level of a ground-floor walkdown, an apartment already one level below that of the street, was as dark and dank as the inside of a bigot's mind. Instead of speleotherms, however, the workshop Simmons had set up was festooned with enough tools to stock an entire aisle of a major home retailer. Very few of them were designed for brute-force work. There were no sledgehammers, no oversized circular saws, no industrial-strength lathes or heavy drill presses.

Instead the well-lit work space was packed with an assortment of gear more suited to an active hobbyist. Dremel accessories and dentist tools decorated most of one wall. A computer-controlled injection molder stood off to one side. Electronic components overflowed from half-shut bins.

Illuminated by overhead lights, a single rectangular worktable dominated the middle of the room. Resting on it, tightly clamped in place and connected to dozens of color-coded wires that fanned out in all directions, sat what at first glance appeared to be a cross between a Koons sculpture and a space engineer's idle dreaming. It had a face, sort of. Only vaguely humanoid, it was as full of menace as an inanimate head-sized object could be.

Entering the basement shop and switching on the last of the lights, Simmons smiled as he walked over to the worktable and patted the head on its head. "And how is my homicidal little friend today? Dormant as ever, I see. That's good." Whistling the old standard "I Ain't Got Nobody," Simmons strolled over to the workbench that dominated one wall, checked one of three computer readouts, tapped a few keys, and turned back to regard the object that was at once his prize and prisoner.

"I think today we'll work on adjusting controlled response as opposed to reflexive hostility. By next week I think I'll have gained enough sway over your cognitive processors to take a chance on restoring visual perception. Then we'll see if we can have a conversation where every other word out of your mouth isn't 'Kill!' What do you say?"

There was no reply from the object on the table. There would not be until Simmons made the necessary repairs and hookups to what he had salvaged from Sector Seven's ruined facility inside the base of Hoover Dam. He was completely convinced that understanding what he had saved ("stolen" was such a pejorative term, he thought) and learning how it functioned would allow him to discover a means for dealing with the invaders.

All of them.

Because despite their actions in defeating the Decepticons and their subsequent insistence that they would forever stand up for the defense of humankind, he trusted the Autobots about as far as he could throw Optimus Prime. If he could learn how they worked, unearth the secrets of their cybernetic brains if not their bodies, then he would know how best to deal with them. How best to protect the planet and its *original* inhabitants. He would see to it that they would cease to be functionally independent organisms and return to being what they were at base. Simple machines, and nothing more. Tools that could be used by mankind, instead of aggressive entities determined to drag the population of the Earth into an ancient intraspecies war being waged by soulless mechanisms. He, Seymour Simmons, would see to that eventuality.

In between taking sandwich orders, of course.

He punched out a few commands on one of the computer keyboards, picked up a small wireless controller, and pointed it at the object on the worktable. "I think I've tapped into the correct synapses. Let's try it and see, shall we?" He depressed a button.

Something sparked in the air above the table and the object atop it twitched slightly. It could not look at him angrily or glare by way of response because its visual perception had yet to be restored. Nor could it speak. It could only fume silently and impotently. It had no choice but to cope as best it could with whatever crude mechanical and electronic manipulations the human chose to inflict upon it.

That would change one day. Change when perception and mobility were restored. Then there would come a reckoning. The human thought he had complete control. At the moment such was indeed the case. But it was only a moment, and the object of Simmons's experimentation was patient. Time was a quantity with which it was far more comfortable than the short-lived organics. Time was a human's enemy and a Decepticon's friend.

Imprisoned securely atop the worktable, deprived of any means to strike back, the partial head of Frenzy tolerated the antics of the disturbed human. While the ongoing delay in defeating the Autobots irritated him almost as much as did the absence of his body, he was not overly concerned.

He knew he was not alone.

* * *

The underground chamber that had been allocated to the Autobots was the single largest open space in the entire NEST complex—or for that matter anywhere on the atoll. It was larger even than the hangars on the main island that had been built years earlier to accommodate the wingspan of B-52s and stealth bombers.

It was not elaborately equipped—yet. At the insistence of Optimus Prime, supplies, tools, raw materials, certain liquids, and specialized apparatus were to be brought in a little at a time.

"What do you need?" NEST's chief supply officer had made the inquiry when the chamber was yet to be completed. "My team and I have been ordered to furnish you with whatever you want."

"We need nothing," the leader of the Autobots had replied. "What we want is time, and understanding."

The supply chief had smiled. "It's my understanding that both items tend to be in short supply in world capitals, but I'll see what I can do."

Now three areas of the vast open space were beginning to fill up. Off to the south vast varieties of raw materials, finished metals, and primitive electronics were being amassed by Ratchet. While each Autobot was capable of a certain minimal amount of maintenance and self-repair, more thorough restoration was the job of the Autobots' equivalent of surgeon, engineer, and metallurgist. It was a task at which Ratchet had never faltered, whether required to make repairs on solid ground or in empty space. Occasionally the humans would, in their ignorance and out of a desire to be helpful, urge some new material or technique on him. He turned none of these offers down, accepting each and every one with equanimity, without commenting on their incredible crudeness or lamentable simplicity.

Behind heavy blast doors a very different sort of inventory was accumulating. Its presence would not have reassured those in Washington, Moscow, or Beijing who continued to voice their suspicions as to the Autobots' ultimate motives. Epps, however, found Ironhide's work endlessly enticing.

"You're sure this stuff is safe here?" he had asked on more than one occasion.

"Certainly." The Autobot weapons master made no attempt to conceal his exasperation. "How many times must I tell you, how many times must you reassure your superiors on my behalf, that this stockpile is harmless unless activated directly by one of my own kind?"

"What did you call it again? Energon?" he repeated.

"Yes, though this form is manufactured from existing energy sources. Energon does occur naturally throughout the galaxy, and in its pure state is extremely dangerous and highly unstable. Indeed there is ample evidence that Energon exsits here on Earth in ample stores, but we have neither the time, nor currently the freedom, to search for it.

"What we have manufactured here is quite safe. For Transformers, Autobots and Decepticons alike, it is a source of energy. You might call it nourishment, though that would be a painfully limited descriptor, and naturally we need to 'refuel' far less frequently than your species. But we require reserves nonetheless, especially if we can expect casualties in the coming days.

"It can of course be weaponized, and indeed forms the basis of our personal arsenals. But your own people could not do so if they tried. This safety factor is a matter of chemistry and design that is beyond the understanding of your weapons' engineers." A massive arm had gestured at the store of uncatalyzed explosives. "It is useless to you, and none of what you see here can 'go off' accidentally."

Epps nodded thoughtfully. "But just for the sake of imagining, just for the hell of it, suppose it did? I'm just talkin', understand."

Ironhide contemplated the substantial stockpile of weapons and related material he had managed to accrue thus far. "The question is purely theoretical?"

"Oh, purely," Epps assured him.

"Something would be lost as a consequence."

The sergeant had nodded understandingly. "The atoll?"

"Yes," Ironhide agreed. "The atoll. Possibly also India."

Epps regarded the mound of material with fresh respect. "Oh."

While both Ratchet's and Ironhide's efforts were notable in their own right and more than worthy of admiration, it was the third corner of the chamber that drew the bulk of attention. Like the other two sections, this one was also filling up.

With Autobots.

They arrived singly from the far corners of the cosmos, drawn to the tiny blue-white globe by the powerful signal being broadcast by Optimus himself.

Scattered by the endless war that had devastated but not destroyed Cybertron, they were each and every one who had thus far found their way to Earth astonished by what they encountered: fellow Autobots not merely living among possibly intelligent organics, but coexisting with them.

"It's not quite as open as it seems." The leader of the Autobots took pains to explain the fragility of the relationship individually to each new arrival. "Here in this place, isolated from nearly all of humankind, we can live and move about in relative freedom. The humans here are specialists, chosen for their adaptive abilities as well as their individual knowledge. They are far more empathetic, more understanding of our situation, than the population at large."

"There are so many of them, and this is such a small planet. How do they manage to survive?" The question came from an Autobot who had taken the identifier Salvage along with the appearance of a not entirely reputable pickup truck.

"With difficulty," Optimus admitted. "They do not understand how to use their resources wisely and for the benefit of all. We can teach them, but we must progress slowly. They are an overly sensitive species and have a tendency to take offense at any perceived slight, no matter how well meaning the commentary. Some of them are wary of us, some are suspicious, and some are openly fearful."

"Fearful!" In the powerful motorcycle shape he had chosen, Knockout revved his oversized engine. "After you saved them from Megatron? After Jazz gave his spark to help protect them?"

Optimus regarded his colleague patiently. "I told

you they are overly sensitive. This tendency sometimes borders on the paranoid. Interestingly, in the reverse of what is normal, the young of the species have less fear of us than do their elders. They are more attuned to our electronic nature. I and the others who arrived here with me have personal knowledge of this, as it was a young human who prevented Megatron from taking control of the Allspark." He held up an admonishing hand to the rumbling cycle.

"Do not underestimate these organics. They are at once intelligent and foolish, fearful and brave. They have a great capacity for improvement, if only they will cast aside their lingering primitive tribal instincts. I think we can help them with that, too."

"Why should we bother?" Salvage asked candidly. "Our war is not theirs."

Optimus did not grunt, but he voiced the mechanical equivalent. "Would that it were so, Salvage. But by allying themselves with us against Megatron, they have made themselves the enemies of all Decepticons. Starscream, for one, does not forget such things."

"Ah, Starscream!" Revving his engine again, the motorcycle roared circles around the assembled Autobots. "If I could but get that misconceived accretion of ego and anxieties in my sights I would blow out his Spark like a twig!"

From off to one side Ratchet looked up from where he had been working. "Be careful what you wish for, Knockout. You might get it."

At this the motorcycle slowed, came to a halt, and began to unfold itself like a pile of metal origami, until Knockout stood dark and gleaming between the repair specialist and the Autobot leader.

"I'm not afraid of any Decepticon, least of all a blowhard like Starscream. Give me one good shot at him, that's all I ask."

"We all would welcome that chance." Optimus Prime's tone was soothing. "Wherever he has fled to, we must find Starscream before he can do any more harm. Either to Autobots or to humans."

"What is this concern for humans?" Knockout was nothing if not impulsive in his questioning. "I understand that they helped you in the fight against Megatron, but surely a few lives among their swarming billions will not be missed."

"You are newly come here, Knockout." Optimus delivered the mild rebuke without rancor. "Humans—that is to say, most humans—mourn every organic life lost, sometimes even those that are not of their species. They keep smaller, less intelligent organics close to them and lament their passing with equal and sometimes greater intensity than they do their own kind."

Knockout sounded dubious. "A strange species with which to ally ourselves."

"This is a path we did not choose," Optimus told him, "but was chosen for us. To fail to protect the humans from the likes of Starscream would be to abrogate our responsibilities as sentient beings."

"Pardon me if I roll out on that." Collapsing back upon himself, Knockout once again assumed the form of the motorcycle he had chosen. With a parting rumble, he vanished down the empty access corridor that lay off to the right, the thunder of his engine echoing around the great chamber for some time after he had left.

"A bit rebellious, for an Autobot." Ratchet voiced the observation from where he was working. "We will need to keep an eye on that one."

"Knockout will be fine." Salvage admired the medical specialist's work. "He's just enthusiastic, that's all. Wants to get on with the business of winding up the war."

"Yes, the war." Optimus turned thoughtful. "Always the war. I wish I were certain that it was 'winding up.' Nothing in this interminable conflict is assured. Not even the help of the humans."

"But you just said—" Salvage began.

Optimus cut him off. "While those humans who know us regard us as friends and allies, there are those besides the suspicious who actively dislike us. They wish us gone or, failing that, rendered inoperative. Their minds are small and their hearts afraid." He sighed heavily. "It seems it is always so with organics. But there are also those whom I am convinced would be our friends under any circumstances. You will have the opportunity to meet with them shortly."

"Yes," said the smaller Autobot, Beachbreak, from nearby. "There's one who while in the water utilizes a supplementary lens to enhance her visual acuity. It is so thick as to render her appearance at such times almost Autobot-like. Though," he added more thoughtfully, "I am not sufficiently conversant with human mores to say whether or not she would find the comparison flattering."

Beachbreak often felt dwarfed by his Autobot colleagues. Standing a little over ten feet tall when in robot mode, he was neither as big nor as powerful as his companions on Diego Garcia. He missed his friend

Bumblebee, not only due to the fact that they were relatively the same young age and enjoyed similar personalities, but also because Bumblebee did not tower over Beachbreak quite as much as the others.

Beachbreak had adopted a rather unique alt mode for himself: when in the open, he appeared as a personal watercraft. The Jet Ski he became resembled nothing that would be found at a resort or public beach. With its dark gray, tapered sides and severe profile it perfectly duplicated the small watercraft that had been developed for use by US Navy SEALs and UK commandos. Appropriate, he felt, because although relatively diminutive in size, he did not lack courage. All he wanted was a chance to prove his valor to his companions.

"There are among them soldiers who take warfare as seriously as us," Optimus continued. "They have proven to be our most steadfast supporters."

This was something Salvage could understand without explanation. "War strips away all suspicion among those who do the actual fighting, and leaves behind only comradeship."

Ratchet indicated agreement. "Under such circumstances the actual viscosity of one's life fluid becomes immaterial."

"You'll meet these individuals also," Optimus assured them. "Soldiers are less interested in the physical makeup of those who stand beside them than whether or not such individuals are good shots. That is a constant among Autobots and humans alike.

"Meanwhile, until and if we are called upon, we have a certain amount of freedom in this place. Within limits, we can roam about as we see fit. This island complex is isolated from the rest of humankind and as a military installation is off-limits to any who have not received the proper security clearance. Even so, I would advise against frequently moving about on the surface in your natural shape. Our arrival on this world has caused enough stress; there is no need to add to it by advertising our presence, even in a place like this. Hence the local camouflage each of you has adopted."

Salvage nodded again as he gestured in the direction of the access corridor. "I'll say one thing for Knockout. You won't have any trouble with him on that score. Sometimes I think he's more fond of his adopted terrestrial configuration than he is of his normal Autobot shape."

"Then he'll blend in well here." Optimus suddenly went quiet. A moment later he explained the pause. "I have been signaled that there is a conference I should attend. Human speech is agonizingly slow, but allows for considerable nuance of expression. Sometimes more so than do our multiple forms of electronic communication. Apparently this involves a matter of some urgency. You will excuse me."

After the leader of the Autobots had departed, Salvage turned to Ratchet. "That noise Knockout generates in his terrestrial guise. It is oddly engaging."

"It is excessively loud," Ratchet objected. "A waste of energy resulting in nothing more than a premature announcement of one's incipient arrival."

"True, true," agreed Salvage. "But engaging nonetheless."

4

Careful Chifungwe squinted into the night and cursed the unknown company motor pool mechanic for his oversight. Surely the man knew that ensuring the delivery truck's windshield wipers were in working order at this time of the year was of primary importance. Their failure in the current storm was going to make him later than ever getting home.

His route was extensive and he was still a long way from Livingstone. At least the truck was empty, the last case of beer having long since been delivered to its rural destination. The rest of the truck was working fine despite the pounding it was taking on the tourist road. Over the years much had changed throughout central Africa, but one mechanical constant held true even in the poorest countries. Public conveyance might collapse, brakeless buses might go over cliffs, and personal transport might be reduced to riding on the back of oxcarts, but come rain or snow, sleet or hail, the beer trucks always got through.

Not always on time, however, even in modern Zambia. And the rain wasn't helping.

While he had known from the time he had made the choice that taking the detour through Kafue National

Park was risky, he hadn't had many options. Not with the main north–south road washed out in two places. There was no guarantee the tourist track would be in any better shape, but there was sure to be less traffic through the park, and no heavy trucks at all. He was certain of the latter because commercial traffic was banned inside the park. If he was caught there would be a substantial fine to pay—and it would come out of his salary. He was counting on the park rangers to be holed up out of the weather, watching football. No one wanted to be out in the storm, including tourists. Kafue being the size of Wales, he felt fairly confident he would not meet any of the latter. If he could just get through these last hundred kilometers without being stopped . . .

A massive shape loomed directly in front of him. Caught in the truck's headlights, it swerved to challenge his approach. Shouting at himself, Careful slammed on the brakes. The truck half slid, half skidded to a halt without making contact.

Elephant.

The matriarch trumpeted at him but did not charge. Startled by the truck's lights, she nevertheless stood guard as the rest of her family group finished crossing the road. With a final contemptuous snort, she trailed after them. As he watched the last enormous gray rump vanish into the rain and darkness, Careful allowed himself a sigh of relief. The brakes had worked. He took a moment to bless the unnamed mechanic whose lineage he had so heartily cursed only moments earlier. The idling truck slipped smoothly into gear as he eased it forward. Elephants notwithstanding, if the road did not get any muddier and he met no rangers or traffic, he might make Livingstone on time despite everything.

An hour later, eyes heavy with exhaustion and mind clouded with sleep, he was forced to slow again to avoid hitting another gray mass that was blocking the road. This time it was a solitary young bull. *Damn elephants,* he thought tiredly to himself. *The government should let us cull and can them, as they do in South Africa.* Evidently the lone pachyderm was finding the road to his liking, because despite the glare of the headlights and Careful's insistent use of the truck's horn he did not move.

Leaning out the driver's-side window into the rain, Careful shook a fist at the recalcitrant creature. "Move! Go find a mopane grove and eat something! I need to eat, too!" Withdrawing into the truck cab, he wiped rain from his face and leaned on the horn anew. When that didn't work, he tried racing the engine. This time the elephant moved. Or rather, was moved.

Something picked it up and set it aside.

Careful Chifungwe's lower jaw dropped as he leaned toward the windshield, eyes very wide, looking out and up into the storm. A shape, a vaguely humanoid figure, was towering above the road. Its eyes shone like those of the demons his grandmother used to tell him about. A modern man, Careful knew there were no such things as demons, unless someone had imbibed too much of his company's product. Yet there it stood, glaring down at him.

Demon or something else, he was not about to linger to ask for identification. Slamming the truck into reverse, he gunned the engine. The delivery truck did not move. Metallic scraping noises came from the back end. Glancing fearfully into the side mirror he saw that another truck, a big powerful pickup, was blocking his retreat.

If he had not been so busy trying to flee, he might have screamed. He did scream, finally, when a hand slammed down on the open sill of his window. Though unsympathetic, the face that appeared out of the darkness was human. The body beneath was clad in military camouflage gear, and the man wore a sodden dark beret. Other shapes, also human, could be seen moving around in the darkness behind him. They carried an eclectic assortment of weapons.

Rebels of some kind. Careful was almost grateful. The worst they could do was kill him. He could not imagine what the elephant-shifting demon might be capable of doing.

"Get out of the truck!" the soldier at the window barked.

Reflexively, Careful shut off the ignition before exiting. Stepping out into the rain, which thankfully was beginning to let up, he found himself confronted by more than a dozen armed men. While most held rifles, a couple hefted more potent RPGs. Not park poachers, then. Poachers didn't go after elephants with rocket-propelled grenades. They tended to spoil the ivory. But what kind of rebels? This part of Zambia had been peaceful for a long time.

Two men returned from having inspected the back of Careful's vehicle. "Empty," one of them reported curtly.

"Too bad." The man who had ordered the driver out of the vehicle looked Careful up and down. "We'll make use of your truck. It will be especially useful. Nobody interferes with beer delivery." He drew himself up. "I am Major General Fellows Mashivingo, of the Human Accessory Force."

Careful was compelled to confess apologetically that he had never heard of either the general or the Human Accessory Force.

Mashivingo flashed white teeth in the darkness. "Few people have. You are among the first. Only a few months ago we were refugees from the Eastern Congo, hunted both by the Kinshasa government and our 'fellow' rebels. Since then we have found more powerful friends and protectors." As if in response, the pickup that had successfully blocked Careful's retreat came rumbling around from the back of the delivery truck. It boasted what in Careful's professional opinion was an excess of lights.

It also had no driver.

When he pointed this out to the erstwhile general, Mashivingo laughed. Overhearing the conversation, several of his subordinates also enjoyed a quick chuckle. "Dropkick has no driver because he *is* the driver."

Careful had no difficulty pleading ignorance. "I do not understand."

"You will." The general looked over at the big pickup. "Show him, Dropkick."

Before Careful's astonished gaze, the truck idling in the rain began to change. Arms appeared as if out of its side, then a torso, and finally legs. The cab became a head, all glistening metal and fiery eyes. Though the resultant figure loomed menacingly over the group of armed, rain-soaked humans, none of them appeared afraid. In fact, a couple of the soldier-rebels raised

their rifles over their heads and cheered appreciatively.

"Starscream was right," the figure rumbled. "Humans are easily impressed."

"I am always right."

Hands still held above his head, Careful whirled as
a second demonic figure appeared behind him. Bigger
than the transformed pickup truck, it was flanked by
still a third mysterious shape: squat, powerful, and
with one arm that terminated in parallel circular
blades instead of fingers.

To the terrified Careful's astonishment, the general
took a step toward the intimidating pair. "His truck is
empty, but looks to be in excellent condition. It will
make good transport. My men are tired of walking."

"Feeble organics." The hulking metal shape that
was standing alongside Starscream spoke in a high-
speed electronic language that only the three Decepticons present could understand. "Must we deal with
them?"

"You are newly arrived on this planet, Macerator,"
rejoined Starscream. "Believe me, I understand your
exasperation. But having engaged them in battle on
the other side of this world I have come to appreciate
what at first glance appears to be their limited abilities. They have courage, if not sense." Gesturing at
the all but worshipful humans gazing up at him, he
continued in the language of Cybertron.

"These here seek to make use of us for their own
purposes. As their wants are those of simple, unen-
lightened organisms, I find it amusing to supply them.
And when we have terminated the last of the Autobots, we will need appropriately submissive subordi-

nates to help us administer this world." Raising his gaze he peered off into the night, his advanced optics allowing him to see far into the rain and distance despite the darkness. "Unlike Megatron, I see no benefit in extermination for extermination's sake. In certain circumstances and under the right conditions properly trained insects can be useful, not unlike drones.

"One reason the Autobots defeated us in battle here was because of the interference of the local organics. We both overlooked and underestimated their capabilities. They have weapons that can harm even Cybertronian bodies."

In an instant of observation Macerator had examined, evaluated, and dismissed the devices being carried by the small group of humans before him. "I perceive nothing here that could mar the polish on my neck, much less inflict damage."

"These are simple weapons, examples of those produced by humans for killing one another."

"Killing one another?" Macerator eyed his superior in confusion. "Do irreconcilable differences exist among them as they do among Autobots and Decepticons?"

"More even than that. The organics are split into dozens, even hundreds of dissenting groups, each convinced it and it alone is in possession of the right path to prosperity, to success, to an imagined afterlife. Apparently they have existed in this archaic condition since they first developed intelligence."

Macerator considered. "From your description it does not sound to me as if they have developed intelligence at all."

"Not as we know it. It is true insect intelligence, where the workers blindly follow the scent trails laid down by their leaders. It is therefore a simple matter to make use of them. Observe."

Stretching out a hand palm-downward, Starscream generated a small flux within his internal synthesizers. An opening appeared in his palm and a minuscule quantity of a particular basic element spilled toward the ground. Taking the shape of small discs, the element gleamed even in the darkness. Cries immediately rose from the assembled rebels. They fell to the ground, scrabbling in the mud, dirtying themselves as each man fought to gather up as many of the tiny discs as he could. Careful was tempted to join them, except that he knew he would be shot.

"You see?" Starscream regarded the vulgar scramble with more bemusement than contempt. "Provide this element in insignificant quantities and the organics further prove their degenerate nature."

Macerator found it difficult to believe what he was seeing. "Even arthropod organics behave more sensibly. They fight only for territory and food. Not tiny bits of metal." Once more he turned his gaze to his superior. "These creatures really can manufacture weapons systems that pose a threat to us?"

"Their slavish devotion to such inconsequentialities as you see before you is exceeded only by their contradictions," Starscream assured him. "We can make use of both." Again he let his perception roam the surrounding forest, empty save for the animals that were taking shelter from the storm.

Using one hand, Dropkick had lifted up the rear of the delivery truck and was studying its undercarriage.

"This is a simple vehicle, even for one of human design. I could mimic it easily."

"Do you *want* to carry humans? Keep the form you have already chosen," Starscream advised him. "Humans are sensitive to exact duplication and react differently to it than we do. They are defined by their differences, not by their similarities."

Dropkick nodded as he eased the multi-ton truck gently back onto its wheel base. "I am fond of the shape I have chosen. It boasts a primitive elegance."

"Aesthete," Macerator growled. "Observe and admire a form far more functional and useful for our purpose."

Dropping forward, he commenced to change. As he had previously, Careful observed the shift with a mixture of fascination and fear. The place where the squat metal demon had once stood was now occupied by a wheeled vehicle of brute force: a trash collector designed not only to gather industrial waste but to shred everything from metal to plastic with the rotating saws that were mounted above and just behind the main cab.

"Primitive." Transforming into his chosen terrestrial guise even faster than his counterpart, Dropkick raced his high-performance engine.

Starscream had to step between them to prevent disagreement from turning into open conflict. In accordance with the plan he had devised to draw the Autobots out of hiding, he and his new companions would make their way southward on this landmass, acquiring more and more human followers along the way. By the time his designs came to fruition they would be in a position to destroy Optimus Prime,

Ironhide, Ratchet, and any other ill-advised allies the surviving Autobots had succeeded in gathering around them. Once that had been accomplished, seizing complete control of this miserable world would be a simple matter of enforcing favorable logistics through terror. Even the self-proclaimed insect "general" who had thrown in his lot and that of his men with the Decepticons agreed that this could be accomplished.

But along the way, Starscream knew, he would have to keep those of his own kind from beating themselves into scrap. It would be incumbent on him to administer the occasional physical as well as verbal drubbing to hotheads like Dropkick and Macerator. They would be of no use to him if they wasted time and energy fighting one another. As with any destructive power their aggressive natures had to be guided, had to be channeled, lest they destroy themselves instead of their enemies. Aiding him in this purpose Starscream had the benefit of experience as well as talent.

Megatron would have had another name for it. He would have called it deviousness. But Megatron was done, finished, dumped in a deep corner of this world's oceans. A figure of vaunted Cybertronian history, but history nonetheless.

As he moved forward to question the clearly terrified human prisoner, he reflected that this was not necessarily a bad thing.

5

While the land for the storage yard at Makoli was suitably flat, a fair amount of local forest had to be cut down to make room for the steady stream of supplies. The project was a cooperative venture of several regional governments, whose intent and hope were to have everything ready for the construction of the third great dam whenever financing and environmental approval were forthcoming.

Downriver from the immense cascade of Mosioatunya, The Smoke That Thunders (better known as Victoria Falls), the mighty Zambezi ripped its way through the black basalt of the Batoka Gorge before being hemmed in and tamed by the two great dams at Kariba and Cahorra Bassa. Though such large dams had long been disparaged by conservation groups and others, both projects were considered comparative successes. The vast lakes they impounded behind them had created fisheries where none had existed before and provided new opportunities for year-round farming in what previously had been depressed regions. Most importantly, their tremendous hydroelectric capacity kept the wheels of industry spinning in more than half a dozen surrounding countries.

Because of all that had been achieved by the two

dams, regional planners had long eyed the steep gorge below the falls as the site for a third. The Zambezi had still more power to give, and it was wanted for their growing economies. So while no formal go-ahead had yet been given for the proposed Batoka dam, several international consortiums hopeful of participating in the giant construction project had spent years quietly preparing for the eventuality by building up the Makoli staging site.

Millions of dollars in machinery and material lay neatly stacked and cataloged on the cleared, hard-packed soil. Huge earthmovers stood like frozen dinosaurs beneath protective tarps. Enormous I-beams and rolls of cold steel reached to the edge of the surrounding forest while pallets of rebar stretched to the near horizon. Mountains of bagged premixed concrete, crates of industrial fasteners, half acres of tools, and carefully labeled specialized supplies baked in the tropical sun. Tubes of industrial sealant lay like artillery shells in their dispensing racks. A humming three-wire strand that carried enough voltage to shock a would-be thief all the way to Cairo occupied the grassless corridor that separated the doubled ten-foot-high, razor-wire-topped chain-link fence that enclosed the storage yard.

Such a massive accumulation of expensive industrial supplies demanded that security be provided by more than the typical private security force. In addition to mercenary expat contractors retained by several individual suppliers desirous of defending their contributions, elements of the Zambian army also patrolled the roadways that separated the mountains of material. These multiple layers of security ensured that theft and graft were greatly reduced. The private security employees watched the mercenaries, the mercenaries watched the army, and the army kept an eye on the private security employees. Everyone who had contributed to the stockpile was happy with the result—except for the private security employees, the mercenaries, and the army, none of whom could filch any of the stored goods without being reported on by their equally frustrated counterparts.

Having worked as a mercenary since leaving Joburg at the age of nineteen, there was little Harin Vashrutha had not seen—or at least heard about. But the arrival of the beat-up beer delivery truck at the front gate of the storage yard was a new one in his experience. Lined up behind it were two far more impressive vehicles: a brand-new large pickup and what appeared to be a heavy-duty garbage truck.

This peculiar convoy was preceded by a jeep in which rode several armed men clad in unidentifiable fatigues. As there were only four of them, plus the beer truck driver, Vashrutha was not concerned. Before he emerged from the comfort of the open-sided guardhouse and its overworked fan, he lowered the volume on the small television he had been watching. He also flipped a silent alarm so that the indicator light above the switch changed from green to yellow. No need, he decided, to go to red. Having followed procedure and prepared for whatever might eventuate, he gripped his Kalashnikov firmly and stepped through the pedestrian portal to confront the unannounced arrivals. The main gate to the supply yard remained closed behind him.

The men in the jeep looked relaxed. An older man

seated in back flaunted stars on the collar of his wrinkled fatigues. Vashrutha was not impressed. Such military insignia could be bought cheaply over the Internet. Of greater significance was the fact that neither the erstwhile senior officer nor any of his soldiers displayed patches indicating that they were members of the Zambian army, the armed forces of Zimbabwe, or any other country participating in the buildup at Makoli. Smiling courteously, the mercenary let one finger gently caress the safety on his weapon as he approached the jeep.

"Can I help you gentlemen?" His gaze rose to the beer truck and the other vehicles idling behind it. For no discernible reason, the pickup truck was racing its engine. Like most men his age, Vashrutha was as fond as anyone of cars fast and fancy. While the pickup's lines were not to his personal taste, its engine certainly sounded impressive. No, more than impressive, he decided. Impatient.

"We are here to pick up certain materials for transshipment." The "general"'s smile widened. "Let us do our job and we won't trouble you."

A strange way to put a simple request, Vashrutha thought. Perhaps the man's English was as irregular as his uniform.

"Most certainly." Cradling the Kalashnikov under one arm, he extended a free hand. "Papers, please."

"Papers?" Leaning forward, the officer spoke to the soldier seated alongside the driver. "Lieutenant Masara, do you have the papers?"

The other man made a show of patting his shirt pockets, then shook his head somberly. "No, General. I have no papers."

What kind of joke was this? Vashrutha took a step back from the jeep, wishing now that he had flipped the entrance gate's alarm indicator to red. Still, without knowing exactly what was going on, it would be best to proceed according to protocol.

"If you have no papers, I cannot let you in. You will have to go into Makoli town and present yourselves to the proper authorities."

"Ah yes," the officer murmured. "The proper authorities. But that should not be necessary, as we have brought our own authorities with us."

Vashrutha blinked, took another look at the beer truck's cab. It was indeed empty except for the driver. "Where are these authorities? In the pickup truck, perhaps?"

"Yes, the 'pickup truck.' " Standing up on the floor of the open jeep, Mashivingo turned and yelled toward the rear of the convoy. "Dropkick! This person will not admit us unless you demonstrate your authority!"

The pickup pulled out of line and came forward. It halted parallel to the jeep, its engine revving loudly. Vashrutha took a couple of steps toward the driver's side but halted halfway.

There was no driver. There was no one in the truck's cab at all.

Peering over the hood, he raised his weapon warily as he once again addressed the occupants of the jeep. "What kind of game are you playing with me? I will have you all arrested. You have no papers, and now you are making fun of me with this remote-controlled truck."

For some reason this produced a rush of laughter

among the men in the jeep. Had Vashrutha taken the time to notice, he would have seen that the driver of the beer truck was shrinking down behind his steering wheel, as if trying to hide himself.

The laughter died down and the officer in the jeep turned suddenly serious. "The truck is not remote-controlled."

"Then who is responsible for it?" the mercenary asked sharply.

A new voice snapped a reply. "I am responsible for myself, as are all who call themselves Decepticons."

Increasingly uneasy, Vashrutha retreated slowly toward the guard hut, holding his rifle out in front of him. "Who—who said that?" The voice seemed to have come from the empty pickup.

The empty pickup promptly stood up in front of him.

Side panels unfolded as the rear bed of the vehicle went vertical. Headlights revolved into the body of the machine. Wheels rotated upward toward what became shoulders. I-beams and crankshaft whirled inward. Ignoring the jeep and its clearly amused occupants, Vashrutha's gaze locked on the mechanical figure that was rising in front of him. It was at once sleek and powerful. And it was looking directly at him.

"We have no more time for this," it declared in the same sharp voice that had previously claimed responsibility. "We have much work to do and we require certain materials in order to replenish ourselves. We will take them now."

Trembling for the first time in his professional career, Vashrutha trained his gun on the towering shape. "You—you cannot come in! You do not have papers! Without the proper papers I will not open the gate."

Eyes flickering with annoyance met the mercenary's shaky gaze as the mechanical figure leaned in his direction. "That will not be necessary. I will."

Pivoting, Dropkick reached out with both hands. Digging into the metal lattice that was blocking his path, incredibly powerful fingers contracted and then yanked. Sparks flew as alarms were tripped. Wrenching effortlessly, the Decepticon pulled up the gate and threw it aside. Mangled and torn, it smashed into several nearby trees.

Reflexes took over as Vashrutha attempted to block the unauthorized entry. The rounds from his Kalashnikov spanged harmlessly off the gleaming metal flanks of the mechanical intruder. When he heard the whine of the jeep's engine, he shifted the muzzle of his weapon toward a more vulnerable target.

"Halt! I warn you, stop where you are or I will—!"

An invisible force sucked the rifle from his fingers. Looking sharply to his right, the mercenary found himself gazing openmouthed at a second mechanical figure. In outline and color it was very different from the one that had ripped apart the gate. It was also bigger.

Glaring down at the solitary human, Macerator popped the automatic weapon he had just snatched from its owner into his mouth, chewed for perhaps a couple of seconds, and then spat. Vashrutha jumped aside as his gun was returned to him. He recognized the crushed, compacted chunk of metal as having been his weapon because a portion of the trigger lay near its surface.

A sudden whine made him look up again, and this time he had to throw himself to one side as a huge multibladed hand descended toward him. It cut through the air above his diving body before neatly slicing the vacant guard station in half. The upper portion of the small building promptly collapsed in on itself. Disdaining the open gate, Macerator advanced by cutting his own opening in the double fence. When his bladed hand contacted the electrified wire that ran between the two outer barriers, a violent electrical discharge flared briefly as it was shorted out, blinding the aghast mercenary. His weight shaking the earth, Macerator followed Dropkick onto the grounds of the vast supply depot.

As the delivery truck motored past where he was lying, a dazed Vashrutha could see that it carried armed men and not beer. They were cheering and laughing as they saw the missing gate and the nearby section of destroyed fencing. One of them hopped off the back of the truck, ran to the collapsed guard station, picked up Vashrutha's television, and hurried back to rejoin his comrades. The mercenary did not try to stop the theft. He had done all that he could do.

Except quit, which he proceeded to announce by climbing to his feet and running as fast as he could for the nearby forest.

At the far end of the storage yard a gathering of private security guards and other mercenaries were already rushing in the direction of the main gate. Some were on foot while others rode electric carts. The gate that provided access to the west side of the compound opened to admit several squadrons of regular Zambian troops. Caught by surprise by the first general alarm in the history of the complex, some of the men were half dressed. Those on foot struggled to pull on their boots. Their more prepared comrades rode in jeeps and Humvees. Several of the latter were equipped with heavy machine guns. Additional support was provided by a pair of tank-like vehicles that mounted heavy anti-aircraft guns instead of the usual howitzer.

Arriving from a different direction and responding to the urgency of the alarm, a third such vehicle decided to sacrifice protocol in favor of speed as it ignored the south gate and bashed its way through the fence line to join the hastily assembling response force.

Shots began to ring out as the rebels in the truck and jeep engaged the first defenders. While the attackers were more heavily armed than the supply depot's security guards, the equation soon changed as mercenaries and soldiers arrived to join the battle. With several of their members hit, the invaders were forced to fall back.

Their retreat did not last long.

Plowing forward, Macerator smashed his way through piles of supplies, scattering building materials in all directions. Security operatives fled before him, but not the rapidly growing group of mercenaries and army troops. Despite the absence of a direct chain of command linking them, in the face of a common threat the two groups joined forces with admirable speed.

"Major Ghiwa, get your men under cover behind

those beams!" a mercenary officer named du Hoit
yelled.

The Zambian officer hesitated, then nodded in response. "See if your people can get around behind
this thing. We will try to hold it until you can flank."

The mercenary snapped a quick salute. "*Ja ek
weet* . . . okay! Be sure your people stay under cover.
We don't want any of you caught in the line of fire."
Whirling, he raced off to rally his fellow hirelings,
shouting commands above the gunfire in a raw mixture of English and Afrikaans.

Ghiwa hurriedly withdrew his forces to the indicated position. "Get that machine gun set up!" he
roared. "Where are the RPGs?" Looking to his left as
he ran for shelter, he cursed in several tribal languages
as well as English. "And where the devil is that heavy
armor?"

The two anti-aircraft tanks were on their way with
the third coming up fast behind, but unlike soldiers
on foot they had to navigate around rather than over
or through the mass of building material.

Ghiwa threw himself down behind the machine-
gun operators, who had finally managed to get the
heavy M60 up on its tripod. What they really needed,
he knew, was a Dillon M134, but the always cash-
strapped government had no money for such advanced
weapons. He had to lean close to the operators to
make himself heard above the racket of small-arms
fire.

"Not there, not there!" To get the gunner's attention he slapped a palm down hard on the man's helmet. "Forget about the rabble around the delivery
truck." Raising an arm, he pointed. "Take out that

recycling vehicle. We don't know what's inside. It might be a bomb. Or even a dirty bomb."

The gunner looked back at him, confused. "Sir, what is a dirty bomb?"

"Never mind. Just shoot!" A dirty bomb, the major knew, would be a device favored in current circumstances not only by eco-terrorists wishing to disrupt the future construction of the Batoka dam, but also by criminals or rebels seeking to extort money from the construction consortium. Setting one off in the depot could contaminate and render useless tens of millions of dollars in supplies. Or the garbage truck could simply contain explosives or additional fighters.

The rumbling, squealing vehicle did not contain any of those destructive elements, however. It was a destructive element all by itself.

As the rebels cheered from behind the protection of their jeep and the delivery truck, the hulking waste collector began to alter shape, rising up on columnar legs until he loomed over the surrounding supply yard. While small-caliber slugs and the larger shells from the heavy machine gun ricocheted off his armored flanks, Macerator studied the local resistance. Though active and defiant, it was every bit as primitive as Starscream had described. Further changing shape and function, arms swiftly became armature.

Construction supplies and bodies flew in all directions as explosive shells began to land among the defending soldiers. Ducking and rolling backward, Ghiwa yelled to his men.

"Spread out! Aim for the thing's head!"

Scrambling to his left, he tried to avoid being blown

to bits as he raced for the gate that led back to the barracks. At the same time he found himself wondering—what could the huge mechanical invaders possibly want with a yard full of construction supplies?

Time enough if he survived to ponder the motivation of assailants whose intentions were as incomprehensible as their appearance. Right now he had to get to the barracks to file an emergency report. Cell phone reception in the Makoli area was intermittent, but there was a broadband connection in his office. If his men and du Hoit's could keep the rebels and their strange war machines occupied, he could sound a warning and call for help.

Something exploded against Macerator's back. Pivoting, he searched for the source of the irritation. A second explosion tickled his chin. Ah, there. More of the tiny organics, firing self-propelled explosives at him. These were far too feeble to even scratch his armor, but the smoke and noise were a distraction. Raising his right arm, he unleashed a small missile. Dirt, powdered concrete, wood framing, and an assortment of human detritus shot skyward as the missile struck home. The irritation promptly vanished. Ignoring the lighter fire that continued to pepper him, he resumed his advance toward the concrete-reinforced building in the center of the compound. While he was surrounded by much that was useful, his perceptors had informed him that the isolated structure contained the choicest prize. Bullets of varying caliber fell from his flanks like dark raindrops.

Questioning whether his mercenary counterpart and colleague du Hoit was still alive, Ghiwa scrambled from behind a three-story-high stack of precast steel arches and sprinted toward the open access gate. No shells or missiles landed near him. If his luck held he would be inside the barracks and online on his computer within minutes. He darted through the gate—only to have to halt sharply as a vehicle he did not recognize pulled up to block his path. He waved furiously at the pickup's driver.

"Move, move—get out of the way! Don't you see what's happening? I have to send word!"

Something creaked beneath the pickup. No, not beneath, he told himself. Within it. Metal began to crumple and fold, to rearrange itself. Staring, Ghiwa slowly backed up toward the gate from which he had just emerged. As he did so it occurred to him that the pickup's driver had looked exactly like a lower-level guard named Vashrutha. *Had* looked like, because now there was no driver. There was no need for one.

Dropkick contemplated the single human retreating before him. "You are not armed. I am disappointed. Even an unequal contest is better than none."

Feeling it was futile but hoping for luck, Ghiwa drew his service pistol and began emptying its clip at the monster. If nothing else, maybe the .45 would distract it. Slugs that would have drilled completely through a human barely made a sound as they bounced off the Decepticon's body. As he fired, the major turned and fled back the way he had come.

In an attempt to make the contest interesting since he could not make it fair, Dropkick did not unlimber any of his main batteries. Instead he reached out, grabbed the nearest section of fence, and pulled. Poles and wire mesh tore out of the ground. When he had extracted a suitable length, the Decepticon rolled it tightly, flung his arm back, and then snapped it forward. The coiled metal unfurled like a flattened whip. The pole at the end struck the unfortunate Ghiwa and sent him sprawling. When his body stopped rolling, it remained still.

It was not what Dropkick had intended. His aim had been to catch the fleeing human in a roll of fence and draw him back. The Decepticon did not dwell on the failure. Turning, he started toward the empty barracks. There would be communications devices inside that needed to be eliminated. There might also be weapons or combustibles. He hoped for the latter. Far from home, and with the Allspark destroyed, it was vital to stockpile potential sources of distilled Energon whenever possible. Depending on the type of material here, it was a potential source, though he wondered if the yield would be worth the effort.

Behind him and within the boundaries of the supply depot, combat continued to rage. He felt neither need nor hurry to join in. Macerator had not called for assistance. Given the feebleness of the forces arrayed against them, Dropkick doubted his comrade would do so.

A series of shells heavier than any that had yet struck him slammed into Macerator's torso. While unable to penetrate his armor, they were powerful enough that the outside possibility existed they could do some minor damage if they happened to strike an especially vulnerable point when he was not paying attention. There being no reason to take chances, while he evaluated the new threat he took a couple of steps to one side and sought temporary shelter behind a small mountain of metal parts.

What he saw would have brought a lump to his throat except that such comparisons with organic reactions were utterly invalid. Grinding in his direction, a pair of armored vehicles were firing steadily at him with quadruple cannons. Their purely mechanical aspect gave them the appearance of a squad of legless representatives of his own kind. While the shells being fired by the multiple Bofors barrels were not of threatening dimensions, they traveled at high velocity and with considerable accuracy. It might prove awkward should one or more of them explode against a joint or a lens. As explosions erupted all around him, Macerator considered how best to counter this latest human assault. He had to admit that if the natives' weapons were not the most advanced, they at least had the virtue of diversity.

He was about to commence his counterattack when the nearer of the two vehicles blew up in a shower of flame and exploding ordnance. Peering out from behind his temporary cover, he saw that the guns had been blown off their mount and were lying on the ground next to the burning vehicle. As the second tank rushed to swing its own guns around, it, too, came under fire from behind. Shells ripped through the top of the machine, tearing away antennas and destroying weaponry. Effectively disarmed, the vehicle's crew abandoned it and bolted in all directions. A couple of them managed to make it to surrounding cover.

Resuming its advance, the third anti-aircraft tank halted alongside the heavily reinforced single-story structure that had been the object of Macerator's attention. As he looked on it rose up off its treads, the dark armor shifting and repositioning itself, until he found himself gazing back into visual receptors that were all but identical to his own. Stepping out from behind the mass of metal where he had momentarily taken refuge, the Decepticon strode forward to meet the new arrival.

"Greetings, Payload. You did well to conceal yourself until your presence was required."

The other Decepticon nodded at his colleague. "When I first arrived on this world Starscream told me I would have no difficulty in choosing an indigenous mode that would reflect not only my personal but also my aesthetic preferences. He was correct." Surveying their surroundings he was disappointed by what he saw, but hardly surprised. "It appears that the natives have now decided to invest in flight rather than fight. A pity. Though hardly much of a challenge, battling them has been a learning experience."

"I agree." Macerator joined his comrade in watching as the surviving humans fled into the surrounding bush. "While individually they are harmless, in packs they can be annoying and, according to Starscream, even dangerous. Underestimating their conjoined capabilities has cost us the Sparks of several."

"So I was informed. Seeing them fleeing like this, it is a hard thing to countenance."

"I was not there myself, of course, but Starscream assures me it was so. Megatron himself was brought low by a single human."

As the volume of small-caliber shells splintering against his body continued to decline, Payload found himself brooding on the seemingly impossible.

"I was told what had transpired, but I believe that

Starscream was given to leaving out certain details. He favors short phrases emphasizing his own contributions, and tends to shout."

"I know. I understand that Megatron's passing was ironic. A Decepticon deceived, was how Starscream put it. No matter. He insists that he has learned more than enough to allow us to take complete control of this world, and that both it and its diminutive but resourceful population can be put to good use. He assures me that when this work is finished we will not only control all of this planet but be in position to destroy the last of the Autobots and regain complete control of Cybertron as well."

Payload was not as much given to contemplation as some of his colleagues, but Macerator's narrative still gave him pause.

"In the past, Starscream has been known to promise many things."

"We must follow his guidance. He is our leader now that Megatron is dead."

Lens locked with lens. "Are you and Dropkick certain he is dead? Should he return and find that we have allied ourselves fully with Starscream, I would fear for my Spark."

Macerator did not hesitate. "Starscream has shown recordings of the great battle that occurred earlier on this world. Megatron's Spark was merged with the Allspark. There is no question that he is dead."

"Then we follow Starscream. For the present." Payload looked toward the building behind which Macerator had been standing. "I sense a source of potential energy within this structure." Arms rose and took aim; one consisted of a revolving cannon, while the other was heavy with missiles of advanced design. "I will make an entrance."

One metal arm came down to restrain another. "That would be unwise. While I, too, am eager to make use of the material within, Starscream warned me that as creative as they are, these humans have not yet learned how to properly stabilize much of their weaponry. I fear that your method of choice might result in the activation and consequent loss of that which we seek to utilize." He stepped forward. "Defer if you will to a more localized and gentler methodology."

Folding in upon itself, a weapons-holding hand gave way to a quintet of incredibly sharp carbon-edged blades. A deep whine filled the air as they began to spin at an impossible speed. Bending forward, Macerator touched his cutting blades to the side of the squat building before him. He proceeded to cut through the thick outer wall of the structure as delicately as a surgeon cracking a chest cavity. Several slices later, Payload joined him in lifting the excised section of roof and setting it aside. The need for the structure's massive, angled concrete walls stood revealed.

Within lay enough industrial explosives to destroy a small city. Or reduce a basalt gorge to transportable rubble.

Gesturing with both hands, Macerator stepped aside. "After you."

"No, no." Payload waved one hand deferentially. "After you. The one who gains entrance always precedes."

"As you wish."

6

Anyone traveling down the southern part of the narrow island's single-lane road of hard-packed coral rubble would hardly have looked twice at the motorcycle and tow truck parked side by side facing the open ocean. Workers from the main part of the atoll or from NEST itself often relaxed by taking short drives away from their respective work areas. While the inner lagoon at Diego Garcia offered quiet water, the ocean side was cooler and richer in sea life.

Had such visitors paused, however, they might have been puzzled to see that no one was snorkeling or diving in front of the parking area. No laughter drifted in on the Indian Ocean wind from picnickers enjoying a day off. No daytime idlers were visible beachcombing for sea glass or shells. The two vehicles sat by themselves, to all intents and purposes abandoned and alone. They were neither, of course. They had each other for company. A visitor might also have noted that no one sat behind the vehicle of the brawny tow truck, and that in defiance of normal motorcycle physics, the powerful two-wheeler somehow managed to remain upright without its kickstand deployed.

"I still don't understand why we weren't asked to

accompany the expedition." Seeking a temporary perch from which to watch for meandering crabs, a seagull settled down atop one of the motorcycle's gleaming handlebars. A sharp blast from the bike's horn sent it squawking seaward.

Longarm was amusing himself by alternately flashing his headlights at a feral cat. The cat would jump at high beam, retreat, then leap at the other, always falling back before making contact. This world was an endless banquet of fascinating organics, the Autobot mused, and in his personal opinion humans were not necessarily the most attractive ones.

"You heard what Optimus said. Sending all of us after Starscream might better ensure success, but if they fail to find him and another crisis should erupt while the bulk of our forces are occupied elsewhere, NEST must be able to draw on at least a minimum of Autobot strength to counter it." The big towing arm swung sideways so that the tip of its heavy hook barely grazed the motorcycle's seat. "That's you and I here, Bumblebee elsewhere."

"But why us? Salvage and Beachbreak are just as new to this world as we are. Why not have them stay behind?"

"I don't know, but I'm sure Optimus has his reasons. My lineage is longer than yours, Knockout, and if there's one thing I know for a certainty, it's that Optimus Prime *always* has his reasons. Keep in mind also that he knows this world and its dominant organic species better than anyone. We are no longer alone in this fight against Starscream and cannot act as if we are."

"Humans. If not out of consideration for them and

their 'feelings,' we could scour this world far more openly. We would already have found Starscream and dealt with him! If he is even *on* this world any longer."

"Do not be so sure of yourself. Starscream's cunning exceeds even his physical abilities. Furthermore, in his Earth guise he can travel farther and faster than any of us. It forces him to appear as himself when he touches ground, but it also gives him great range and the ability to conceal himself in many places."

"*I'd* find him." Coming to life with a roar, the motorcycle lofted an impressive fishtail of beach sand as it wheelied toward the water. At the last possible instant it spun around, kicking sand and dirt into the sea, and returned to rejoin the tow truck.

"You shouldn't do that." Longarm would have shaken his head had he been presenting one. "Even on this island across from the humans' main base we're not supposed to reveal ourselves or our abilities unless it's absolutely necessary."

"What abilities?" Knockout flashed his headlight. "I haven't altered my appearance."

"No, but there is no driver on your seat. It is not normal for human vehicles to move about under their own power without a guiding human on board. When we are out like this, even on the island that is headquarters for NEST, we need to be careful not to draw attention to ourselves."

Knockout rumbled sullenly. "So much time spent underground. Nowhere to explore. I chose this guise for its aesthetics and mobility, but also because it can cover long distances at high speed. I want to make use of it, not be strangled by it."

"As long as there are Decepticons to worry about, we must restrict our activities and our actions." Longarm spoke sternly to his compatriot. "Our other objective is to protect our human allies. It is not to go gallivanting about this new world as though all were right with the cosmos."

"But it's such an *interesting* world," Knockout objected. "Even some of the humans, those not constipated by self-importance and a surplus of gravity, are interesting. I want to see more of their home and meet more of them."

"Collective survival must perforce take precedence over individual satisfaction." Longarm's tone was somber. "There will be ample time for exploration and enjoyment once our aims have been accomplished."

" 'Our aims.' " The motorcycle roared petulantly. "How many more long cycles must we wait before these are accomplished? Is existence until then to be restricted to nothing more than waiting and fighting, waiting and fighting?"

"Until the last fight, it must always be so."

"And will there be a 'last' fight?"

Engaging its engine, the tow truck started to back up toward the road. "Optimus thinks so. Megatron is finished. Terminate Starscream on this world and manage the journey back to Cybertron. Then we can at last begin to rebuild that which was destroyed, and recover all that was lost to us." With the motorcycle hastening to catch up, the truck turned and rumbled out onto the island's single track.

"Meanwhile, Optimus Prime is our leader and we

must do as he says. I have never known him to err in judgment."

"There's always a first time."

The truck's brakes locked up. "What? What did you say, Knockout?"

"Nothing." The motorcycle's engine revved loudly. "Race you back to the base!"

Longarm did not even make the attempt. The other Autobot's capacity to accelerate exceeded that of his own heavier guise by several orders of magnitude. Sand and gravel spit backward by the cycle's rear tire clinked off Longarm's grille and windshield. These did no damage either to his local form or to his ego.

Knockout was impatient. Such eagerness could be channeled, such energy needed to be utilized. But as he followed his comrade back to NEST headquarters at a more leisurely pace, Longarm could not help but reflect on his earlier words.

If there was to be a fight soon with Starscream, he would have wanted to be in on it, too.

"I don't get it."

Riding in the cab of the big diesel that was Optimus Prime's chosen terrestrial form, Lennox directed his bemusement not to Sergeant Epps, who though seated behind the wheel never laid a hand on it, nor to Kaminari or Petr who occupied the wide seat behind them. Instead he addressed himself to empty air—or more precisely, to the perfectly smooth dash in front of him. The response, when it came, issued from speakers that filled the truck cab with sound. When he spoke thus to those he was transporting, Optimus was careful to lower his voice to a comparative whisper so as not to damage fragile organic auditory apparatus. To Kaminari it sounded as if the cab were inhabited by a resolute ghost speaking in a perfectly normal tone of voice.

"It is evident that other Decepticons have arrived on Earth," the leader of the Autobots remarked. "Just as the signal I have been sending out has drawn others of my kind such as Salvage and Beachbreak, Longarm and Knockout to your world, so Starscream must have been propagating a call for assistance."

"Unless it is Megatron's doing." Sitting behind Epps, Petr was intent on an inch-long iridescent green beetle that had flown in through an open window and was now tentatively exploring the back of the Russian's left hand.

"Megatron can't send a damn postcard." Though he was sitting behind the wheel, Epps made no attempt to manipulate the "controls" laid out in front of him. Like his companions, he was only a passenger. The cord dangling from his right ear connected to the powerful portable computer resting on his lap. "He's done, dead, and drowned."

"I concur." Optimus's reassuring voice drifted softly through the cab. "Therefore these new Decepticons must have been drawn here in response to a call from Starscream. Which in turn confirms the suspicions raised by the initial reports of an aircraft matching his chosen terrestrial mode overflying this region. He is here, somewhere, and we will find him."

"What about these new Decepticons?" Kaminari shifted in her seat. "Do we know anything about them?"

Leaning to her right, she glanced in the side-view

mirror. An ambulance and two pickup trucks kicked up dust behind the diesel as the small convoy rumbled down the dirt road. While an unusual group of vehicles for the area, it was not so outrageous as to attract more than casual attention from the driver of the occasional other oncoming vehicle or the occupants of the small villages through which they were passing. Any casual onlooker would have seen just a trio of trucks, heading south toward the river.

"I wish we had images." Lennox spoke without turning, his attention fixed on the road ahead. "But while the cell phone coverage in this part of the world is adequate, it can be intermittent. And soldiers and mercenaries locked in the middle of a firefight usually don't have time to whip out their phones and take snapshots." He looked back at her. "So all we have to go on are the confused reports of a few frightened survivors."

"Three of them, to be exact." Epps put his feet up on the dash. Optimus did not object. "What I don't understand is that according to the reports, they didn't get bombed. That's Starscream's modus operandi: strafing and bombing. But according to what we were told, all the action was confined to the ground. Guns and missiles goin' off all over the place, but nothing raining down from above." A slight electrical charge tickled his feet and he hastily took them off the dash. His attention returned to the screen of the laptop that was positioned on his upper thighs.

"Yeah," Lennox agreed. "And none of the descriptions of the three Decepticons that participated in the attack match up with Starscream's natural body shape." Reaching forward, he tapped the truck console. "So what gives, big guy?"

"Knowing Starscream," Optimus replied, "this might be his way of luring us into a trap. If so, he has succeeded. We are indeed coming for him. Whatever he has planned, I do not think he can defeat five of us operating with human assistance. That is why it is important there are only four of you. Were we to try to confront him with a massive contingent of human soldiers and weapons, I am convinced he would not risk an appearance. Not after his defeat at Mission City. But against myself and a few Autobots, with only a quartet of humans to back us up, I think he will risk whatever he has in mind for the chance to destroy Ratchet, Ironhide, and myself."

"Of one thing we can be certain." Sticking his hand out the open window, Petr let the wind carry away the iridescent beetle.

"Yeah, what's that?" Epps had reluctantly traded his music player for a communications headset.

"We will soon find out," the Russian replied.

Edging forward on the bench seat, Kaminari accidentally bumped into Lennox and was quick to murmur an apology. He was still trying to figure her out. The scientist, whose name meant "thunder" in Japanese, was more than a little strange. As Epps had pointed out, an idiosyncratic combination of geek and warrior. But how would she and her experimental weapon work in the field? As Petr had just said, they would soon find out.

"Where do you think they're heading?" she asked.

"No telling." The captain grabbed a handgrip as Optimus hit a bump that jostled his passengers. Apologizing, the Autobot slowed his speed in an effort to smooth out the ride. Lennox continued.

"It's pretty clear from the reports of those who survived the confrontation at the construction staging depot that whoever these Decepticons are, they were after potential sources for synthetic Energon. According to Optimus, based on what was taken they should have adequate power for the time being. But why they would remain in this area we simply don't know. There's nothing of vital strategic importance in the region where they were last seen heading. No military bases, no population centers—nothing but scattered small villages and a lot of wildlife. Which is good for us."

"Right," said Kami. Her expression hardened as she settled back on her seat. "Because when all hell breaks loose, collateral damage will be minimized."

Their conversation was interrupted by Epps. Staring at his laptop screen, the technical sergeant straightened. The excitement in his voice was palpable.

"All right! We have contact."

As he ignored the road in front of them, his fingers began to dance over the computer keys. Though word of the Decepticons' presence in this area had been kept as quiet as possible to prevent panic among the local population, the authorities were well aware of what happened at the construction site supply compound. Hasty instructions had gone out to all regional authorities to be on the lookout for the invaders. While a garbage truck and a pickup might not draw much attention, the presence of an anti-aircraft tank rumbling through a town was certain to attract notice.

A uniformed policeman in just such an insignificant village had personally witnessed the three-vehicle procession as it traveled at high speed through his community. As soon as it was safely past, he had reported its presence via his phone. The alert had gone to the nearest district police station. From there it had been relayed to Lusaka, then to Zambian military headquarters. An officer there had activated a special signal that had sent the information upward to a communications satellite, which in turn had forwarded it to the nearest of six recently launched NEST satellites, which had simultaneously provided the relevant information to Diego Garcia and the operations team that was on the ground rolling through southern Zambia.

Leaning to his left, Lennox joined his fellow soldier in studying the data displayed on the screen. "We're close." Straightening, he compared the road immediately ahead with the detailed map that had appeared on Epps's GPS-equipped computer.

"If this is correct, they're barely two kilometers in front of us, Optimus. Turn left off the main road." Behind him, Kaminari scrambled for something to hang on to as the diesel began to rattle and shake.

"This is a main road?"

Reaching across, the Russian gave her a playful shove. "This is not Yokohama freeway, *miloshka.*"

She glared at him. "It's not Yekaterinburg, either. Don't touch me again."

Grinning, he slowly advanced one outthrust finger in her direction.

"I'm warning you," she told him irritably.

"What are you going to do?" he challenged her. "Give karate demonstration from seated position?"

Changing conditions put a stop to such horseplay as Optimus led the team off the north–south road onto a side track that was barely wide enough to accommodate a wayward jeep. Despite the Autobot's best efforts to anticipate the increasing number of ravines and hillocks, a certain amount of bumping and jouncing inside the cab was inevitable. Behind him, Ratchet, Ironhide, and Salvage hewed to the new route with determination. Trees and brush slapped against the sides of the careering diesel. Any human-driven truck of comparable size attempting to negotiate the upgraded goat track would by now have blown tires, busted axles, or crashed into the surrounding brush.

Like the soldiers up front, Kaminari and Petr were too busy trying to keep their heads from slamming against the roof to waste energy arguing. Lennox stared as Optimus smashed through several trees whose trunks had grown sideways across the track.

Where on Earth were the Decepticons going, and why?

Somehow Epps managed to stay focused on his computer readout. "Closing fast!" He had to shout to make himself heard above the chaos of the truck as it crashed through increasingly dense brush. "Almost on 'em. Why aren't they moving faster, trying to get away? Surely they know by now that we're on to them?"

Raising an arm, Lennox pointed. "Maybe because they're out of road."

A moment later the view ahead cleared. The vista

thus revealed was breathtaking. Blue sky shone above the line of forest green that dominated the bank opposite. Directly ahead of the slowing diesel, a herd of wildebeest were hurrying to one side while a clutch of hippos were rushing to get out of the way of three large, singular metallic figures. Unable to cross the wide, powerful, deep river in their Earthly forms, the three Decepticons had reverted to their natural shapes. There were no humans around to record their presence, no scouts to report on their appearance.

Optimus screeched to a halt as the rapidly shrinking road vanished into a sandbar. "Autobots, transform!" he bellowed, barely giving the four humans he had been transporting enough time to vacate his cab. While Epps shut down his laptop and abandoned it to Optimus's care, Lennox and the others were on the ground and running back the length of the big truck.

Befitting his specialty as the group's weapons expert, Ironhide was already on his feet. In front of him, the ambulance was shifting to reveal itself as Ratchet. Salvage waited until the humans reached him and idled patiently as they removed several tarp-covered devices from his truck bed. Meanwhile Beachbreak hummed impatiently on his back. As soon as the humans had taken what they needed, the pickup truck rumbled to life and crashed off along the bank, its four-wheel drive keeping it level and moving forward.

Freed of the need to monitor the laptop, Epps was once more in his element as he hefted a backpack crammed with special, recently developed sabot shells. Lennox hoisted the launcher itself. As for Petr, the captain did not recognize the rifle-like device the stocky scientist was unwrapping. He knew only that it was something innovative that had been hastily developed by the Russian Academy of Sciences working in conjunction with the weapons specialists at NEST. Kaminari had drawn her own unique weapon from an oversized holster strapped to her back.

The Earth quivered slightly as Optimus came up alongside him. His weapons systems fully deployed, Ironhide flanked the humans while Ratchet brought up the rear and stood ready in reserve. Frowning as he ran, Lennox looked around anxiously.

"Where are the others? Salvage and Beachbreak?"

The African sun glinted off bright lenses as Optimus looked down at him. "Hurrying to position themselves, according to my instructions. If all goes well their assistance may not be needed." The Autobot's gaze rose to lock on the hulking bipedal shapes that were presently attempting to cross the river. "It seems that we are three against three, but when two of those three are myself and Ironhide, the odds are very different from the actual numbers." Incredibly advanced visual perceptors focused. New imagery was matched against old memory.

"We are facing Macerator and Dropkick. They are good fighters, but can be taken. Payload will be more of a problem, as his area of expertise is akin to that of Ironhide."

As Kaminari and Petr hurried to try and keep up, Ironhide rumbled expectantly.

"Akin to, perhaps, but *far* from equal." Raising his voice, he bellowed a challenge across the white water. "Payload! Inheritor of futility! Turn and fight!"

That was Ironhide, Lennox thought as he ran. Never one to mince words. Only opponents.

The nearest Decepticon was quick to turn and respond. "Ironhide! It will be a pleasure to watch your component parts detonate one by one!" This comment was punctuated by a puff of smoke from the vicinity of the challenging Decepticon's left shoulder.

"Incoming!" Epps shouted a warning as he dove for the nearest pile of water-worn, car-sized boulders. Payload's missile landed just behind them. The ground where it struck shook as it vomited sand and dirt skyward.

Shells and missiles tore into air, earth, and water as the three Autobots advanced into the roaring river to engage their Decepticon counterparts, each combatant seeking a weak spot on the part of the other. Meanwhile the humans had been forced to halt on the riverbank. While Petr knelt and began making adjustments to the peculiar gun he carried, Kaminari could only watch and wait in nervous anticipation.

"Why do they have to fight in the river? Why can't they come over here? I can't reach any of them this way!"

Petr glanced up at her. "What—can't you swim?"

"Look at this river, you idiot! Look at the way the current is flowing. This isn't some gently meandering Siberian salmon stream. This is the Zambezi! Besides the current, it's full of hippopotamuses and crocodiles."

"Not at the moment." He pointed.

It was true. From where they stood on the riverbank it looked as if every living thing within half a kilometer was racing to get as far as possible away from the scene of battle. Hippos, crocs, buffalo, even elephants were fleeing upriver or into the bush, leaving the water to the half dozen towering mechanical combatants.

Lennox hurried to activate the launcher he carried. Despite Optimus's confident claim, the initial stages of the fight did not appear to be going nearly as well for the Autobots as their leader had envisaged. For one thing the river here was fast and deep enough to inhibit the movements of Autobot and Decepticon alike. Had that been the Decepticons' plan all along: to lure their opponents into the water, hoping that it would equalize the odds? If so, either Optimus had not considered the current and depth factors, or else he was convinced he and his comrades could overcome them. After all, the Zambezi was nobody's ally. It slowed Decepticon and Autobot alike. It also made it much more difficult for Lennox to lock onto a target with his own weapon.

The tube he was balancing on his right shoulder was a modified Stinger ground-to-air missile launcher. Unlike its predecessors, which were designed to be discarded once used, the lightweight titanium-and-carbon-fiber device the captain struggled to aim could be reused multiple times. That was important because Epps's backpack contained a dozen highly compact self-propelled rounds. Each was tipped with the new armor-penetrating sabot round that had been developed by American and Israeli members of NEST working in conjunction with Ironhide. At NEST's underground testing range on Diego Garcia, the two men had had plenty of practice in firing the new weapon.

Unfortunately, none of it had involved firing at a target that was locked in close physical combat with an ally in the midst of a wide, fast-flowing tropical river.

"Loaded and locked!" Slamming the back of the launcher shut, Epps gave the captain a slap on the shoulder to indicate that he could fire at any time. While the launcher's weight had been pared to the minimum it was still considerably more difficult to aim than, say, an ordinary rifle. Furthermore, the Zambezi's flow was powerful enough to push all six combatants steadily downstream.

"Fire—Captain, sir!" Epps shouted.

"I can't get a clean line!" Lennox glanced up from the launcher's electronic tracker. "Every time I get a clear sight, one of our guys stumbles into the view-finder and I have to reset." Shouldering the launcher, he found himself scrambling to keep pace with the ongoing battle, running along the shoreline or jumping from rock to rock. Picking up the backpack full of shells, Epps followed.

Out in the middle of the river, cannon fire and missiles had given way to hand-to-hand fighting. The bots were massive and heavy, but the Zambezi was stronger, especially out in the center of the current where the water was deepest. Optimus and Ironhide were locked in combat with the two largest Decepticons, Macerator and Payload, while Ratchet engaged Dropkick. Every time one of the Autobots tried to disengage in order to fire a weapon, its corresponding foe would leap forward to wrestle it back into the water. To Lennox it looked as if the Decepticons were not trying to strike debilitating blows so much as they were fighting some kind of incomprehensible holding action.

To what end? It struck the increasingly winded Lennox as a losing strategy. Each time a Decepticon attacked, the Autobot he was confronting had time to adopt a solid defensive stance. By now Ratchet had suffered only a few glancing blows while Ironhide and Optimus were largely unhurt. In contrast, one of Dropkick's arms was hanging loose. As for the belligerent Payload, unable to bring his heavy integrated weapons systems to bear, he was being ferociously pounded by his relentless counterpart Ironhide. And despite absorbing one crushing blow after another, Macerator clung tenaciously to Optimus, seemingly indifferent to the damage that the leader of the Autobots was inflicting. While the outcome of the clash was far from decided, it was apparent to anyone that the Decepticons were losing, as a group as well as on an individual basis.

Then Payload let go of Ironhide, swept around in a wide circle, and slashed with all his strength. Ironhide did his best to dodge the blow. On land it would have missed completely. But the water shoving him downstream interfered with his footing. Fluids spurted and the Autobot staggered.

"Damn it." Cursing softly, Lennox dropped to a crouch and tried to steady the launcher. The combatants were even farther away now and the roar of the rushing river much louder where he had stopped. Furthermore, the slowly drifting fighters were approaching a fog bank that made singling out potential targets even more difficult. If the battle was swallowed up by the fog, then . . .

An inability to successfully lock onto a target was not the only reason the captain suddenly straightened. "Oh my God," he muttered in abrupt recognition. An anxious Epps came up alongside him.

"What is it, Captain? What's wrong?"

Lennox didn't look over at the tech sergeant. His gaze was mesmerized by the mist that was about to envelop the mechanical combatants.

"I just realized how far downriver we've come."

He was about to elaborate when a sound between a roar and a hiss caused both soldiers to look upstream. Something was rocketing in their direction, moving fast and sending up a fishtail of water behind it.

Beachbreak, finally in his element. And he wasn't alone.

Seated in the driver's seat but freed from any need to steer was a sweating Petr Andronov. Despite the rocking and bouncing, he was trying to balance something on the stealth Jet Ski's front. Lennox was able to make out the strange weapon the Russian had brought with him. Seated directly behind him in the passenger's seat was Kaminari Ishihara. As the two men on shore looked on aghast, despite the danger she rose to a standing position and began sighting her own weapon.

Putting down the launcher, a frantic Lennox began waving his arms to try and draw attention to himself. Not from the new arrivals, who thanks to Beachbreak's abilities were reasonably safe, but in an attempt to alert the other Autobots. It was becoming increasingly, dangerously clear why the Decepticons had chosen to forgo the use of heavy weaponry in favor of hand-to-hand combat. Their choice had nothing to do with tradition, custom, or an inbuilt need to physically demolish their opponents.

They were not called Decepticons for nothing.

Ratchet was first to realize the gravity of the changed circumstances and try to break off the fight. Turning, he began struggling against the current as he fought to make his way toward the shore where the two human soldiers continued to gesticulate wildly. Dropkick fired one shot after him. On land it would have struck the retreating Autobot square in the lower back. In the river, however, the force of the detonation was swallowed up by the now raging, foaming current that reached to Ratchet's shoulders. Frustrated but realizing that pursuit would expose him to whatever surprise the land-based humans might have waiting, the Decepticon also turned away and began fighting to make his way to the opposite bank.

Farther downstream, Payload and Ironhide were still locked in combat. With one shoulder damaged, Ironhide was having a hard time fending off the increasingly potent attacks of his enemy. Payload was reaching back to deliver still another ferocious blow when suddenly he began to twitch, then to shake violently. Turning and looking down, he saw that something had attached itself to his left side. As he reached for it, Petr fired his weapon again. A second small flat object fastened itself to the Decepticon's flank, at which point Payload's contortions intensified. Bringing down his massive fist, he tried to pulverize the small craft that was racing back and forth just upstream from where he was standing. But the Jet Ski was far too agile, and the intended deadly blow crushed only water.

As the Decepticon's fist descended beneath the surface of the river, Beachbreak zoomed in anew. The Russian was reloading, but nothing prevented Kaminari from leaning dangerously over the side. Clinging with one hand to her grip on Beachbreak's back, she extended herself as far as possible and fired her EMP. She and the designers she had worked with at Tsukuba hoped that the sharp pulse generated by the device would be capable of interrupting the energy flow of any internally powered machine. It had only been built with the aid of computer simulations, however. Trying it against something as powerful and alien as a Transformer was not like testing it in a lab.

Payload reacted as the pulse hit his right leg. Though the contact impacted no vital circuits or components, it was powerful enough to generate the mechanical equivalent of a brief muscle spasm. This proved irritating enough that despite the orders he had been given he broke off the fight. Twitching and jerking from the effects of Petr's rifle and Kami's blast, and having to make a conscious effort to maintain his balance, he turned and tottered off in Dropkick's wake.

Once again free of restraining Decepticon arms, Ironhide prepared to unlimber his heavy weapons. He would have a clear shot at the retreating Payload's back. But before he could ready himself, much less take aim, he was confronted by Beachbreak and the smaller Autobot's two human passengers.

"Get back, get back to shore!" Kaminari was yelling at him.

"Why?" The big Autobot looked longingly at Payload's unsteady flight. "I can follow and finish him."

"If you don't get out of this current you'll be finished yourself!" Kaminari gestured into the mist that had already swallowed Optimus and Macerator.

"She is telling you the truth. We must get clear of this place." Having divested himself of that warning, Petr regarded his small rifle with satisfaction. "My colleagues will be pleased. This really does disrupt Decepticon internal current flow."

The Autobot weapons specialist hesitated a moment longer. Then, with a last reluctant look at the stumbling, fleeing Payload, he turned and started toward the shore where the humans Lennox and Epps were jumping up and down and waving at him frantically. What was upsetting them so? Even if they had not destroyed the opposing Decepticons, at least two of them had been seriously damaged and before the fight was over Optimus would surely put an end to Macerator. Ironhide looked into the mist but in his haste could not see either his leader or the clinging Decepticon.

It was indeed difficult to advance against the current. More so than he had anticipated. How many Earthly rivers commanded such an imposing flow? One that seemed to increase with every step. Startled, he discovered that he could not make any progress against the current. He was holding his ground, but he was not moving forward.

"Here!" A metal cable appeared, unreeling from the back of Beachbreak.

Divining his comrade's intent, Ironhide grasped it with both hands. The smaller Autobot was noted for his agility, not for his strength, but despite his unpretentious size he boasted a powerful internal engine. It roared full-out now.

Slowly, progressively, and with Beachbreak's help, Ironhide was able to raise a leg and put one foot forward. Then another, and another. The closer they came to the riverbank, the lighter the current became, until at last Ironhide was able to let go of the cable and proceed the rest of the way through the water on his own. As the bigger Autobot emerged from the river, Beachbreak spun around to allow first Kaminari and then Petr to jump off onto the bank.

Eyeing the peculiar rifle the man was holding, Epps immediately confronted his Russian colleague. "What the hell does that thing shoot, anyway? I didn't see any explosions."

"It's a battery-powered gun that fires—batteries. More or less." Petr proceeded to explain. "Coated in special adhesive, they attach themselves to a Decepticon and instantly deliver a full discharge. You would be astonished at the amount of energy that can be crammed into a battery pack these days. Enough to at least momentarily disrupt a Decepticon's internal flow." Turning, he squinted across the river. "The discharge is not enough to kill one, but rendering it unstable allows other, more lethal weapons to more easily be brought to bear. Not to mention those mounted by an Autobot."

"I could have finished Payload." Looming over them, water and dark green plants dripping from his limbs and sides, Ironhide gazed longingly across the river. Then his eyes dropped to Kaminari. "That was a fine blow you struck."

She bowed slightly. "Thank you. But it was more important to save you."

"Save me?" Had he possessed the appropriately

flexible features, Ironhide would have frowned. "Save me from what? Being swept downriver? I would eventually have regained control and made my way to shore."

"Not necessarily."

The Autobot's attention shifted to the captain, then back to the river and the mist that now completely obscured its surface off to their left. "Where is Optimus? And Macerator? Have they been swept downstream?"

"Worse than that, I'm afraid."

A new sound drew his attention and he looked upward, squinting into the sun. An aircraft was approaching from somewhere over the distant low hills. As it drew closer the captain was able to make out the silhouette. Not civilian. Definitely military. Sweptback wings, sleek fuselage, twin engines. He knew he should not have been surprised.

Starscream had arrived. Just as Optimus and Macerator, locked together in hand-to-hand combat, were about to be swept over the rim of Victoria Falls.

7

The dense, swirling mist obscured everything except the Decepticon he was fighting. Something about this contest was not right, Optimus reflected even as he aimed another powerful blow at his opponent's head. Macerator had ample opportunities to strike back, yet the thickset Decepticon was not taking advantage of them. His only objective seemed to be to hold as firmly to his enemy as possible.

Concentrating on the fight, Optimus did not realize that the intensifying roar that had enveloped them along with the mist had grown far too loud to be generated by the river alone, no matter how fast its flow or how great its volume. There had to be another source. It revealed itself seconds later, too late for him to do anything about it. In any case, the forcefully clinging Macerator would not permit it.

"Victory!" The Decepticon let out a triumphant yell as, entwined together, they tumbled over the edge of one of the most formidable waterfalls on the planet and plunged downward into a rocky gorge of unsurpassed danger.

At virtually the same time a roar of a different kind could be heard, just loud enough to make itself audible above the thundering waters. Finally releasing his grip on his opponent, Macerator pushed himself away. As they tumbled in tandem, Optimus could see the Decepticon falling downward just to his left. And then . . .

Then he was gone, snatched clear of the water by a streaking aircraft whose outlines he knew only too well. As Starscream bore Macerator away to safety, the bellowing of the Decepticon's engines left in their wake an echo of mocking laughter. Attempted along the face of nearly any other great waterfall on Earth, the split-second rescue would have been impossible. But the gorge into which Victoria Falls spilled was a straight line nearly a mile and a half long. Plenty of room to allow Starscream to line up on his target, dive down, cruise along the face of the falls, fine-tune his position, and snatch the tumbling Macerator from destruction on the water-pounded rocks below.

It was one such rock that saved Optimus now.

Protruding out from the torrent halfway down the cataract, it was the only solid object amid a surge of spray. Extending an arm decisively, Optimus got one hand on it. A human's hand would have slipped off, or its owner would have been swept away like a fly under a faucet by the force of the falling water. The Autobot's grip was far more powerful. Even so, it required an extra burst of energy to the relevant servos to enable Optimus to grab hold and hang on.

A bad moment followed when he thought he heard the stone giving way beneath his weight, but it was only the sound of water striking the top of the stony projection. The rock to which he was clinging was not a boulder that had been washed over the top of the falls to embed itself in a crevice: it was part and parcel of the underside of the cascade itself.

He was not injured, but neither could he escape. Thrusting an arm into the cataract in an attempt to reach bedrock, he found that the sheer weight of the falling water forced him to pull back. Processed through his visual perceptors, a glance downward indicated that it was another two hundred feet to the base of the falls. He might well survive such a drop, but the power of the water crashing down atop him would pound him into the jagged black basalt. As he continued to analyze his surroundings and contemplate his options, he realized that letting go might be the only way out. Peering through the dense mist, he searched for the smoothest possible drop site beneath him. Any shock-absorbing sand had been washed away centuries ago, while the fast-flowing water itself promised an uncertain cushion at best. A flat rock would have to do.

He was just about to release his grasp and take his chances when a closed transmission gave him pause.

"Optimus! Hang on. We have your position."

Tilting his head back, he did not try to see straight through the falling water. But like his companions he possessed means of perception beyond the mere visual. The strength of Ratchet's signal was enough for him to pinpoint its location. Even though he could not "see" the medical specialist, Optimus knew where he was.

So he waited, dangling by one hand from the projecting spear of stone, until something dark and thin came whipping past his face. He caught it on the second swing. A military-grade cable fashioned of special alloy, reinforced and virtually unbreakable. Where had that come from? Ratchet did not carry it as integrated equipment, and surely it was not part of Ironhide's inventory. Then he remembered.

Beachbreak. By himself, the little aqueous Autobot was not strong enough to get Optimus out of this fix. But he could supply the means to do so, while Ironhide, Ratchet, and Salvage provided the muscle.

His concern was that even if they could haul him upward through the water, the pressure of the falls would put a tremendous strain on any cable, no matter how strong or tightly braided the strands of alloy. He transmitted as much.

"We know." This time it was Beachbreak speaking. "Your position clear of most of the water will allow you to swing outward. We are on an island in the middle of the river not far to your north. If you let go, you will drop and should eventually cease swinging directly beneath the island. The flow below it is greatly reduced from elsewhere. Once you have stopped swinging we can pull you up."

It was a good plan, well conceived—with one possible flaw. A little elementary geometry showed that there might not be enough room at the bottom of the proposed arc to allow him to clear the rocks beneath. In which case he would slam into the base of the falls with as much force as if he had simply let go and dropped. Taking a moment to consider both options, he finally settled on the former. At least that way if the line proved too short and he hit bottom, he would be entangled with the cable and they could haul up his battered body.

"We are all ready here, Optimus." Ratchet's tone was encouraging.

"We won't let you fall." That was Ironhide. If anyone could pull him to safety it would be the indomitable weapons expert, Optimus knew. Carefully, he studied the raging river that filled the gorge as he calculated the length of the fall and the angle of his forthcoming swing. Had he been capable of doing so, he would have taken a deep breath.

"Letting go," he transmitted simply as he released his handhold on the protruding rock.

He had wrapped several turns of the cable around his left arm. No matter what happened, he would not let go of it. Would it hold his weight? Plunging down and forward, he felt his mass being taken up by the line. As he dropped, the rocks below rapidly grew larger in his vision.

He wasn't going to make it, he saw. The relevant calculations were just slightly off. Reaching up, he grabbed the cable with his right hand and pulled hard. He drew his legs up toward his chest. The bottom of the arc approached. A part of him that was not vital struck sparks off a chunk of basalt and sent gravel flying.

He swung clear.

It took several minutes for him to stop swinging. Each time he fell back toward the bottom of the arc he had to pull his legs up to avoid smashing them into the rocks. He did not have to tell his compatriots when he had stopped swinging or when to begin hauling. Beachbreak could tell from the stable tension on the cable. Had he tried to halt Optimus's fall or pull him up on his own, the larger Autobot's weight would have dragged the stealth ski across the island and over the edge. But though he was straining with all his might, he was not operating in isolation.

On the heavily vegetated island that split the river, three Autobots stood hauling on the cable while in a quiet eddy near the far end the grimly determined Beachbreak methodically took up and reeled in the slack. The strain on his internal systems and servos was terrible, but somehow he maintained a steady pull on the line. Four anxious humans followed the procedure from their position on the near shore. While any of the Autobots could have taken them out to the island, their presence there was not necessary. They would only be in the way, Ratchet had pointed out, and the feeble amount of organic muscle they could contribute to the process of hauling was not worth the risk that one of them might slip or otherwise fall over the edge of the falls.

Epps pointed excitedly. "There he is! They've got him!" Lennox and Kaminari joined in the cheering as a gust of wind momentarily pushed aside the cascade-clinging mist and the battle-hardened shape of Optimus Prime emerged into view near the front edge of the island. Andronov did not join in the celebration. He was preoccupied with trying to identify the genus of a flowering water plant that was sprouting from a nearby mud puddle.

The process of getting back to the shore was relatively simple for the Autobots: they jumped. The distance from the shore to the small outcropping was roughly eighty-five feet, and with the exception of Beachbreak it was an easy leap for all. Beachbreak, after his successful rescue plan, was enjoying that which he had longed for: a chance to prove his worth. Given the circumstances, he was no longer ashamed at having to be carried across on Ironhide's shoulders.

But the victory was short-lived. Starscream, after having deposited Macerator on the far shore, had circled back to gloat over the demise of Optimus Prime. Enraged by the sheer dumb luck of Prime, and the pathetic heroism of the little Autobot, he screeched in for his revenge. As Ironhide leaped the short distance of the falls, Starscream streaked low and knocked Beachbreak off the weapons specialist's shoulders.

Even in Jet Ski mode, Beachbreak would never have been able to fight the current so close to the precipice. In robot form, the point was moot. He gave a single startled cry and disappeared over the rim. There was nothing anyone could do. With a shriek of triumph, Starscream disappeared.

Moments later the remainder of the team was once more reunited on shore. The suddenness and shock of the tragedy left them all speechless.

Kaminari in particular had focused her pre-NEST studies on and had reserved her admiration for the bigger, more powerful Autobots like Optimus and Ironhide. But over the past weeks she had come to love the little Autobot, not only for his spirit but also for his undaunted courage. If not for Beachbreak's chosen terrestrial configuration and quick thinking Optimus might well have been lost, or at least seriously hurt. Until this point she had not considered her own feelings toward their Cybertronian allies, but she realized now that a bond stronger than she had expected had been forged. She would mourn more than a lost comrade: she would mourn a lost friend.

Wiping Zambezi and tears from his face, Lennox peered up at the leader of the Autobots. "He was a brave soldier, Optimus. He will be missed. But our situation is still dangerous. How are you feeling? Do you need time to rest?"

"I'm feeling tired, frustrated. We should have been better prepared. Now Beachbreak has paid the price for my own failure." The powerful metallic shape considered. Turning, he looked toward the south, across the top of the falls. "It was all a trap, from the very beginning. Fearing he could not defeat me in battle, Starscream sought to do so with trickery. The raid on the construction supply depot was a distraction meant to draw us to this part of the world. Knowing we would be advised of it, and would respond, the Decepticons employed it to lure us here. The intent all along was to draw one or more of us into this river and trap us in its flow so that we could then be forced over the falls. My failure to see this and to lead effectively has cost us dearly."

Moving up beside his leader, Ratchet joined him gazing southward. "We saw Starscream emerge carrying Macerator to safety. Given the margin for error, a terrible risk to take with an ally."

Ironhide was openly derisive. "As if that would have given Starscream a moment's concern." He was looking across the river. "Payload and Dropkick are over there, somewhere. If there is a road, they will by now have shifted into their terrestrial modes."

Optimus nodded. "Very likely. But in local guise Payload cannot move very fast, and his appearance is distinctive. Dropkick and Macerator can blend in with local vehicles, but not him." Tilting back his head, he looked upward. "Sergeant Epps, is there a NEST satellite in position to scan the surrounding territory?"

"I'm on it, Optimus." Settling himself atop some nearby rocks, Epps opened his armored laptop and went back online. He shifted the computer on his lap until the satellite antenna that was integrated into the back of the clamshell cover had acquired a sufficiently strong signal. He looked up at his companions. "But it'll take a while for thrusters to adjust its orbit so that it can scan this area with sufficient resolution. Until then, we're blind."

"We will have to wait." Ironhide's tone indicated that he was itching to shoot at something.

"We could go into Livingstone and wait there," Petr pointed out. "At least then when satellite locates the Decepticons we will be in better position to respond quick."

"Yes," Kaminari agreed. "Except that Dropkick and Payload are on the other side of the Zambezi, and unless they use the old railroad bridge just below the falls to try to cross back, they'll have to head either up- or downstream for quite a distance until they can ford easily. In addition to which we don't know where Starscream is headed." She turned to Epps. "We need that information."

Leaning back against a mist-slicked slab of basalt, the tech sergeant crossed his arms and shrugged. "Can't reach out and push a satellite any faster."

"I could," Ironhide grumbled, "if I was up there."

So they waited. Off by herself, Kaminari sought solace in reciting ancient samurai precepts while executing Jodo moves in the direction of everything from rocks to small trees. Epps had his earbuds in and while monitoring the satellite tracking system was listening to music only slightly less discordant than the thoughts running through his mind.

Lennox was left to sit down and try to recover alongside Optimus. Even with his legs folded into a seated position, the Autobot towered above the human soldier.

"They're going to meet up somewhere." With fighting temporarily in abeyance Lennox was able to admire the beauty of their surroundings.

"Without doubt. They have struck a blow against us, they will not give up yet." Save for the occasional water plant that still clung to his gleaming metal frame and a few scrapes and scars that had been incurred in the clash with the Decepticons, Prime's tough metal body was undamaged. "It is not like Starscream to leave so abruptly. I should have thought he would have to at least fire a few missiles in my direction."

Lennox nodded thoughtfully. "Yeah. Unless—he had something else he wanted to do."

"Yes, but what in this part of your world would be sufficient to so draw his attention?" A hand waved at the far side of the river. "This is mostly open country. Attractive, to be sure, but without the potential to benefit his intentions in any way that I can envision. After all, he has spent the last year someplace where we could not find him, and was unable to move against us until other Decepticons arrived on Earth to reinforce him. As a consequence, he still knows little of your world beyond what he learned prior to and subsequent to the encounter at the big dam."

Lennox's eyes widened and he leaped to his feet. "The fight at the dam. Hoover Dam!" Whirling, he stared at the leader of the Autobots. "That's one thing Starscream *does* know about our world. The importance of large dams. He knows how vital they are to our industry—and how dangerous they can be if damaged."

Optimus was fully engaged. "This relates to our present situation how?"

Raising an arm, Lennox gestured southward, past the falls. "Downriver from here on the Zambezi are the Kariba and Cahorra Bassa dams, the second and third biggest in Africa. If Kariba were to go, the flood would take out Cahorra Bassa below it. The entire industrial base of southern Africa would be thrown into chaos by the loss of the hydroelectric power." His voice tightened. "I can't imagine the destruction and damage that would result from the amount of water that would be released. Tens, maybe hundreds of thousands of people would be killed."

Optimus considered solemnly. "I see your point. By showing that he is capable of causing such devastation and that the Autobots were unable to prevent it, he might force human authorities to bow to his demands. At the very least, it might induce your governments to insist on neutrality in our ongoing war."

"Which would mean the end of NEST, and the end of any cooperation between your people and mine against the Decepticons."

Optimus nodded slowly. "Starscream would never be satisfied with an arrangement of 'neutrality' on a permanent basis. If he and his fellow Decepticons succeeded in defeating us and winning the war, they would sooner or later make Earth a slave planet of Cybertron. It is not in the nature of Decepticons to regard any organics, even those as clever as your kind, as equals. But I fear that in the face of an overwhelming terroristic threat, some or all of your governments might choose to take the easy way out."

Lennox's expression darkened. "Wouldn't be the first time."

Epps let out a shout. "NEST Five is in position and scanning." As the humans crowded around the technical sergeant's open laptop, the Autobots hung back. Their stance did not prevent them from being able to see the information and images that were coming up on the screen.

"There." It was the acutely observant Petr who first spotted the strange shape moving down the small road. "Hold on that traffic."

Epps looked over at him. "What do you think you see? The image isn't clear enough for a positive ident." He indicated the screen. "That could be a logging truck."

"Those cannot be logs," Andronov insisted. "But they could be the barrels of guns."

Epps challenged the Russian's analysis of the image they were watching. "What makes you so sure?"

"Because there no trees of that size left anywhere in that part of Zimbabwe."

Lennox was practically leaning on Epps's shoulder. "Can you enhance the resolution any more, Sergeant?"

Epps shook his head. "Hey, you're looking at real-time video beamed from a low-orbit satellite straight to the middle of Africa. This ain't HBO, Captain."

"Direct the camera to move farther down the same

road as the vehicle you are discussing, " Ratchet suggested. Epps complied.

As the camera advanced, tracking along the road, it picked up several other vehicles utilizing the same route and traveling in the same direction—but only one was driving at exactly the same speed as the suspect "logging" truck.

"That's Dropkick." Ratchet straightened.

Epps frowned at the imperfect image. "Can you be sure? There are several pickups on the road."

"But no other ones traveling at the same speed as the truck," Ratchet pointed out. "Why should a pickup truck capable of much greater speed travel neither faster nor slower than the vehicle behind it, but at exactly the same velocity?"

"Ratchet is right." Optimus straightened. "The two vehicles are moving in tandem but apart, so as not to draw attention to themselves." One massive finger lightly touched Petr on the shoulder. "When considered together with the preceding botanical observation, I think the identification is accurate. We are looking at Payload and Dropkick."

"And they're heading south," Epps pointed out. He looked up from the computer. "Kariba and Cahorra Bassa are south."

"Then we must go there as well." The leader of the Autobots turned his attention back to Lennox. "Even if your supposition is wrong, Captain, we cannot take that chance. This sounds like something Starscream would do. The deaths of thousands, of millions of your kind, would not disturb his conscience for one moment, and all the better if he felt it would advance his cause or help the Decepticons to win the war."

Lennox nodded. "It's decided, then. We'll head back north to the air base outside Lusaka, and they can fly us down to the airstrip nearest Kariba."

"No." Reaching across, Optimus put a finger on the human's shoulder. "I have already calculated the distance and times involved. We will get there faster in our terrestrial modes." As he rose, his gaze took in his expectant companions.

"Autobots, transform and roll out!"

The guards barely looked up from their station when the garbage truck appeared. Since the winding road to the top of the dam descended through thick forest, they had only just noticed its approach. Taking a break from the card game that occupied his three colleagues, one of the men rose to peer curiously at the oncoming vehicle. What he saw caused him to frown. It did not look like the regular garbage truck. For one thing, it was outfitted with more than just a dumpster lifter. The heavy blades tucked against the top of the vehicle just behind the cab were an accessory he had never seen before. Increasingly intrigued, he picked up his rifle and stepped out of the windowless, open-sided guardhouse onto the hot pavement, leaving the card game behind. He was losing anyway.

The truck was not approaching very fast. The guard's attention perked up when it appeared as if the vehicle was going to head out onto the roadway that ran across the top of the dam. Then it stopped, backed up several feet, turned to the right, and headed for the tree-shaded corner of the parking lot that was backed by several big dumpsters. The truck's operator seemed oddly disinterested in his work, but that did nothing to raise the soldier's suspicions. Had he been forced to drive a garbage truck for the miserable wages such labor paid he, too, would have spent as much time as possible ingesting the locally available narcotics.

He kept an eye on the work until the truck had methodically picked up and tossed the contents of two of the four dumpsters into its back end. As it did so the purpose of the mysterious five aligned blades became clear. Whirring smoothly, they reduced the refuse to tiny fragments before depositing it in the back of the collector. Why it should be necessary to do this on-site instead of at a waste plant or dump the soldier did not know. Something to do with new recycling regulations, no doubt. Reassured, he turned and walked back to rejoin his comrades, sufficiently satisfied that he did not even bother to check the license plate on the pickup that had pulled up alongside the bigger truck.

As a result, he did not see the thick stream of minced trash that was ejected from the front of the garbage truck to cover the rear corner of the parking area, nor did he hear the exclamation of disgust the vehicle emitted.

"Pfagh!" A front bumper rose unnaturally to wipe at the spewing orifice that had momentarily replaced the truck's grille. "These humans, they foul their own nest."

"An entrenched excess that will be appropriately addressed once we have assumed control of this world." Dropkick spoke with confidence. "Starscream, we are ready to proceed as ordered."

A voice echoed simultaneously inside the minds of

both Decepticons. "Move out, then. Payload is in position and waiting for you to begin." High overhead, a jet contrail slashed across the otherwise pollution-free blue sky. The white line began to arc back on itself, circling. No commercial aircraft in this part of the world would have any reason to describe such a flight path. The guards at the dam might have remarked on it, had any of them bothered to look up. But like that of the technicians and engineers responsible for the operation of the great dam, their attention was attuned to more Earth-bound concerns.

Dropkick led the way, pleased with the human simulation he had projected into the pickup shape's front seat. He thought it an excellent likeness of one of the soft-bodied creatures. Macerator followed close behind. Together they approached the gate that blocked the road across the top of the dam. There was a second, smaller guard post on the lake side of the road. As the Decepticons drew near, a single soldier emerged. While one hand rested on the short-barreled automatic weapon slung across his body, the other rose in a palm-outward gesture Dropkick knew meant that he should halt.

No foot was necessary to depress the truck's accelerator. In fact, no accelerator was necessary. With a roar, the pickup leaped forward. Behind it, Macerator's throaty engine rumbled as the garbage truck shifted gears to follow its smaller brethren.

The guard's eyes went wide. To his credit he did not panic. Raising his weapon, he dodged to one side and opened fire. A moment later the shots from his rifle were joined by the louder chatter of the machine gun mounted inside the guard station. Slugs that would have shredded normal automobile sheet metal bounced like pebbles off the two oncoming trucks.

Dropkick didn't slow as he smashed through the gate. What he did not destroy was crushed and mangled beneath Macerator's weight. Their path now unimpeded, the two vehicles cruised out onto the top of the dam. Automatic-weapons fire continued to rattle behind them.

Cards were forgotten as the soldiers in the other guard post scrambled for their weapons and rushed to join the fight. Inside the gate guard post, a frantic corporal was jabbering wildly into the local intercom. From a barracks located on the nearby hillside several dozen other hastily roused soldiers were piling into waiting jeeps and open trucks.

Machine-gun fire now began to hit the pair of rolling intruders from opposite directions as the guard post on the other side of the dam opened up. Burning rubber, Dropkick screeched to a halt and parked himself sideways in the exact middle of the crossing. Lining up behind him, Macerator did likewise. Positioned grille-to-tail, they were now in a position to block traffic coming from either direction.

"The humans' firepower here is puny." Ignoring the noisy torrent of small-arms fire, Dropkick paused to admire the view down the gorge. "I assume it is having no effect on you?"

"I am feeling little in the way of actual contact," Macerator replied as a torrent of .50-caliber slugs ricocheted off his armored flanks. "It does not matter. We will not be here for long."

"Interesting." Raising a front wheel, Dropkick pointed down the dam-top roadway in the direction they had been heading before they had come to a halt. "It would appear that they do have some heavier weapons here."

Showcasing the result of regular drilling, a squadron of soldiers had stopped just inside the far gate and were pulling the protective tarps off a truck whose bed was equipped with a multiple rocket launcher. Inside the truck's cab, the gunner activated internal electronics to aim the multibarreled weapon at the pair of motionless and seemingly indifferent intruders. Moments later the first of nine available missiles erupted from its launcher as nearby troops covered their ears. The projectile struck Macerator broadside, rocking the big truck slightly back on its wheelbase.

"I did feel that." The Decepticon's tone darkened. "I believe my exterior may have incurred a slight smudge. The audacity of these insects astonishes me."

A portion of the middle of the garbage truck shifted, flowed, and changed shape. Appearing out of its flank was a tightly bound cylinder containing multiple barrels. The sound they made as they fired in unison echoed across the impounded lake below. Shells ripped into the truck-mounted missile launcher, tearing it to shreds. The heat they generated also ignited the remaining eight projectiles where they sat in the launcher. A few exploded in place, sending shrapnel flying in all directions and mowing down every soldier unfortunate enough to be standing too close. Several missiles launched, flying wildly in all directions. One exploded in the air while another struck the lake, a third the forest behind the guard station, and a fourth the road itself, adding to the completeness of the confusion that had enveloped the dam and its surrounds.

The teams of soldiers from the barracks arrived on the other side of the dam. Deploying to cover and without waiting for orders from their superiors, they opened up on the two trucks parked in the center of the road. Panicked technicians were fleeing from the dam's installations. Piling into their own vehicles, the guards stationed in the gorge below were now racing as fast as possible up the switchbacks that led to the top in order to join in the fight to save a national treasure.

As soon as the last of them had departed, Payload began to move.

No ordinary vehicle could have made its way down into the gorge without utilizing one of the access roads, but Payload's treads and low center of gravity enabled him to avoid detection, mowing down brush and trees as he descended. Concealed by the canyon's thick vegetation, he had waited motionless and hidden until Macerator and Dropkick made their move. Now, with all the defending human forces converging on the two Decepticons parked atop the center of the dam, he pushed forward out of the bush unopposed. No one challenged him as he settled himself on a nice, level piece of beach beside the lake and elevated his multiple guns. Requiring only a few seconds to calibrate distance, he opened fire.

The large-caliber anti-aircraft shells were not aimed at the human defenders; nor did they land within reinforced structures. Instead Payload's salvos were directed at just one spot—the exact center of the lower portion of the dam. They did not penetrate: the concrete there was too thick for that. But they did make a start, steadily and inexorably, at chipping away the thick curved wall.

Firing desperately from behind the crumpled security gate, the soldiers situated there turned as a new sound rose above the constant chatter of small-arms fire. The noise was loud, intermittent, and oddly familiar. As they searched, the source revealed itself. Forced to scatter at its approach and knowing nothing of the newcomers, they fired wildly in their direction.

Blowing his horn, Optimus Prime came barreling down the hilly access road. In the absence of identification, the guards assumed the wildly careering diesel was another trespasser. They also unloaded on the two pickup trucks that were following, but ceased fire when the ambulance appeared. Skidding to a stop, Ratchet unloaded his human passengers in a safe area before spinning around in a most un-ambulance-like manner to hurry after his friends.

Recognizing the American flags stitched in place beneath the NEST insignia on the soldiers' shoulders, a Zambian lieutenant hurried over to confront the new arrivals. Breathless and sweating, he did his best to explain what was happening. Epps didn't linger to listen. Hearing the steady *ack-ack* of heavy fire echoing through the gorge, he rushed to a vantage point and pulled out his compact monocular. By the time Lennox, Petr, Kaminari, and the Zambian officer joined him, the tech sergeant had already made a guess as to the Decepticons' intentions.

"You were right, Captain! They're trying to bust the dam."

"Bust the . . . ?" Horrified realization flushed the Zambian soldier's face. "Catastrophe! Thousands will die. If the flood of water reaches Cahorra Bassa, the entire Zambezi basin will be washed into the Indian Ocean!"

Andronov was hefting his singular rifle. "If I can get down there I can—"

He was interrupted by a tremendous crash. All eyes went to the crest of the dam.

Racing along the top, Optimus had smashed into the two parked trucks, knocking Macerator sideways and sending the lighter Dropkick spinning. As the latter howled in fury and began to change shape, so did the pickup that had followed the diesel out onto the top of the dam. The smaller Decepticon barely had time to rise on two legs before the black dually assumed the form of Ironhide and slammed into him. As the two skidded down the dam-topping road toward the far gate, the soldiers there scattered in all directions.

Behind the humans, Ratchet had also shifted shape. Stunned by the sight, the soldiers nearby had stopped shooting. There was nothing they could contribute anyway to the battle now raging atop the dam, and their light weapons would do no harm to Payload even if they could shoot with accuracy that deep into the gorge. Having recognized the danger, the Zambian officer had retreated and was trying to regroup his men.

Lennox saw them piling into their vehicles. He shook his head regretfully. "They'll never get down there in time. And Payload's on the other side of the river."

Ratchet had moved up alongside the captain. "I will climb down and engage him."

Lennox knew he could not stop the Autobot from doing as he pleased, but he felt he had to try. "I've seen you in combat, Ratchet. You're a good fighter— but it's not your specialty. I don't think you can take Payload, and I'd hate to lose you." Having already singled out the largest freestanding structure in the dam administration complex, he started toward it. "Stay here and back up Optimus and Ironhide. Sergeant, Petr, come with me!" As the three men headed for the building, a frowning Kaminari called after them.

"Hey, what about me?"

Lennox half shouted back to her, "Stay with Rachet and Salvage. If any Decepticons try to escape—you know what to do!"

A heavy shell slammed into Optimus's shoulder. Shrugging it off, he fired repeatedly at Macerator, knocking the now altered enemy backward and over the side of the dam. As the Decepticon grabbed hold of the edge and prepared to pull himself back up, Optimus loomed over him. The Autobot's right arm transformed into a weapon as ancient and traditional as it was lethal: an enormous shining sword.

"Your time is done, Macerator. You've caused enough harm on this innocent world."

Clinging to the inner dam wall, his body dangling over the sheer four-hundred-foot drop, the Decepticon glared up at his foe. "Not as much as you, Optimus."

The leader of the Autobots was momentarily taken

aback. "Your cognitive circuitry has been damaged. What you say makes no sense."

"Megatron and the others came here for the Allspark. Had we been allowed to recover it, we would not be fighting you now and therefore these creatures would not be involved in our battle."

Sword raised high to catch the sun, Optimus hesitated. What Macerator said was true enough—as far as it went. Megatron had come for the Allspark. Other Decepticons had followed, and likewise the Autobots to prevent them from regaining it. Because of them, this world now found itself unwillingly involved in the ancient war. Much as Optimus wished to ignore them, Macerator's words resonated.

He stared down at the Decepticon. "I know Megatron. I know all of you. You would not have taken the Allspark and left this world in peace. You would have subdued it and made slaves of its people. Even in the absence of the Allspark, my conscience and that of my friends could not have allowed that." The great sword descended.

It pierced Macerator's chest armor, plunging directly into his Spark. The lights in his eyes flashed, then went out. Maintaining its grip even in the absence of direction, one hand of the Decepticon's decapitated body continued to cling to the edge of the dam. Using his foot, Optimus pried up the metal fingers. They left deep grooves in the concrete as they were snapped backward. Falling free, the body of the dead Decepticon struck the lower curve of the dam once, twice, before sending a geyser of water upward as it struck the calm surface of the lake. The metal corpse appeared to float there for a moment before sinking swiftly beneath the surface and out of sight.

Far below on the face of the dam a damp stain had appeared at the point where Payload was keeping up a steady fire. A trickle of water appeared, then another.

Having located a service elevator and descended into the depths of the complex, Lennox and his companions were searching frantically for a technician. Their location rendered them unaware of the expanding leak—which was just as well.

"Where the hell did everyone run to?" Clutching his rifle, Lennox scanned the empty rooms. "*Somebody* had to stay behind."

Those standing on the lookout high above and to one side of the access road finally saw what was going on. It was Kaminari who noticed it first. Her assessment was harsh.

"They're taking too much time." A glance over at the dam roadway showed that while Optimus was in the process of finishing off Macerator, Ironhide was still fully entangled with the less robust but more agile Dropkick. "They're going to be too late. The dam's going to go, and everyone is *inside* it."

Ratchet foresaw the impending tragedy at the same time as the human. Turning, he confronted Salvage. The pickup truck had also changed into its robot form.

"Can you throw me?"

Salvage regarded the older Autobot uncertainly. "What?"

"Can you throw me? I am used to patching lesions, though this will be on a somewhat different scale."

"I don't underst—yes, I can throw you. But throw you where, and at what?" By way of reply Ratchet raised an arm and pointed. Salvage blinked at him. "You want me to throw you at Payload? I don't know if I can . . ."

"Not that far." Pivoting, Ratchet indicated the expanding weak spot in the dam. "There. Throw me there. If your aim is a little high I can slide down. A little low and I will climb up. Quickly now, before the holes become too large to fix. We must stanch the— bleeding."

"What is 'bleeding'?" Salvage was visibly confused.

"A human medical term." Ratchet extended both arms toward his fellow Autobot. "Just get me as close as you can."

Kaminari ran up beside him. "You can't do this, Ratchet. If you stay in one place on the face of the dam you'll be completely exposed to Payload's weapons! He'll be able to concentrate all his fire on you."

Looking down at her, Ratchet's voice softened. "Repair is my strong suit, Kaminari. My armor should sustain me against Payload's fire—for a little while, at least."

"And then?" she pressed him.

" 'Then' is a relative term, for Autobots as well as humans. Events will determine what happens. But there is no more time. I must act to prevent a greater misfortune than my possible death. As a healer, I cannot stand by and let thousands of humans die." He turned back to the waiting, staring Salvage. "Compute carefully, my friend. Mass, angle, and distance."

Nodding gravely, Salvage took a firm grip on the other Autobot's wrists. Then he began to spin. Faster and faster. Kaminari hastily retreated. As the increasing centrifugal force lifted Ratchet off the ground, the wind generated by his whirling mass forced her to turn away.

Spinning a fully extended Ratchet around him, Salvage had become a blur. A human athlete would have collapsed in a nauseated heap long before the Autobot had achieved anything close to his current velocity. Shielding her eyes, Kaminari could not imagine how Salvage could even maintain his stance, much less determine the exact moment when to release his compatriot. Like a Greek god heaving an Olympian discus, Salvage let go at the precisely optimum moment and angle.

Flung outward in a soaring arc over the four-hundred-foot-deep gorge, Ratchet seemed to hang in the air for a moment. Then he began to fall, steeling himself for the impact. His entire internal system sustained a shock as he slammed up against the curving face of the dam. A check ran instantly and automatically. To his relief nothing was broken and all his parts remained in working order. Digging feet and fingers into the concrete a hundred feet above the river below, he leaned his head back as far as he could in order to assess his immediate surroundings. The result of Salvage's throw could not have been better. It stood as a perfect tribute to Autobot ability.

Ratchet had landed directly beside the damaged portion of the dam.

Internal generators went into overdrive. The Autobot's hand began to glow softly, then more intensely. On contact with him, the leaking water turned to steam, hissing as it rose upward. Straining internally, Ratchet continued to put out more and more excess heat. The outside of his metal body now blazed white hot.

Around him, cracked concrete and the rebar within began to melt and flow, forming a sealed whole that was stronger than the material it replaced. The now molten metal and re-forming building material also sealed the small cracks that had appeared in the dam face. The ominous trickles of water dried up; puffs of steam faded away. Always the healer, Ratchet had halted the nascent structure failure by using internally generated heat to reseal the concrete and metal area beneath him.

Below and on the opposite riverbank, an enraged Payload continued firing steadily. Frustrated in his efforts to crack the dam, he concentrated on trying to hit the hardworking Autobot. First he would terminate the interloper. Then he would resume his assault on the human edifice whose structural integrity Ratchet had managed to temporarily preserve. A surge of satisfaction washed through the Decepticon. Not only would it not take long to conclude the task at hand, but he would have the added pleasure of finishing off one of the hated Autobots as well.

One shell after another slammed into the area around Ratchet. Even as he continued the work of repairing the dam face, he managed to dodge most of them. But not all. He winced when the occasional heavy round detonated against his back. His armor could only take so much. Nevertheless, he would hold out as long as he could. If he could repair the dam while occupying Payload's attention, it would give Optimus or Ironhide time enough to intervene.

Someone finally did, but it was not one of the other Autobots.

Deep within the dam control center Lennox, Epps, and Andronov finally encountered a senior technician. Panting hard, Lennox challenged him.

"How come you didn't flee with the others?"

The white-haired tech adjusted his glasses. "This dam is my pride and the pride of my country. If it goes, so do I."

Epps was peering out the heavy glass window that ran the length of the room and looked out over the gorge below. Payload had not moved and was continuing to pump shell after shell into the dam face. "He's still there!"

"Good." Lennox's attention had shifted from the technician to the wide, complex console in front of him. "I've been in a place like this before but I don't know how to operate anything here." He looked over at the elderly tech. "Do you have an emergency release?"

"Emergency . . . ? Yes, certainly, but I cannot even think of triggering such a thing without authorization from Lusaka."

Standing nearby, Petr raised his rifle. It did not fire bullets and in any case he had no intention of using it on the old man—but the technician didn't know that.

"Here is authorization, Russian-style. Activate emergency release."

"Do it now," Epps added. "As one tech to another,

I'm telling you that it's the best thing. You gotta do this—fast."

The senior technician hesitated, his gaze darting between Epps and Lennox. "I take no responsibility for the consequences. There will be damage downriver."

"There'll be nothing at all downriver if you don't," Lennox told him. *"Do it."*

Andronov gestured with his weapon. Lips tight, the tech reached for the console and flipped several switches. Green telltales above each switch went to red. The hip-hop bleat of an alarm filled the control room. There followed a moment of further hesitation. The technician raised a protective, transparent plastic cover to expose two red buttons beneath. He pressed one. Lennox knew enough from the time he had spent at Hoover to encourage the tech.

"Both of 'em," he ordered. With a regretful sigh, the man complied.

His movements restricted by the need to complete his repair efforts, Ratchet felt himself steadily weakening. Another direct hit from Payload's multiple guns might penetrate his deteriorating armor and split his back. A follow-up shot would tear into his vitals, destroying essential components and interdicting critical circuitry. Nevertheless, he was determined to keep working as long as possible. With the repairs complete, it would force Payload to begin the process of destruction all over again somewhere else.

A rising rumble filled his aural pickups. Had he already suffered a fatal blow, one that was distorting perception of his surroundings? His vision must be going as well, he decided. The blue sky before him, visions of river below flanked by steep hillsides and green forest, had also disappeared. Now he could see nothing but whiteness.

This is wrong, he told himself. If his senses were failing, everything should go to black, not white. Nor should the white be in motion. It was then that he recognized what he was seeing. There was nothing wrong with his senses, auditory or visual. What he was seeing above him, in front of him, and all around him, was water. An immense, unrestrained rush of water. And it did not spring from a massive leak or a failure of the dam.

The emergency floodgates had been opened.

Released by the override, thousands of tons of water burst from Kariba's two floodgates directly above the Autobot. Under pressure from the enormous lake behind them, the twin discharges shot an incredible volume of liquid into the narrow canyon below. Sweeping up trees and sand and huge boulders before it, the man-made flood thundered down the gorge.

Payload saw it coming. Realizing instantly that he could never escape the flood in his present terrestrial guise, he started to change shape. The wall of water struck him as he was only partway through the process. Unable to get a grip on anything solid, the Decepticon found himself picked up like a leaf and swept downstream. In the crazed, roiling current he was sometimes shoved upward toward the surface of the flood only to be thrust immediately straight downward by its roiling currents. By the time he had fully shifted into his normal shape he had been slammed time and time again into the unyielding rock of the riverbed. His cognitive systems had been battered to the point that it was all he could do to maintain consciousness.

High above, Starscream saw the flood race madly down the canyon. For an instant he felt the triumph rush through him, only to have the sensation turn to fury as he saw that the dam was still intact. At almost the same time he lost Macerator's signal. When Payload also failed to respond to repeated requests to report, the frustrated Decepticon considered diving and strafing the Autobots who were clearly visible and exposed atop the dam itself. But as soon as he dove within range of them, he would likewise find himself in range of their own weapons. This was neither the time nor the place to confront the despised Optimus and his deluded companions with a final challenge.

"Get out of there!" he broadcast crossly to Dropkick. "Macerator has ceased all contact and I cannot raise Payload. Retreat to the agreed-upon meeting place!"

"I comply, Starscream."

Below, Dropkick dodged a blow from Ironhide, backed up, and altered. As the Autobot weapons master fired, his adversary spun and shot away. The explosive shell detonated just behind the squealing pickup truck. Dropping into a crouch, Ironhide sighted along the top of the dam and prepared to unleash a stream of missiles in the wake of the fleeing Decepticon. A metal hand came down on his arm.

"No," Optimus told him. "You cannot shoot. The far side is crowded with humans, and our friends are somewhere over there as well. Anything you fire that misses is liable to kill others."

Temptation tugged hard at the veteran Autobot. "I have a clear line of sight, Optimus."

"Clear enough so that you can be sure every shot will hit home instead of streaking past?"

Ironhide hesitated. Then, muttering under his breath, he straightened. His gaze followed the accelerating, fleeing Decepticon. "It pains my internals to let him escape. There are debts yet to be paid."

"I feel the same." Optimus gestured behind him. "But we cannot risk the injury to many humans." Tilting his head back, he scanned the sky. "Starscream has fled. We have won the day, and struck a heavy blow against our enemies. Macerator is dead and Payload is at least injured." He nodded in the direction of the escaping Decepticon. "Dropkick cannot do much harm on his own, and we will eventually run him down." Looking to the far side, he found himself studying the terrain with increasing anxiety. "I see Salvage, but where is Ratchet?"

"That old complainer?" Ironhide grunted derisively. "Probably sitting in the shade watching the battle and waiting to see who gets hurt."

Dropkick, in the meantime, did not know why Optimus Prime and Ironhide were not firing at him, but he was more than willing to accept that which he did not understand. The encounter had not gone as planned. Macerator was gone, probably killed, and Payload had failed to bring down the human construction. But he, Dropkick, was still alive and relatively undamaged. The ruined gateway lay just ahead. As he drew near, traveling at high speed in his terrestrial guise, a few of the surviving human soldiers noted his approach and resumed shooting at him.

The occasional small-caliber slug bounced harmlessly off his exterior.

Then he noticed that a single human was running *toward* him. Deranged, he wondered, or simply brainless? For a moment he considered shifting his course just enough to one side to run the figure down. It would provide some small measure of recompense to see it go flying, broken and dead, to the pavement. But Starscream had ordered him to save himself, and he reluctantly decided to hold to the quickest course.

As he sped past the human, the figure thrust something toward him. It could do no damage, of course, and so he ignored it. Then he felt himself lurch as a pulse slammed sharply against the driver's-side door.

On the access road just off the dam, the pickup truck skewed wildly in surprise, barely regaining control as it started up the first slope that led out of the canyon. Halfway up it changed. Looking down at himself, Dropkick saw the small dark spot where the end of the stick had contacted his epidermis. He felt slightly—drunk. Too startled to retrace his route and confront his unexpectedly unsettling attacker, he pressed one hand to the discoloration and resumed working his way up out of the canyon. With each step he increased his stride. Soon he was out of sight. But he would not forget what had happened.

Below and behind, Salvage had rolled up alongside a panting, sweating Kaminari. She held her weapon at her side. Depressing a button, the apparatus ceased humming.

"Well struck, Kaminari!" In his excitement Salvage was about to give the female warrior a congratulatory shove, until he remembered that such a push risked fracturing her fragile human bones. "That's one Decepticon who will think twice before passing so close to a human."

She holstered the weapon in the lightweight sling on her back. The sling was actually composed of a single long, flexible linear battery that would recharge the weapon while it rested against her spine.

"Well, it knows what one human with two advanced degrees and training in martial arts can do." With the Decepticon now out of striking range, she turned her attention back to the gorge. "Ratchet!"

They waited while the battered Autobot climbed up the face of the dam and over the side wall to rejoin them. Safe again among friends, human as well as Autobot, the limping Ratchet proceeded to analyze his own injuries.

"Nothing that can't be fixed," he finally announced.

"If I but had a tiny fragment of Allspark for every time I've heard you say that." Ironhide's tone was gruff as always, but there was no mistaking the affection that highlighted the observation.

Around them, the Zambian guards and technicians were beginning to recover from the shock of the attack. Soldiers attended to their wounded while techs and other personnel embarked on preliminary cleanup efforts. Ratchet turned his gaze skyward.

"What of Starscream?"

"Fled, as is his habit." In contrast with that of his friend, Optimus's attention was directed downriver. "We need to find Payload. I'm sure that he's injured, though to what extent it is impossible to tell. In his terrestrial form he cannot move fast, and among local vehicles he stands out. In full Decepticon mode he will attract even more attention. If we can get to him before Starscream does, we will be able to rid ourselves of yet another foe."

"I don't think Starscream in his local mode is strong enough to lift Payload." Ironhide had moved up alongside his leader to join him in staring down the gorge. "Certainly not for any distance."

"A positive thought. We should proceed on that assumption." Turning, Optimus looked back at his human allies. "Will all of you ride with me this time? Better if Ratchet is left to heal unencumbered."

"This riverine forest holds many wonders that I would like to examine at length," Petr began, "but . . ." He shrugged. "I have a feeling that there will be other opportunities for studying of such things."

Optimus nodded. "Among my kind learning is also a continuous and unending process. It is one more sign of the cerebral, if not physical, relationship that bonds us together."

Simmons was only halfway through the copy of the ancient monograph and finding it hard going. Untrained in anthropology or archaeology, he was forced to continuously switch back and forth between the material and a translating codex.

There was so much to learn, he had come to realize. Trying to put things together, to come to some kind of understanding about these alien machines. Despite being dismissed from the service, his interest in the invaders—and they were all invaders to him, Autobots and Decepticons alike—had never flagged.

As chief agent for the now disbanded Sector Seven, he had always been more a man of action than academics. Required reading for his job had usually involved skimming manuals explaining the use of surveillance equipment or surreptitious communications gear. Fieldwork required training in the use of weapons, not library catalogs. Since Sector Seven's dissolution and replacement by NEST, much of his time had been devoted to working in his mother's deli. Not that he needed the money: his government pension covered all his basic needs. No, he needed something to do, to occupy his hands and body while his obsession with the aliens occupied his mind. So he sliced and diced pastrami and brisket instead of the enemies of the United States and the planet.

Were they enemies? It was one of the mysteries he was trying to unravel. About the Decepticons neither he nor anyone else had any second thoughts. The battle at Mission City had resolved that. It was the Autobots who puzzled him. They claimed to have come to Earth in search of the now vanished Allspark. All well and good. But why remain? Because they had no means of leaving, or because as their leader Optimus Prime claimed their presence was necessary to dissuade further depredations by the Decepticons, who if given the opportunity would make slaves of humanity?

In the convoluted (and sometimes convulsive) mind of former agent Seymour Simmons, something simply didn't add up. While he was willing to give Prime and the other Autobots the benefit of the doubt, that doubt still remained.

Fortunately, between the Internet and the plethora of libraries and universities in the Greater New York area, he had access to more material than he could hope to process. That did not stop him from devouring everything he could find that he felt bore the slightest relevance to Earth's new residents. The monograph copy he was currently laboriously deciphering, for example, was ancient Greek. Prior to discovering it, the only thing Simmons knew about ancient Greeks was that a retired couple ran a gyro restaurant down the street from his mother's deli.

Occasionally he would look up from his work to cast a hopeful query or a casual curse in the direction of the gleaming metal entity that was firmly clamped to the table in the middle of his basement. Regardless of their nature, comments on his part received no response. What remained of the head of Frenzy sat as stolid and immobile in the center of the table as an overpriced sculpture by Moore or Hirst, and about as comprehensible.

"If you could only talk." Simmons rubbed at his tired eyes. "You miserable broken excuse for a Rosetta stone. Not your fault that you ended up a cross between a computer and a salad tosser." In his wilder moments, of which Simmons had always had plenty, he had even considered bringing the alien skull to the deli and mounting it on the wall along with the hundreds of other donated and found objects that decorated the family restaurant.

What secrets the disembodied head must hold, he mused. What revelations, what knowledge. Only by deciphering all it contained might he learn the truth about the two contesting groups of alien robotic life-forms.

What, after all, did mankind know of them and their origins? Practically nothing except what little Optimus had chosen to divulge. The Autobots had been reluctant to speak of themselves and were even more closemouthed about their advanced technology. Because of the personal relationship he had established from the beginning with one of the Autobots, that smart-ass kid Sam Witwicky probably knew more about them than anyone, and he wasn't talking, either. In fact, the last Simmons had heard, the kid had turned down all offers to work for the government in favor of going to college. And the authorities couldn't press him on his choice because doing so would only compromise further their frantic attempts to cover up the true nature of the alien visitation. Not to mention the fact that if they came down hard on him, he could always go to the media.

So a reluctant government had to back off and watch helplessly as their main interlocutor with the alien visitors headed off to university. Simmons thought it just as well. Though he'd gained a lot of respect for the Witwicky kid in the course of the confrontation with the Decepticons at Mission City, he still could not escape the feeling that the youth was sneering at him behind his back. And as for the kid's choice in female companionship, the less said the better.

Not that Seymour Simmons was dating anyone better than Witwicky's foxy car thief. For one thing, he felt he couldn't spare the time on fripperies like a social life. *Someone* had to try to make sense of what was going on. Someone had to be ready to save the world. In between serving corned beef on rye, of course.

"Without mustard." Every time he thought of it, his blood pressure rose.

Princeton! The Witwicky kid was going to Princeton. Something didn't jibe with that, either. The youth's background, his family history, all pointed to him getting into a local small college, maybe going to a JC first. A state university at best. Not Princeton. Was he channeling Einstein's ghost? So much to learn, Simmons thought. So much to try and figure out. And that car of the kid's. It wasn't talking, either.

He returned to his labors. If there was one estimable quality Seymour Simmons possessed, it was persistence. Set him to a task and he was, his mother had often said of her son, like a dog with a bone.

Consider that cracker Archimedes. Another ancient Greek who just happened to be the subject of the monograph the former agent was currently translating. Just where had *he* gotten all those advanced notions?

Something sputtered in front of him. He looked up. Nothing amiss, nothing changed. He returned to his translating.

The sound was repeated. It was coming from the alien head mounted on the small table. A tinny, crackling voice issued from the remnant of a mouth. It was speaking Decepticon, which Simmons knew as well as anyone in the world.

"Body." Sparks flew from the sides and top of the head as it spit and popped and flared. "Where body? Gone, gone, taken, gone. Bring it back. So far away, taken . . ."

Rising slowly from his chair, a captivated Simmons approached the head. In addition to the sparks, several lights were flaring deep within the alien construct. The formerly intact Decepticon had been a metal homicidal maniac that had done its best to slaughter him, the secretary of defense, and several other people deep within the bowels of Hoover Dam. Immobile and disembodied, it had sat harmlessly on his basement table ever since he had snuck it home. And now it was trying to talk.

If its murderous instincts were sufficiently moderated, it was just possible he might be able to persuade it not only that he was a friend, but to supply him with some answers.

"What are you trying to say? Are you asking about your body? I don't know where it is, chrome dome. Maybe if you gimme a hint, I can look for it. Give you your body back, yeah, but without the Cuisinart capability, if you know what I mean." He drew nearer, unafraid of the lights or the sparks. After all, he had lived for nearly a year with this mechanism in his basement without suffering any adverse consequences from its proximity. It wasn't as if he was hiding the body of Megatron in a garage.

"Body missing," the head sputtered. "Not fair. Frenzy do his job. Perform all tasks, obey all orders. Accumulate requisite information . . ."

Simmons sidled closer still. "Yeah, information. Vital information. Tell me." His tone turned coaxing, and he switched on the recorder he always kept ready in one pocket. "Any information is good information. Tell me about the Autobots. Tell me about the Decepticons. This war of yours—what's it really all about? What do you animated cuckoo clocks really want from us? From Earth?" Cautiously, he extended a hand toward the imprisoned head. "Tell Uncle Seymour all about it."

"Need full body, remaining neural components to—" The voice broke off abruptly. When it resumed, it was at the level of a shriek. "*Insect!* Ambulatory macrobiotic pulp! Frenzy chop!" Atop the table the head started to shake and vibrate furiously. The lights that had come on within began to flash like the window in an uptown nightclub.

"Hey, easy there, take it easy." Halting his approach and raising his hands to show that he meant no harm, Simmons made placating gestures without knowing if the Decepticon skull could even perceive the movement, much less understand the meaning behind it. "I'm not gonna hurt you. I'm not the one who took your body. All I want is to ask you some ques—"

"All humans must submit!" the head screamed. "Release Frenzy or suf . . . or suf . . . !"

The lights in the basement went crazy. A subtle tremor shot through the floor. Startled, Simmons felt it through the soles of his shoes. A faint rumbling grew audible. In front of him, the table holding the clamped head began to jump and bounce lightly on its four legs. While he had been careful to secure the skull to a wooden table so the Decepticon remnant could not control the platform on which it rested, something was clearly going on.

Turning to his right, he rushed to the wall and fumbled for the circuit breaker that controlled the multiple power cords he had connected to the skull. As soon as his fingers wrapped around the switch, a blue flame erupted from the wall socket. A jolt of electricity shot through his fingers. Fortunately, the breaker only controlled a 110-volt line and not the 220 he had hooked up. So the surge sent him stumbling backward but didn't put him on the ground.

Behind him, the table holding the head of Frenzy was now bounding violently as the Decepticon continued to spew a stream of alien gibberish. It was also bouncing in one direction—toward the electrical transformer into which several live leads had been plugged. Simmons instantly deduced what was happening. Having revived sufficiently to sense the proximity of the larger power source, the Decepticon was struggling to reach it. If the diminished alien intelligence could make contact with and draw upon the apartment building's full electrical load . . .

Simmons charged the opposite wall. Screeching atop the hopping, bouncing table, what was left of Frenzy focused single-mindedly on reaching the source of revitalizing energy. It was within a yard of doing so when the former agent grabbed the industrial-capacity cord connecting the transformer to the wall and yanked the heavy-duty plug out of its socket.

All power was cut to the basement. The Decepticon's electronic howling ceased, as did the banging of the wooden table legs against the bare concrete floor. Fumbling in the darkness, Simmons located one of several flashlights he had stashed around the room. Following its beam, he cautiously approached the worktable.

It was devoid of movement. No sparks flared from the alien skull, no lights flickered within its depths. Reaching down, he carefully touched one of the wires that ran from it, felt nothing. Moving from point to point around the room, he unplugged each and every cord one by one. Returning to the transformer, he plugged it back in and flipped the master switch. The lights in the basement came back on, but the head of Frenzy remained inert. Walking back to the worktable, Simmons picked it up and returned it to its former location in the center of the room. Taking a deep breath, he reached out and touched the alien metal. Nothing. A second touch turned into a prolonged exploration of the skull. There was some lingering residual heat that was rapidly fading.

"You guys are always full of surprises," he muttered softly. "Should've known better than to let down my guard. That won't happen again."

A sudden loud pounding on the floor above at the door to his apartment caused him to jump slightly.

"Now you stay right there," he told the head, "and don't move." The admonition was half joke, half command.

The figure standing in the hallway facing his apartment was almost as intimidating as a Decepticon: his landlord, Carlson. The man's language was more comprehensible than Frenzy's, though no less hyperactive.

"What are you doing in there, Simmons?" Short and squat, the landlord struggled to see past his taller tenant.

"Just reading," Simmons told him. "Why? My rent's paid. You want to borrow a cup of sugar or something?"

"Yeah, right. I'm baking cookies. Not that I could if I wanted to, because a couple minutes ago every light in the building went out and every appliance went nuts." He gestured upward. "Mrs. Berkowitz in Six-C, she was in the middle of her favorite soap when her TV went out—and it's Friday. You should've heard the ration she gave me." His expression tensed. "Surge came from your place. I got blown lightbulbs all over the building that I gotta spend half a day replacing!"

"You should switch to LEDs." When circumstances dictated, Simmons was quite capable of controlling his temper.

"Wise guy. Maybe I'll do that, and tack the bill onto your rent."

"Okay." Simmons smiled broadly.

His ready acquiescence took the landlord aback. "Really? You'll pay for the replacements?"

The former agent shrugged. "It's just a few light-bulbs. If I'm responsible, I'll pay, sure."

"Well—okay then." His anger if not his curiosity assuaged, the older man turned to leave. "But whatever you're doing in there, if it happens again, I'm gonna have a city inspector check out any modifications you've made to your wiring. And if they're illegal, you're out, Simmons. I don't care if you *do* pay your rent on time. I ain't gonna let you burn down the building."

"No problem, Carlson. Not to worry." The ex-agent smiled as he closed the door behind his grumbling landlord.

Not to worry. This was what he was forced to cope with: ignorant fools like his fellow apartment dwellers who had no idea that the man in 1B was devoting all of his spare time to trying to save the world, and them, from total destruction. One thing the recent episode in the basement had made clear: he could not continue his work here. As inconvenient as it was going to be, he was going to have to move not only the heavily wired Decepticon head but all of his research material somewhere else. To a place that would afford safety and privacy as well as access to a more secure supply of electricity. He couldn't take the risk that the increasingly suspicious Carlson might enter his apartment while Simmons was at work, much less that the landlord might do so in the company of a city inspector.

What he needed was a commercial venue with

commercial-grade wiring and power sources, but one to which he could be sure only he had access. Renting office or shop space wouldn't work, as doing so would risk the same potential unauthorized visit by a landlord. He had no close friends, so that option was out. Where could he go? Where could he take his materials and feel safe leaving them unguarded even if he needed to go out of the city for a while?

Eventually it came to him. Without mustard.

While Technical Sergeant Epps's head bobbed slightly and steadily to the beat of the music that was blasting from the docked music player sitting on the shelf in front of him, it had no apparent effect on the enormous Autobot who was crouched close behind and peering over his shoulder. Like the rest of the Autobots, Ironhide had done his best to try to comprehend how humans derived pleasure from listening to the sharply modulated soundwaves generated by such devices. It sounded nothing at all like the music he enjoyed back on Cybertron. Periodic exposure had bred, if not familiarity, at least a modicum of understanding.

For him, however, it could not compete with the unleashing of a suitably devastating explosion or the pleasure to be had from admiring a weapon well designed.

The human's passion for oddly mutating sound waves notwithstanding, Ironhide had discovered a common bond with the human named Epps. Flaunting a build similar to that of the Autobot, though on a much smaller scale and with weaponry externalized instead of integrated, Epps shared Ironhide's fascination with advanced ordnance. The pair had spent many a pleasant hour by themselves secluded in NEST's weapons facility discussing the efficacy of an assortment of volatile elements while debating such military arcana as line-of-sight versus guided-arc delivery. On numerous such occasions Epps had also insisted on showing off pictures of his mate and three offspring.

Leaning away from the workbench, Epps admired the short-barreled, large-magazine weapon he had been working on. "She's finished," he declared proudly. "What do you think? I started with a Protecta, which is an upgraded model of the old Striker Street-Sweeper, reinforced the barrel and other components, and enlarged the magazine to hold the smallest sabot rounds currently in production."

Ironhide examined the lethal-looking device. "May I?" One immense metal hand reached forward.

"Please do. I'd be interested in your expert opinion."

With two fingers, the Autobot carefully picked up the weapon and brought it close to his face. After a moment's inspection, he held it alongside his right hand. A series of loud metallic clicks and whirs filled the room as the hand melded into an enormous multibarreled missile launcher. Next to it, Epps's project was dwarfed.

"What d'you think?" The tech sergeant gazed expectantly at the Autobot weapons specialist.

What is it that Optimus keeps telling us to keep in mind when dealing with humans? Ironhide mused. *Oh yes—tact and diplomacy.* Unfortunately, tact and diplomacy were not among Ironhide's specialties, his mind being more fort- than forte-oriented. His replies tended to be as straightforward and unvarying as his aim.

"Very nice toy," he ventured hesitantly.

Extending a hand, Epps uttered a word the Autobot had not yet assimilated into his English vocabulary. "Thanks," he muttered. "Give it back, man."

"I am not a man. I am an Autobot. We are autonomous robotic lifeforms from the planet . . ." He broke off, seeing that his human friend was not listening. "Oh, I remember now. A linguistic colloquialism."

"Yeah." Epps clamped the weapon back onto its workstand mount. "You know what you can do with your colloquialism."

"No, I do not. Perhaps you can tell me," Ironhide inquired ingenuously.

"Don't tempt me." Donning his safety work glasses, the sergeant had leaned forward and was studying his project anew. "You know, I'm open to suggestions."

"In that case . . ."

They worked together for more than an hour before Epps finally rose from his seat. The tech sergeant lavished one more loving look on his sabot-firing Protecta before heading for the door. Halfway to the exit he paused and glanced back.

"You know, there's one thing that's been on my mind ever since we took down Megatron and the other Decepticons at Mission City. No matter how heavily or how long you and your buddies were engaged, you never seemed to run out of ammo. The energy beam stuff I can sort of grasp, but not the repeated use of heavy explosives. How does that work?"

Always happy to expound on a subject that was near and dear to him, Ironhide explained. "We have within ourselves the ability to ingest raw materials and rapidly reproduce a wide variety of necessary resources depending on the necessities of the moment. Our advanced design and construction demands that each of us be able to repair and replenish much of which we are composed and which we use. All of us have these abilities, though some are more adept at certain aspects than others. Mine is weaponry. Ratchet's is repair." He shook his head, utilizing the simple human gesture with the ease of practice.

"Bumblebee could explain it better, but since he is not here I shall try my best. As a technical weapons specialist I presume you possess a basic familiarity with the principles of nanoengineering, quantum alteration of volatile compounds, and metaflux metallurgy down to the subatomic scale?"

Epps pursed his lips, stared at the Autobot for a long moment, and nodded. "Let's just say that now I understand why I sometimes see you guys eating scrap, and leave it at that. Makes sense if you think about it. Like energy, real yield has to come from somewhere. I get it now. You have to be able to alter more than just your shapes." He grinned to himself. "I remember a robot that could reproduce bourbon, but he wasn't real." Hand on the door, he squinted back at the looming angular shape that filled much of the workroom with its bulk. "What about Optimus Prime? What does he specialize in?"

Ironhide did not hesitate. "Leadership."

* * *

"We've got *two* indications of activity, sir."

Lennox stared at the screen in front of the technician. The team had only just returned from Zambia and had barely had enough time to clean up and begin repairing the damage to Ratchet—and now this.

"We've never had two simultaneous hits at the same time." He stared closely at the readouts beneath the screen. "Are you sure about this, Cabrillo?"

"Yes sir." The tech pointed at first one portion of the screen, then another. Her fingernails, Lennox noted absently, were very long, and the ends were decorated with little American flag decals. They reminded him of his wife, and home, from which he had been too long absent. You could only say so many times to your life partner that your absence was necessary for the safety of the world before she no longer cared. He'd already missed his daughter's birthday one too many times.

"Satellites confirm both Gamma readings. We've got a hot spot in southeastern Peru and another approaching Oobagooma and moving south."

"Where the hell is Oobagooma?" Lennox muttered. "You sure you're not making this up?"

The tech looked up at him. Her tone was dead serious. "No sir. It's in far Western Australia, sir."

The captain did not try to hide his bafflement. "Western Australia. Southeastern Peru. What could there possibly be in such remote places to attract the attention of the Decepticons?"

"I can't imagine, sir." The tech looked up at him. Her eye shadow, he noticed, was nearly as thick as the polish on her nails. "Maybe they're diversions, to draw our attention away from somewhere else."

"Might be," he murmured thoughtfully. "But we can't take that chance. We're going to have to split our forces in order to find out. Thank you, Cabrillo."

When informed of this new development, Optimus concurred with the captain's conclusion. Speaking in the huge underground chamber that was the main Autobot living area, he rested an arm on one knee as he knelt before Lennox.

"We have had experience with Starscream dividing his forces before. He is an expert in the use of misleading tactics. I agree with you that we cannot allow him to operate unchallenged regardless of how isolated are the areas on which he seems to be focusing. I have of course memorized every detail of your planet's surface. This Western Australia is much closer to our base here and so I will accompany you to confront him there." He rose. "Ironhide and Salvage will come with us. Ratchet, I fear, is too badly injured to risk another confrontation so soon. His strength is dangerously depleted, and he has to rest. Who else can we muster?"

Lennox considered. "We'll take Kaminari with us. Petr can go to Peru, and I'll put Epps in charge of that operation." He looked up at the Autobot leader. "Do you think Longarm can deal with this by himself, or at least make the necessary on-the-ground observations to find out what's going on there?"

"All Autobots are prepared to survive and fight on their own, yet it is always better to have backup. Though I am hesitant to do so, I will send Knockout with him."

Lennox frowned. "Why the hesitation? I've seen Knockout in both his terrestrial guise and natural Autobot form. He doesn't look any different or less competent than the rest of you."

"He is young as Autobots go and therefore lacks experience." Optimus was clearly unhappy at the choice that had been left to him. "Still, he should go, if only to cover Longarm's back. And Longarm is a veteran. I am sure he will keep Knockout in line." The Autobot leader sounded more confident. "It will be good seasoning for Knockout to have to deal with a minor Decepticon incursion. Perhaps he may even have the opportunity to engage a Decepticon. That is an experience he longs for, though I wonder if he will feel the same after the fact."

Lennox concurred. "Epps will help Longarm keep an eye on him. And Petr will be there to analyze—if Epps can keep his attention from being diverted from the task at hand by some interesting bug."

"We must leave as soon as possible," Optimus exclaimed. "Though few humans appear to be in imminent danger in either location, Starscream and his minions do not expose themselves for nothing. We must learn why they are now operating in such empty places."

"I know, I know." Lennox sighed. "I'll alert Command to get a couple of C-17s ready."

"You yourself are always ready, Captain Lennox, to defend us as well as your own kind."

But Optimus was wrong. At that moment Lennox was thinking not of the challenge to come, but of his daughter.

* * *

Longarm had to use his tow arm to physically restrain Knockout when the ramp at the rear of the big
cargo jet dropped down and open. The noncorporeal
rider the transformed motorcycle had projected onto
his back wore black leather, heavy shades, and chains.

"Hold him there." Puffing from the sudden exposure to high altitude, Technical Sergeant Epps hurried
to the back of the plane to catch up to the two Autobots. Pausing to catch his breath, he planted himself
directly in front of the idling cycle.

"Get out of the way, Sergeant!" The cycle roared,
its big engine deafening within the confines of the
fuselage. Around them, NEST operatives dressed as
relief workers occasionally glanced in the direction of
the two machines. Used to being around the Autobots
while back on Diego Garcia, no one stared.

"Man, look at yourself." Epps shook his head as
Petr, preoccupied as usual, strolled past him. "You
cannot go out here lookin' like that, wheelie dude."

Knockout's rumbling dropped to a purr. "Why
not?" The human image on his back did not move,
did not change expression, did not breathe. Knockout
had scanned it from what seemed to be a suitable
source subject in NEST's main research library. "Me-
chanically I know that I am perfect, and my 'rider'
provides the necessary camouflage."

"Says who?" Epps gestured as he spoke. "This is
highlands Peru, South America. Your 'rider,' my machine, is lifted from an early 1950s American film.
That image was standout then, and if *anybody* here
were to recognize it now we'd have ourselves one instant big-ass riot. Even if the right-on image did not

happen to be a human icon, it's way too North American for this location." He cast a critical eye over the rest of Knockout's ensemble. "Additionally, that getup is era-inappropriate and way too flashy for this part of the world. You don't even begin to look local."

Stopping alongside the idling bike, Longarm could only concur with the human's assessment. "Do not take it to heart, Knockout. Many of us needed to have our initial vehicular transformations refined in order to blend in properly among the humans. Even Bumblebee did so. Humans are not like the inhabitants of Cybertron. Conditions, habits, customs all vary greatly on this world depending on location. They are not consistent, not even within designated tribal boundaries."

There was silence for a moment save for the sounds of efficient NEST operatives busying themselves with cargo pallets. The delivery of very real earthquake relief supplies provided the necessary cover for the arrival of the unmarked C-17.

"I suppose you're right, Longarm." Knockout gave in reluctantly. "If Optimus can take criticism from an adolescent human, I certainly can accept it from an adult technical specialist."

"Flattery is nice," Epps commented. "Compliance would be better." Once again he singled out the projection that was "riding" on Knockout's seat. "Close, but try again." Obediently, the face of the bike rider morphed to fulfill the cosmetic instructions. "Costume should be poncho over jeans and a lighter-weight jacket. Leather is okay. I'm told they do up a lot of good leatherwork here. If we get time between bustin' Decepticons I've gotta try and get my lady a jacket." He continued to analyze the projection. "Not so much metal in the jacket and on the body. Lose the chrome studs. This ain't LA."

"But I *like* the metal highlights," Knockout protested.

" 'Course you do. You're an Autobot. But your 'rider' ain't. He's supposed to be a spittin' image of local flesh and blood."

The big bike shook visibly. "Don't remind me." Once again the outlines of the human simulation on his back shifted and flowed. This time when it stabilized it looked much more like a well-off young Cuzcano than an early American film icon. The bike would still be likely to draw attention from the locals, but at least now its rider would not.

Epps pulled his own NEST-issued poncho tighter around him as he accompanied the two altered Autobots down the back ramp of the cargo jet. Petr Andronov was already standing on the tarmac admiring their surroundings. At over eleven thousand feet, the air around the ancient Inca capital of Cuzco was considerably thinner than at sea-level Diego Garcia, or even that of southern Zambia.

Running to meet the plane, a local NEST contact affiliated with the Peruvian armed forces greeted the two men in lightly accented English.

"Welcome to the Andes, Mr. Andronov, Sergeant Epps. I am Lieutenant Pierre Morales, S.A. NEST technical adjutant."

Epps blinked at him. " 'Pierre'? If you don't mind my pointin' it out."

"Not at all." The officer smiled. "I am used to it.

My mother was a French agronomist. After working much of her life in these mountains, she married my father and retired here." He held out two cups and a thermos. "Have some coca tea. It will help with the *soroche*."

"Altitude sickness," Petr explained as he accepted the thermos and one of the cups.

Epps took the other and eyed his companion appreciatively. "Man, is there anything you don't know?"

"*Da*. I cannot rap."

Epps raised a hand. "Hey, don't look at me. I like the classics."

Steam issued from the thermos as Petr filled his cup with pale golden tea. "Russian? Tchaikovsky? Glinka? Scriabin?"

Epps shook his head as he took the thermos. "American. Brown. Gaye. Green."

Morales stared as the driverless tow truck accompanied the motorcycle and its slightly rezzing rider down the ramp. "Are those—Autobots?"

Epps nodded. "Longarm and Knockout. The experienced and the energetic."

"*Soprender* . . . amazing! They look like perfectly ordinary everyday vehicles."

"That's good. 'Ordinary' is exactly what we're after." He lowered the cup from his mouth and smacked his lips approvingly. "Nice flavor. Real delicate. How many cups do I have to drink to get a buzz on?"

"At least a hundred. I have only seen Autobots in my training videos. Will I—can I—see them change?"

"Sorry." Handing back the cup, Epps shook his head. "Outside authorized NEST perimeters they only do that when it's necessary, and it's only necessary when something bad is happening, and so—you really don't want to see them do it."

"*Que lastima.* Ah well. Come." Turning, Morales led the way across the tarmac. Betraying no hint of their true identities, the two vehicles followed. So did Andronov, pausing now and then to examine the occasional weed that thrust an emerald shaft up through the paving. As they walked, the Peruvian officer filled them in.

"The activity that was detected by NEST's tracking satellites is still centered on some Inca sites to the southeast of here. The ruins in question are substantial, but not famous like Ollyantaytambo or Macchu Picchu. We have overflown the area in helicopters but seen nothing. Only local residents, some tourists, and ordinary vehicles that—" He broke off. "Ah. 'Ordinary.'" He glanced back at Longarm and Knockout. "How does one tell a Decepticon from an everyday run-of-the-mill machine? My squad and I find ourselves looking cross-eyed at every truck, every taxi."

Petr nodded. "It can be mentally unsettling to not know if bus you board is going to take you to your destination or take your life. Tracking satellites can pick up evidence but still have difficulty resolving the specifics of individual vehicles, as we recently saw for ourselves in Africa. And errant Decepticon signals are only intermittent." He jerked a thick thumb in Longarm's direction. "The Autobots will know."

Morales looked behind him, in the direction of the big cargo jet that continued to unload a steady stream of supplies. "This is it? You are the whole team? Two humans and two Autobots?"

"Hey," Epps chided him. "I was at *Mission City.*"

"We are more than enough to handle one Decepticon signal," Petr replied. "Unless, of course, it is Starscream."

The officer's eyes widened. "Starscream! You don't think *he's* here, do you?"

Epps looked back at the tow truck that was following them. "Hey Longarm! You hear that? You think ol' Starscream might be messin' around hereabouts?"

"Since you ask my opinion, Sergeant Epps, I do not. It would be highly uncharacteristic of Starscream to engage in any terrestrial operations by himself."

"Yeah, that's what I thought." Epps turned back to Morales. "We don't even know for certain yet that we got us a Decepticon here, Pierre."

"*Verdad,* my friend. Hopefully you will find out later today."

"Not today." Sucking the thin air, the sergeant regarded the pale, leaden sky. "Nobody's blowing up any local infrastructure, so there's no immediate emergency. This Decepticon, if that's what the signal is coming from, doesn't know we're here. So the only thing Petr and I are gonna roll out of tonight is bed." He patted his stomach. "Any suggestions for dinner?"

"I can recommend," Morales told him. "Would you like to try some local specialties? I know an excellent place for *cui.*"

"I'm up for anything that sounds cute," Epps replied enthusiastically.

"Not myself, I think."

The sergeant eyed the Russian. "Why not? You know something about this 'cui'?"

Andronov shook his head. "Who, I? *Nyet*, nothing. I just want some real tea, is all. Something stronger and sweeter and blacker than this flavored water we have been given." He eyed his cup of pale liquid with obvious distaste.

Epps shrugged. "Suit yourself. I'll eat your portion, too."

But he did not.

🔰 10 🔰

The following morning dawned cold and rushed. Rushed, because an angry Epps spent a number of minutes chasing the guffawing Andronov several times around the NEST compound's offices.

"What is the matter with you, my friend?" Panting hard, the scientist sought shelter behind a long, wide desk.

"I'm gonna kill you, man!" Facing him, Epps finally paused and straightened. "Maybe later, when I can catch my breath. Cuí! I'm gonna cuí your . . . !"

"Did you not like the taste of guinea pig? The 'rabbit of the Andes,' it is called. A staple food of the Incas and is still so today." He was grinning hugely. "The little hairs, are they not so nice and crunchy when they have been burned?"

"Shoulda told me I'd be eatin' some kinda big rat." Epps saw Morales approaching. "Kill you later. Gotta resolve us a possible Decepticon sighting today."

Despite the tech sergeant's chronological disclaimer, Petr continued to maintain some distance between them as Morales offered greetings. By the time they had left Cuzco behind and found themselves heading in the direction of the suspicious signal, memories of Sergeant Epps's gustatory calamity had been put aside as he came to see the humor in it. Leastwise, his mind did. His stomach was still not entirely assuaged.

Riding in a civilian Hummer so that local operatives could maintain NEST's usual low profile, they were followed by a four-wheel-drive van carrying half a dozen of Morales's heavily armed colleagues. Epps would have preferred more backup, but because this was not a part of the planet where the Decepticon threat had ever loomed large, NEST's presence was recent and correspondingly slight.

In his tow truck guise Longarm brought up the rear, but he was unable to keep Knockout from zooming ahead of the others or taking side trips onto dirt roads. Every time the younger Autobot took off on his own he did so with a roar and a flourish, sending dirt and gravel flying. Local farmers tending their herds and ancient fields looked askance at this odd convoy, but because of Longarm's presence assumed it had something to do with repair or construction farther along the route.

They were grateful to see that something was being done. In this part of the country there was only the one road running eastward through the mountains, and it was always in need of maintenance. It looked as if the government was providing a road crew to maybe do something about fixing the important route. At least it was a change from the usual somber convoy of ambulances and hearses.

Cresting the pass near the turnoff to Tres Cruces, the convoy slowed as it began its descent. Despite the altitude it was soon impossible to see anything except the trees that began to shadow the road. After a while even they were swallowed by the perpetual mist.

From his seat behind Morales, Epps leaned out his open window. The air had rapidly grown so moist that it seemed as if it were raining *up*.

"Damn! This is like San Francisco on a bad day. We could be surrounded by Decepticons and never even see 'em. When does it clear up?"

"It never 'clears up,' my friend." Turning in his seat, Morales looked back at his passengers. "This is cloud forest. One sees the sun here but rarely. It will be like this for another thousand meters or so of steady descent until we reach the first foothills of the rain forest."

Opening his computer Epps positioned it on his lap as best he could, but was unable to pick up a signal. The lack of contact was not unexpected. They were dropping down into an incredibly steep, winding canyon on the eastern slope of the Andes. In places the rock seemed to overhang the road. Not the likeliest spot to locate a satellite signal even with the best equipment, much less with his laptop's small integrated antenna. Frustrated, he closed the clamshell. They were heading for the last recorded location for the Gamma pickup. As the Hummer slowed to a crawl in order to negotiate increasingly tight curves and switchbacks, the question that had been bothering him and Lennox as well as Optimus Prime ever since this signal had been detected rose once more to the fore.

What on Earth, pun intended, had drawn so much as a single Decepticon to this isolated corner of the planet? There was no technology here to adapt, no supply of metal, no population to terrorize. Only scantly inhabited mountain and rain forest. Had they overlooked something before the sergeant and the others had been dispatched? Or was the satellite pickup simply an error—a computer glitch or false reading?

Regardless, Epps knew it had to be checked out. No Decepticon signal however questionable could be allowed to go uninvestigated.

He glanced to his left. If the Russian scientist had any better theories, he wasn't voicing them. Instead, Andronov appeared completely engrossed in the wall of green that was sliding past the Hummer. Epiphytes clung tenaciously to overhanging trees while mosses and other hydrophilic growths covered even the bare rock from which the road had been laboriously chiseled.

Chiseled and blasted, Epps told himself as he studied as much as he could see of the winding route ahead. He found that he was increasingly thankful for the dense cloud cover. The single-lane dirt road, which provided the only access from the highlands to the Amazon basin for hundreds of miles in either direction, had not a single guardrail. He sensed rather than saw the sheer drop on his side of the Hummer.

Leaning forward, he tapped their guide on the shoulder. "What happens if you meet somebody coming up? A truck, or a bus?"

Morales didn't smile. "They back up until we find a place where one or the other can pass. Traffic descending always has the right-of-way."

A plainly dubious Epps peered out the window

again. "I don't see anyplace to pass. Unless you're a bird."

"There aren't many such places. It all depends on the relative sizes of the confronting vehicles. I once heard of a petrol tanker that had climbed halfway up to the pass only to have to back all the way down to Pilcopata. Took both drivers hours to complete the trip."

Epps contemplated the mist. "Anybody ever go over the side here?"

"Oh, frequently." Morales spoke as if it were the most normal thing in the world, like a traffic sigalert on the Los Angeles freeways. "The canyon below us is littered with the corpses of dozens of trucks and buses."

The sergeant swallowed. "'Dozens'?"

"Maybe hundreds. Nobody knows for certain because no one keeps track of such things and because so much of the canyon is inaccessible without special mountaineering equipment. You can't use aircraft in here, obviously, because of the narrowness of the canyon walls and the permanent cloud cover. Also, many of the accidents are not reported because the truck is carrying illegal or smuggled cargo, or the bus has improper brakes, or any one of a number of other reasons." He smiled reassuringly. "Do not worry. We are in a new vehicle with four-wheel drive, as is the van behind us. And I assume your Autobot friends do not have issues with traction."

Leaning far out the window, Epps looked back up the treacherous road. Longarm's reassuring shape was clearly visible behind the van. He could not see

Knockout, but he could hear the rumble of the smaller Autobot's engine. He eased back into his seat.

"If they do, none of 'em has ever spoken about it to me. Though even an Autobot can only survive a fall of so many hundreds of feet."

"Then it is best that they keep to the road. There are drops in places here that are considerably greater than a hundred meters."

Finally, something that drew Andronov's attention away from the local biota. "A hundred *meters*, you say?"

"Yes, but such drops will grow smaller and more infrequent as we continue to descend."

Epps was about to ask the Russian if he would care to switch seats when a sudden shout from Knockout rose above his concerns as well as above the steady growling of gears and engines.

"There—there they are! I've got them on my perceptors!"

"Hey, wait . . . !" Epps yelled out the window. Either his admonition was too late, its subject did not hear him, or else he was simply being ignored.

Cutting so close to the edge of the roadway and the clouds below that his rear tire sent dirt and gravel spinning out into emptiness, Knockout came roaring past the Hummer to vanish into the mist ahead of it. Within seconds his exhaust had been swallowed up by the clouds. An alarmed Epps leaned forward.

"Stop! Hold up right here."

Morales passed the order to the Hummer's driver. The officer's translation was unnecessary, as the driver had already hit the brakes—"stop" being one

English word that was recognized pretty much every-where across the planet.

With the Hummer in park and the oversized brake set, Epps dragged his launcher from behind the seat and climbed out, taking care to move to the front of the vehicle while keeping well away from the lethal drop on his side. Armed only with a pistol, Morales joined him. Showing that despite his continual dis-tractions he could shift his attention quickly from aphids to enemies, Petr emerged behind them grip-ping his special rifle.

As the three men peered down the cloud-swathed road, a rumble approached from behind. Skirting perilously close to the edge, his tires kicking pebbles off into emptiness, Longarm had squeezed past the van to come up behind the Hummer. As he did so, one of his rear wheels actually hung out in open air for a moment before regaining contact with the roadbed.

Humans and Autobot listened intently. Though the bends in the road and the heavy mist combined to mute noise, the sound of Knockout's engine receding into the distance could still be heard.

Clutching the launcher, Epps looked back at the tow truck. The tech sergeant was quietly fuming. "All of a sudden he just went zooming past us, shouting something about having 'them' on his perceptors."

"I know," the truck replied. "I of course received his broadcast the instant it was generated."

"I yelled at him to stop. He ignored me. Or pre-tended he didn't hear."

Longarm sighed heavily. "Knockout is smart, but

impulsive. I myself am presently sensing nothing directly in front of us."

"Good!" The sergeant raised the muzzle of his weapon. "Won't hurt him to admit he's made a mistake."

"That is what concerns me. We rarely make such mistakes." Longarm spoke absently, the bulk of his attention focused on the section of canyon just ahead. "Utilizing different wavelengths and instruments that are more sensitive than human oculars, I can see reasonably well through the water vapor in which we are currently enveloped. But I cannot see through solid rock—at least, not very far—and the twists and cutbacks in this route prevent me from accessing Knockout's present position." A moment passed during which the only sounds were those of idling engines and unseen rain forest birds. Then . . .

"Ah, he is returning. Perhaps you were right after all, Sergeant Epps. A false alar—"

"Weapons up, weapons up!"

They heard Knockout before they could see him. In contrast, no one had any difficulty detecting the explosions that erupted in the motorcycle's wake. Chunks of road and cliffside flew in all directions. Epps started to run to his right to take cover, realized that the only cover available in that direction lay hundreds or thousands of feet below, and threw himself down beside the Hummer. *We're in a helluva position,* he thought as he raised the launcher. Trapped on a narrow road between sheer cliff on one side and sheer drop on the other. Sitting ducks, though ducks would have been better off in the wet and the clouds.

Had this been the Decepticons' intent all along? he

found himself wondering. Send out a barely perceptible signal, just enough to draw a minimal reaction, and then corner NEST's responders in an indefensible location? But the narrow, winding mountain route was no less inaccessible to the enemy than it was to Longarm and Knockout. There was no more room here for Decepticons to maneuver than there was for Autobots. Whoever was pursuing and shooting at Knockout would be restricted to the same single, precarious roadway.

Unless . . .

Unless the Decepticons here had chosen terrestrial guises specifically intended to be able to deal with such difficult surroundings.

The familiar sound of metal changing its shape resonated behind him. He did not need to look around to know what was happening. Further confirmation came from the awed reactions of the operatives who had by now piled out of the van. A moment later a pair of gleaming metal legs strode past, stepping easily over the Hummer that occupied most of the roadway. The fully altered Longarm had his weapons systems out and activated.

Exploding without warning from the cloud cover, something struck Longarm hard on his right shoulder. The blast sent him spinning in that direction. One leg fought for solid purchase before sliding off into empty air. Stunned, Epps reached instinctively toward Longarm. The gesture was little more than that. He could no more grab hold of and prevent the Autobot from falling than he could have saved Optimus from a similar plunge.

As he tumbled over the edge, Longarm reached

back. Metal fingers slammed into solid rock and dug in, breaking the potentially fatal fall.

"Get behind the bend!" Andronov held his rifle while searching the mist for a target. His knowledge of battlefield tactics was revealing the Spetsnaz training in his background to an appreciative Epps. "Behind rock!" With his free hand he waved wildly.

The local NEST fighters were unable to understand his heavily accented English, but Morales translated as he joined the Russian in retreating. They managed to get behind the nearest twist in the road just before a series of explosions tore the van to shreds. Striking just beneath the Hummer's front bumper, another shell blew it into the air and sideways into the cliff face. The concussion also lifted Epps off the ground and sent him flying—again to his right.

As if in slow motion, he saw the side of the road shrinking above him. While he fell he wondered if he would land in a moss-cloaked tree and if it would be soft enough to break his fall—or his back. Of course, if a thousand feet of cloud lay between him and the rain forest below, it wouldn't matter what he landed on. As it turned out, he struck on something hard and unyielding—but after falling only a few feet.

"I have you, Sergeant Epps!"

Safe in Longarm's grasp, Epps found himself rising upward almost as fast as he had dropped. After setting the human safely back on solid ground, Longarm shoved forcefully with both hands. The effort boosted him high into the air, and he landed beside the sergeant hard enough to send a quiver through the roadbed. Seconds later a shape burst through the swirling mist and came barreling toward them. It was

Knockout, moving fast. As another explosion sent fiery yellow and orange flame rippling through the clouds, he changed shape. By the time he reached their position and came to a halt in front of Longarm, he had fully resumed his natural form.

"I was right! My perception was correct. The Decepticons are—!"

Reaching out, Longarm slapped him hard and deliberately across his face.

A stunned Epps stared openmouthed. Never before had he seen an Autobot strike another. He had never even *heard* of such a thing. Longarm's open metal palm carried enough force to send Knockout stumbling into the cliff face.

"You have acted recklessly, endangering not only yourself and me but the humans as well! What have you to say for yourself?"

"I . . ." Clearly stunned by the senior Autobot's reaction, Knockout's thought processes had been shocked into temporary stasis.

"Leave it for later." Longarm dropped into a fighting stance. "Here they come!"

Kneeling, Epps aimed his launcher down the road. He resolved to make the shot a good one. As he took aim, he wondered what—no, not what, he corrected himself, *who*—they were facing. At least no shrill whine was echoing through the cloud-enveloped chasm. If Starscream was anywhere in the vicinity, he was flying too high to be heard.

But a dangerously similar sound was rising up the canyon, increasing in volume as it drew nearer.

It was high-pitched but uneven. Nor was it alone. A softer yet even more familiar clamor accompanied it.

As a sudden breeze cleared the mist slightly, Epps squinted just above the launcher's sightline. He knew *both* sounds. It was his present unfamiliar surroundings and uncertain expectations that had momentarily thrown him off. Looking up from where he knelt in the cold mud he yelled a warning to his companions—mechanical as well as human.

"Incoming! Osprey—chopper!"

As he turned from the road to face the abyss, the Decepticons emerged from the clouds off to his right. The Osprey came up parallel to the road, the better to bring its side guns to bear. Spitting out more than a thousand rounds a minute, the rapidly rotating miniguns chewed up rock and vehicles alike. If the Peruvian NEST fighters had not taken cover behind the upper bend in the road they would have been turned to hamburger. Only Epps's kneeling stance saved him as the swarm of slugs tore through the air above his head.

In addition to reducing the Hummer and the remains of the van to even finer scrap, the heavy fire drove Longarm and Knockout toward the dripping, fern-covered rock face. Both Autobots answered with weapons of their own as the chopper hovering farther down the canyon let loose with rockets. With chunks of stone, roadway, and sheet metal flying all around him, Epps was unable to take proper aim with his launcher. It was all he could do to bury his face in the mud, try to squirm as deep down into the roadbed as he could, and work to keep from being blown off the thoroughfare. He dared not even look up to see if Petr or Morales were still alive. As if the din of multiple explosions were not deafening enough, each one echoed repeatedly off the narrow canyon walls.

Backs pressed against the sheer, sodden rock behind them, Knockout and Longarm kept up a steady fire on the two aircraft. A lucky shot from the larger Autobot struck the Osprey in a vulnerable spot and sent it reeling downward.

Got one of the bastards! Epps thought exultantly. Raising his head, he tried to swing the launcher's muzzle up and around. If the two Autobots could keep the chopper occupied and he could get off a clean shot with the sabot round . . .

The mist parted. Propelled by powerful metal hands, an enormous metal body swung itself up and over the side of the road directly in front of him. Rolling madly downslope, Epps just managed to avoid being stepped on. Too close now to let loose with heavy weapons, the converted Osprey stood confronting the two Autobots. Its right shoulder joint was still smoking where Longarm's missile had struck home.

"I will carve both of you up with my bare hands!" So saying, the big Decepticon spread his fingers wide. The Osprey's twin rotors had become huge blades spinning at metal-cutting speed, their whine clearly audible above the rain that had begun to fall. Holding both sets of rotating blades out in front of him, the Decepticon started forward. Where the blades struck the roadbed, deep grooves appeared in the mud and in the bedrock beneath.

"Greetings, Ruination," Longarm yelled back. "Be careful while boasting that you don't lose track of what your hands are doing and accidentally cut your own throat." Dropping into a squat, he proceeded to leap higher than a surprised Epps would have thought possible.

Inclining backward at an angle that would have snapped any human spine, Ruination raised his spinning blades upward to fend off the expected plunge. Instead, now that the Decepticon's lethal hands were pointed upward, Knockout hit him from beneath, nearly taking his legs out from under him. Stumbling, Ruination struggled to keep his balance on the narrow roadway. As he lowered his arms the raging Decepticon tried to bring his blades to bear on the smaller Autobot, who was now clinging tightly to his legs. One razor-sharp edge sliced into the back of Knockout's left foot and the Autobot yelled in pain.

Which was when Longarm finally landed hard on their assailant from above.

Wrapping his legs around the bigger Decepticon's waist, he began pounding the enemy from behind with both fists. Engaged from behind and below, Ruination flailed wildly but was unable to bring his cutting rotors to bear on the Autobot who had fastened itself to his back.

Looking on as Longarm and Knockout began to get the better of the brawny Decepticon, Epps was about to let out a jubilant yell when a sudden thought struck him.

Where's the other Decepticon?

Blademaster showed himself a moment later. Still in chopper guise he came roaring up the road, waiting to change until the last minute before reaching down to grab Knockout's legs. Yanking hard, he dislodged the Autobot from Ruination's ankles and began dragging him backward through the mud on his ventral side. As Knockout struggled desperately to right himself and bring one of his weapons, any weapon, to bear, one of Blademaster's rotors morphed into an enormous killing blade that he raised high over his head. Twisting around, Knockout could only thrust up both arms defensively.

Blinking away water, mud, an assortment of minuscule cloud forest inhabitants, and who knew what else, Epps took the best aim he could with his battered launcher. Like the sergeant, it was soaked and full of grit. Would it still fire? Locking down on his target, Epps squeezed the trigger.

With a hiss and a whoosh, the compact missile burst from the launcher. Though it missed the Decepticon's face, which had been Epps's target, it struck Blademaster in the neck. Any joint being more vulnerable to attack than flat armor, the sabot round burned furiously as it struck home. Blademaster let out a cry of distress and grabbed at his throat with both hands as he staggered away from Knockout. Saved, freed, and only lightly injured, the smaller Autobot immediately rose to his feet and pressed the attack, throwing himself at his injured foe. Though momentarily disoriented, Blademaster was still able to strike out with one hand and knock the smaller Autobot aside. As he did so, a new figure emerged from the mist to charge the tottering Decepticon.

Not only was Dr. Petr Andronov built like a linebacker, Epps decided from where he lay on the roadway: he moved like one, too.

Taking aim with his singular rifle, the Russian got off several shots in quick succession before the mass of interlocked metal that was Ruination and Long-arm came rolling in his direction to send him scrambling back to the safety of the bend in the road. Having regrouped beneath a rocky overhang, the Peruvian NEST operatives were now firing steadily from there, though their small-arms fire was little more than a distraction to Decepticons.

Petr's sortie, however, had a much more immediate result. Already hurt by Epps's sabot round, knocked backward by the charging Knockout, Blademaster now found himself suffering from the effects of several powerful electrical discharges against his body. The combination was sufficient to momentarily destabilize his internal systems. Tottering backward, he took one step, a second—and the third saw him step off into empty air. Arms flailing wildly, he fell backward into the clouds. As he did so he fought to shift back into his terrestrial guise. But due to the disruption he had incurred he was only able to partially change. Half Decepticon, half helicopter, he fell out of sight, the air whistling around him as he plummeted. Rolling to the edge of the roadbed a filthy, soaked-to-the-skin Epps listened intently. Moments later he was rewarded by the faint echo of a distant *clang*.

He wasn't the only one who heard the sound that marked the end of Blademaster's uncontrolled dive. Off to his right, the enraged Ruination let out a ferocious alien snarl. Reaching back over his shoulders, he got a solid grip on Longarm, pulled him off his back, and hurled him against the cliff face. Shards of rock went flying and Epps had to cover his face as the already injured and exhausted Autobot slumped to the roadbed. Cutting blades whirling, Ruination started toward the barely moving Longarm, only to find his advance blocked by a much smaller but grimly determined figure.

Scored, dented, and limping on one foot, Knockout regarded the much bigger Decepticon out of fiercely glowing eyes.

Epps held his breath as Ruination glared down at his audacious challenger.

"Impudent pile of circuits, I will carve you into equal segments suitable for easy disposal." Both hand blades abruptly rotated from vertical to horizontal. "But not now. Another time."

As Epps and the others looked on, the big Decepticon changed back into his Osprey guise. The VTOL aircraft showed plenty of damage, but nothing serious enough to prevent it from retreating straight back and dropping downward. From his position at the edge of the roadway Epps was able to follow the Decepticon's progress as he descended into the mist below. As he did so, the NEST operatives raced from their place of concealment to the side of the road and began pumping automatic-weapon fire into the clouds below. Rolling over and rising to a sitting position, Epps was too tired to tell them that they were wasting their time.

Across the road and downhill, Knockout was tending as best he could to the injured Longarm. The older Autobot peered up at his cohort. One eye was blinking intermittently as if the light behind it was threatening to go out.

"You—saved my life. I am grateful." Creaking, groaning, and with Knockout's support, Longarm struggled to his feet. As soon as he was standing by himself the smaller Autobot released him, stepped back, and turned to look out into the clouds that had swallowed their enemies.

"I was trying to decide whether to go uphill or down, and found myself positioned between you. That's all."

Longarm joined his comrade in peering down into the mist. If anything, it was growing thicker as the afternoon progressed and the air heated up. One hand rose to rest on the other Autobot's shoulder. Its middle finger was bent completely backward. An equivalent injury would have left a human moaning in pain, but Longarm had simply disengaged the relevant neural sensors and would leave the broken digit disconnected until Ratchet could repair it.

"I am sorry that I struck you earlier." The bigger Autobot's tone was contrite.

"You shouldn't be."

Utilizing his perceptors at maximum, Knockout was frustrated that he could not locate either of the two Decepticons in the chasm below. Had they flown off together, utilizing their terrestrial modes? Or had Ruination been forced to carry the more seriously hurt Blademaster away to safety? The latter course seemed the most likely. Both Decepticons had been damaged, Blademaster seriously. It was unlikely that they would seek to continue the fight. Knockout turned to face his friend.

"Though we are individuals, we serve the same cause. Inexperience and excitement had led me to forget that. It will not happen again."

"That," declared Longarm approvingly, "is truly the voice of experience talking."

While the two Autobots lapsed into the fullness of their own electronic language, conversing at speeds no human could follow, Epps turned to find Petr staring at him.

"Don't look at me like that," the sergeant growled. "I'm not one of your damn bugs."

"No," the Russian agreed affably. "The majority of insects I study tend to be considerably less soiled. You could do with a *dooshim*."

Epps blinked up at him. "A *what*?"

Petr hesitated, then smiled understandingly. "Ah, I forget. Word in my language that sounds like something entirely else in English. In Russian, *dooshim* is a shower."

"Oh." Epps's blood pressure subsided. He started brushing at himself, realized the futility of it, and stopped. Blinking at the road ahead, he pondered their next move. It was still raining, though it was difficult to tell where the rain began and the clouds and mist fell off. "This whole region is one big shower, but I don't feel any cleaner for it."

"You need *garyacha vada*. Hot water. And soap." Petr's gaze considered the technical sergeant from head to foot. "Lots of soap."

Epps made a face at him. "How about if I take that rifle of yours and . . ."

Smiling afresh, Petr raised an encouraging hand. "Today has already prove to be a more than sufficiently electrifying experience, thank you." He nodded past the other man, at the permanently saturated roadway. "You are in charge. What are your orders? Do we pursue?"

Epps mulled the options, then turned to the two Autobots. "What do you think? Should we go after them?"

A newly respectful Knockout waited for Longarm to respond. "Blademaster has been gravely, perhaps mortally injured. We cannot of course accurately gauge the extend of the damage he has suffered without another, closer look. If Ruination has flown him away that will prove impossible." Raising an arm, he reflected briefly on his injured finger, then looked down at himself and over at Knockout.

"Both of us have likewise sustained damage. Unlike these Decepticons, we have no localized flight capability. Whatever their intentions in this region, it is my considered opinion that neither Ruination nor Blademaster is presently capable of carrying them out. If they hold true to form, they will retire to a place of concealment and safety where they can undergo restoration."

Alongside Epps, Petr spoke up. "We know they are here. They know that we know they are here. Given such mutual awareness, they are likely to abandon whatever brought them to this part of this continent. If is one thing we have learned about these Decepticons, is that they do not function optimally while under scrutiny."

Epps considered all that had been said before making a decision. "Right. We go back to Cuzco." He turned to Morales. "In addition to enhanced satellite surveillance, NEST will provide you with additional support, Lieutenant, so that you can continue to properly monitor the situation here. You've seen how fast our people can respond. If these intruders show up here again, you can bet we'll be back. With more firepower next time."

"*Gracias por su ayuda,* Sergeant. We will keep on top of the situation." He paused briefly. "Your *compadre* is correct: you do need a shower."

Epps eyed the soaking-wet officer. "You aren't in any shape to slip the slipper on no señorita yourself, Lieutenant."

Morales offered a smile in return, then turned to look uphill. "Our vehicles are destroyed and we are on foot now. Though the vegetation around us is tropical, we are still in the mountains and it will get cold tonight. We should start walking."

"All the way back Cuzco?" Slinging his rifle over his shoulder, a doubtful Petr offered a mild curse in Russian.

Morales started up the road. "Do not despair. As I mentioned before, this is the only road for many miles in both directions from the highlands down into the *selva.* A bus or truck will come along and we will acquire a ride."

"Can't be soon enough for me." Epps kicked the empty and therefore useless missile launcher over the side of the road and watched as it was swallowed up by the clouds below. It was unlikely to change the balance of power among the local monkeys. "I've had enough for one day."

As they trudged upward, the scientist came up alongside him. "Cheer up, Sergeant. At least you are not in desert, *da*?"

Epps shot him a look. "For a Russian, you're a pretty funny guy, Petr."

His companion's attention dropped to a burst of blue flowers that was sprouting from the center of the roadway. "All Russians are funny, Sergeant. It just take a little tragedy and misery to bring out the humor in us. Did you ever hear the one about the *slivoki* and the pig farmer?"

"No." Arching his back and stretching, Epps found that some of the soreness was beginning to fade from his legs and back. "Why don't you enlighten me."

The scientist proceeded to do so.

11

There is the Outback, and then there is Beyond the Outback. Looking down at the endless stretches of raw red earth below the descending transport, Lennox knew immediately that they had arrived at the latter.

Oobagooma. It didn't even sound like a real place. What lay here, among this interminable expanse of exhausted, erosion-sculpted hills and boot-piercing spinifex and lethal serpents, to attract the likes of Starscream? The only landing strip in the area was small, dirt, and quite incapable of handling an aircraft the size of the C-17. They would have to parachute in.

They could have started from Perth, he knew, but even traveling at high speed it would have taken the three Autobots days to reach this isolated part of this country that was also a continent, and where time and Decepticons were concerned, leisurely travel could not be allowed to enter into the equation. Not if they wanted a chance to catch Starscream or any of his cohorts before they could cause any real damage.

But what damage could they do here? Lennox wondered as he leaped spread-eagled from the back of the plane. Not only were there no sensitive facilities in the immediate vicinity, there was nothing of consequence for a thousand miles in any direction. Certainly nothing that seemed likely to draw the interest of a single-minded Decepticon, much less Starscream himself.

As he floated toward the red ground below, tugging occasionally on the chute's control cords, he wondered how Epps and Andronov were doing in South America. Then Kaminari Ishihara shot past him, a black-haired torpedo free-falling until the last possible moment, and the ocher surface that was rising rapidly toward him drew his full attention.

Optimus, Ironhide, and Salvage were already on the ground and had changed into their favored terrestrial guises: two pickups and one husky diesel. Prior to departure both Optimus and Ironhide had been concerned that their rolling shapes might be too flamboyant for the backcountry where they were headed. An Australian officer posted to Diego Garcia had promptly set them straight.

"She'll be right, mates. The farther you go into the Outback, the more vehicular customization you'll encounter. Not much else to do in that bloody backcountry. One bit of advice for Salvage and Ironhide, though. Change your identifying insignia to a local auto manufacturer. Be less likely to draw attention that way."

Though the recommended modification seemed too insignificant to be worth the bother, both Autobots had taken the advice to heart and instituted the recommended adjustment. Lined up on the wide dirt road, it seemed even less necessary than ever. Not a single car or truck had passed their way since they had touched down.

Like Epps in Cuzco they could have called upon NEST forces to bolster their strength. But with both Optimus and Ironhide on-site the addition of a squad or even a division of armed humans seemed superfluous. Human soldiers wouldn't be of much use against Starscream. Besides, the nearest NEST post was located in Perth, more than a thousand miles to the south. Additionally, the presence of a large number of trained operatives in such an underpopulated part of the country would be likely to draw more attention from local prospectors, tourists, and locals than suited NEST. In this part of Australia, trucks were a more common sight than groups of strangers.

Peculiarly enough, an overflying F-22 Raptor would draw less attention than a squadron of armed men and women. The empty Outback was often used by military aircraft to practice everything from tactical maneuvering to low-level bombing runs. Lennox knew any other intruders would by now have adopted innocent Earthly forms such as trucks, cars, or commercial vehicles. A Decepticon who chose a more blatantly aggressive shape like Payload would quickly find himself the unwanted subject of hasty cell phone snaps or hurriedly recorded videos.

Still, he told himself as the shock of landing ran up his legs, one could never predict what a Decepticon might do. The question here, he mused as he gathered in his chute, was what they hoped to achieve in such a desolate, uninhabited wilderness. Whatever it was, it was his job to find out and put a stop to it. There was only one problem.

The Gamma signal originally detected by one of NEST's surveillance satellites that had brought them here had disappeared just before they had left Diego Garcia.

It was not the first time a signal had been picked up only to be lost soon after. Fully aware that the Autobots and their human allies were hunting them around the clock, the Decepticons had developed ways of masking their presence as they traveled. If it were otherwise, every Decepticon on Earth would have been located and suitably dealt with immediately following the clash at Mission City. It was only when they were expending an unusual amount of energy in a location that happened to pass beneath the sensors of an orbiting satellite that they could be detected. So Lennox was not surprised that the transmission that had brought them here had subsequently gone missing.

It would make finding whoever had generated it difficult but not impossible. If the source was still in the immediate area Optimus and his companions would be able to sense even low-level transmissions once the originator was on the move again. If he, or they, had journeyed out of range, well, it wouldn't be the first time NEST had missed a chance to take down one or more of the Decepticons. Eventually though, they would get them all.

They had to, Lennox knew.

Kaminari had already slipped out of her harness, packed up her chute, and begun striding toward the waiting vehicles. The order of travel had been determined earlier, on board the transport. Ironhide would lead the way with Optimus following and Salvage bringing up the rear. The humans' individual gear, including the scientist's inimitable Jo stick and Lennox's more prosaic sabot launcher, had been carried down on Optimus's back. They would find it in the big truck's cab along with the minimal necessities for human survival: food, drink, and personal communications gear.

Donning dark shades, Lennox adjusted the side flaps that were designed to keep out the Outback's maddeningly persistent flies as he contemplated the sky. Clouds to the north, bright sunshine elsewhere. The temperature was mercifully and unexpectedly congenial. When transporting humans Optimus and his companions were perfectly capable of generating internal air-conditioning, as they had done in Zambia. Lennox disliked having to trouble them with such details. Such requests made humans appear even weaker by comparison, and were probably distracting as well. All of the Autobots' concentration and energies needed to be focused on locating and destroying Decepticons: not on providing for the comfort of their human companions.

He was not so preoccupied with such thoughts that he failed to chide the scientific member of the team for engaging in unnecessarily dangerous extracurricular activities before the search had even begun.

"This is not a vacation jaunt, Dr. Ishihara. That extended free fall you just took was unwarranted."

Removing her drop helmet, she shook out her long black hair. "Why, Captain, how thoughtful of you to be concerned for little me," she replied tightly.

He grunted. "Got nothing to do with the kind of concern you're talking about. You're here because of your skills and I'd be disappointed to lose them."

"Ah. So if I were to die your regret would be wholly professional?"

Optimus interrupted the conversation. "If it would not constitute too much of an imposition, might I remind both of you that we are here to look for Decepticons whose signal has been lost and who may be moving farther away from this location with every minute that you both stand here jockeying for individual social dominance?"

Lennox let it lie as he climbed up onto the running board on the driver's side of the cab. "Never mind. Let's move." Peering across the truck's hood, he gestured at the expedition's other human. "If you're ready, Kami-sama?"

She looked startled, started to say something, then nodded and headed for the door on her side of the truck. As soon as she had settled herself into the seat beside him, three engines revved as one and the trio of vehicles started off in the direction where the last confirmed Gamma signal had been detected. Once under way, the scientist double-checked to make certain all of her gear was present in the cab. Satisfied that nothing had been overlooked, she sat back down beside him.

They were heading for a line of low, heavily eroded hills and gullies that dominated the horizon off to the northwest. This part of Australia was home to some of the oldest rocks on Earth. Also to some of its more peculiar plants and animals, all of which had been forced to adapt to an unrelentingly harsh environment. More than anything, the terrain reminded him of the American Southwest. That thought in turn brought back memories of the battle at Mission City.

Peering out the window, he surveyed the austere countryside. If that kind of clash was fated to be repeated here, at least no innocent civilians would be put at risk.

Eyeing their stark surroundings, the red rock and sandy ground interrupted only intermittently by clumps of struggling brush and the isolated gum tree, he found himself wondering yet again what a Decepticon would seek here other than isolation. If the latter, the planet boasted locations even more remote that would be better suited to concealment. It didn't make sense. Starscream and his ilk had to be after more than just seclusion.

Halfway around the world, Epps was probably wondering the same thing. The Decepticons had to be searching for something besides solitude. Unless of course their presence in the jungles of Peru and the Outback of Australia was just a coincidence involving their quest for something as yet undetermined.

No, he corrected himself. That didn't stand to reason, either. Nothing they did involved coincidence. Like all machines, sentient or not, Autobots and Decepticons always operated with a set purpose in mind. Based on what he had learned and the knowledge he had acquired from a year of living and working among the Autobots, it was impossible to imagine someone like Ironhide, for example, engaging in a previously unresearched activity on the spur of the moment, or Starscream doing anything that smacked of the spontaneous.

The team advanced northward all the rest of that day and on into early evening. The Autobots, of course, could have continued searching operations around the clock, but in deference to their human allies chose to rest during times of darkness. There was no need for a campfire or, for that matter, a lantern. Soldier and scientist consumed their self-heating, ready-to-eat meals while illuminated by the soft yellow glow of Optimus's fog lights.

As she ate, Kaminari amused herself by pointing at the eastern horizon and slowly working her finger westward. One by one, she began identifying stars. Given the clarity of the Outback night, she had not made much progress when an impressed Lennox finally interrupted.

"Do you know the name of *every* star in the sky?"

She looked at him over a forkful of food. "Certainly not. For one thing, these heavens are far less familiar to me than those of the Northern Hemisphere. Learning the names of the stars is an amusement, a diversion."

He spooned up beef stew. "I'd think your areas of expertise would be more than sufficient to fill up your brain without the need for any additional stimulation."

Her head went back slightly as she laughed and her hair was lost against the night. "I have a big hard drive. Plenty of unused space." Her eyes twinkled in the truck's lights. "How about you, Captain? What occupies your thoughts in your spare time?"

He swallowed. "My family. Ways of eliminating Decepticons. Football." He dug into his remaining food. "Must seem pretty plebeian to someone of your accomplishments."

Her smile vanished and she turned serious. "It's 'plebeian' people like you, Captain William Lennox, who keep people like me safe from things like Decepticons." Her playfulness returned. "Also, any career soldier who can use 'plebeian' in a sentence garners my undying admiration."

He smiled through the steam rising from his spoon. "Then I'll try to keep thinking of things you don't think I'd think about."

His response was punctuated by a chorus of canine yips in the distance that were simultaneously mournful and hopeful. "Dingo," he commented. Tilting the disposable, biodegradable container to his lips, he sucked down the last of the stew. As he did so, something much nearer than the wild dogs let out a nasal bellow. Kaminari had ignored the yips, but the new sound made her jump.

"What was that?"

"Wild camel, I think. Not sure what subspecies. Can't tell without looking at its fur."

She stared. "How do you know so much about camels?"

He crumpled the empty food container and set it aside. "Spent some time in the Gulf States about a year ago. Too much time." He rose. "We ought to get some rest. You take Optimus's cab." He nodded across the illuminated area where they had parked for the night. "I'll get in Ironhide's backseat."

"That's not nearly as comfortable," she pointed out.

"It suits me. On the verge of a potential battlefield situation I don't like to get too comfortable. Try to get a good night's sleep. We've got a lot of ground to cover tomorrow, Kami."

She met his gaze. "Not 'sama' anymore?"

"I'll decide later. This expedition is just getting started."

Ironhide's faux interior was more than accommodating to someone who had spent plenty of nights sleeping in a tent or on bare ground. As he let consciousness slip away while gazing out the windshield at the spray of stars overhead, a strange new sound reached him where he lay. Not dingoes or camels this time. Something far more jaunty but almost as alien: Japanese girl band pop music.

Sealing the cab while still allowing for a sufficient free flow of air to keep his guest alive, Ironhide proceeded to soundproof his interior. He also shut down his own aural receptors. Optimus could not politely do likewise since he was the one playing host to the human with the pounding music player.

One more reason why Prime was the leader, Ironhide reflected as he settled down to wait for sunrise. Had the female human's irritatingly repetitive sound device been present in his cab, he would readily have turned one of his lesser weapons on it and blasted it out of existence.

The first light of dawn in the Outback was as brilliant and sharply defined as the southern stars had been the night before. Lennox was both surprised and relieved to see that Kaminari was already eating her breakfast when he emerged from the back of the black dually.

"I know scientists tend to be early risers, but I'm still impressed," he told her.

"One learns nothing while sleeping." She indicated a small lizard with a blue tongue that was sitting on a nearby rock catching the first warming rays of the rising sun. "Petr would like it here. The way I feel about it, I can sleep when I'm dead."

As his coffee warmed he opened his laptop and amused himself by initiating a search for the word "Oobagooma." The site had been well researched prior to their departure from Diego Garcia, of course, but he was still in waking mode and the scientist had pushed him to do something useful. Or at least to give the appearance of doing so.

Nothing new appeared on the screen. There was nothing more about their inhospitable surroundings to see on the Web than there was in person. They were in a part of the world that had no population to speak of and no developed industrial facilities. Nothing to offer except isolation and remoteness; two qualities that the region shared with the far greener southeastern Peru.

He punched in the specific coordinates where Epps was operating. Physically at least, the two regions could hardly be more disparate. One was windswept semi-desert, the other lush tropical forest. One was flat or hilly at most, the other steep and mountainous. Their present location was dry except in monsoon season, the other perpetually drenched and humid. Neither boasted much in the way of a human presence. Both featured protected natural areas. He studied the lines of information keenly, looking for something, anything, that might provide a link between the two seemingly unrelated corners of the planet. There was also . . . there was also . . .

He sat up straight, leaning forward and away from

the dually's front tire. Ironhide responded to the sudden movement.

"You react sharply." Concern underlay the truck's response. "A muscle spasm?"

"No, a brain spasm." The fingers of Lennox's right hand moved over the keyboard. "Or maybe a brain fart—I'm not sure yet."

Kaminari noted the exchange. "What have you found, Captain?"

"I was thinking about coincidence last night. How the Autobots and Decepticons never do anything that's just coincidental. It got me to wondering. Our surveillance satellites pick up two strong Gamma signals in two locations as utterly different as any two on Earth can be. According to machine logic, that can't be coincidence. Which means that even though research didn't come up with anything, there *has* to be something that links the two signal sites. Maybe they were concentrating so hard on prior Decepticon motivation they overlooked something that would otherwise have been obvious." He tapped the reinforced screen. "I think maybe I've found it."

Bending slightly forward so that the tip of the scabbard slung across her back wouldn't dig into the ground, she crouched down beside him to stare at the laptop. "You are looking at a summary of what is known about this area. I have studied it closely. I do not see any similarity with the part of South America where Sergeant Epps has been sent."

"Not overtly." There was excitement in his voice—or at least as much as Lennox ever allowed himself to show. "You have to cast a wide net to make the connection." He tapped the screen again. Two maps appeared, side by side. They displayed geological schematics accompanied by summarizations in small print.

"Look at this part of northwest South America, Kami. Not only the area where Epps, Petr, and the two Autobots are hunting Decepticons, but the regions to the north and south as well. What do you see?"

She scratched at one ear. "It's a geology map. Surveyors' reports. What am I looking for? Roadways and population centers show up much better on a political map."

"Look here, and here." He tapped the screen. "These are all exploration blocks that have been leased out to various companies. For prospecting and mining gold, silver, copper, nonmetals, and—hydrocarbons."

She drew back slightly and shifted her gaze from the screen to the soldier. "So? Are you thinking the Decepticons are into recreational prospecting?"

"No," Lennox replied, "but looking at these maps and this information I have the feeling that they are after something."

She eyed him blankly. "I don't understand." It was the first time since making her acquaintance that he had heard her use that phrase.

"What minerals is this area, where we are now, noted for?"

She shook her head. "I have no idea. I didn't think a knowledge of local geology was required groundwork for hunting Decepticons."

"Neither did I. Until I started thinking about coincidences." Closing the armored laptop, he tucked it under one arm as he stood. "Optimus!"

Starting up, the big diesel came closer. "Captain Lennox? You have found something?"

"Maybe. You Autobots are especially sensitive to radioactives. Are you aware of any around here?"

The leader of the Autobots was silent for a moment. "As a matter of fact, there are significant ore bodies scattered throughout the ground as far as I can perceive."

"Of course there are." Lennox turned back to the still bemused Kaminari. "*That's* what Oobagooma is noted for. That's the *only* thing Oobagooma is noted for. A big uranium deposit that the local government is still debating whether or not and how to exploit. But," he concluded triumphantly, "the Decepticons wouldn't hesitate.

"Consider what's happened recently. First the Decepticons move on the Kariba–Cahorra Bassa dam complex in southeast Africa. A place capable of generating enormous quantities of hydroelectric power."

"But their intent there was to destroy the two dams and cause as much damage, death, and disruption to local economies as possible," she argued.

"Ah, that's what *we* thought. That was the human interpretation. You have to think more like an autonomous robotic lifeform. Suppose that was their secondary objective, their backup? What if their *initial* purpose was to find a way to make use of all that energy? To accumulate power from an outside source? More power than they themselves could generate. If they have a way to store it . . ." He looked past her to where the big diesel sat idling. "Optimus?"

The leader of the Autobots considered. So did Iron-hide and Salvage, who had moved closer to listen. "Such a thing is possible," he finally conceded. "Iron-hide?"

"It could be done," the weapons specialist concurred. "Connection to an abundant external power source, if one could be found, could bloat an individual's internal capacity to the point of overload. Of course, consequent discharge to another point of reception would relieve the overload and alleviate the danger."

Lennox nodded slowly as he repeated the Autobot's explanation. " 'Discharge to another point of reception.' Like, to another Autobot?"

"Or to a Decepticon, yes. But there is no need to accumulate more energy than one of us can use. Each of us is amply powered by our individual Spark. Excess energy, like excess heat in humans, would simply be radiated away by our bodies. Yet I sense you are not engaging in idle speculation to pass the time, Captain Lennox."

"Damn straight." He turned a slow circle as he spoke, addressing each of the Autobots as well as Kaminari. "Consider what's here, in this supposedly 'empty' part of the world. Uranium. For Decepticons, a potential source of more power than they need simply to live. Just as exists at the Kariba–Cahorra complex. Now, according to the maps and information I just pulled up, what underlies the whole eastern face of the Andes? Oil and natural gas. Another potential source of a big external energy burst." He paused briefly to let his words sink in.

"Hydroelectric, fissionables, hydrocarbons. All vast,

concentrated sources of energy. All located far from populated areas where exploitation of similar resources would draw attention from nearby human residents. Localities where Decepticons operating undercover could exploit and draw on whatever they find. And the *only* thing that links all three otherwise highly diverse locations with Decepticon activity."

"But why? To what end?" Kaminari challenged him. "The Decepticons' energy needs are no greater than those of the Autobots, and we don't see them hoarding great stores. Just enough for emergencies. Why would they need to overload themselves, as Ironhide just pointed out, with a potentially dangerous surfeit of power?"

Lennox eyed her fixedly. "I'm sure Ironhide's right. They wouldn't need the supply of excess power for themselves. They'd store it up for something else. Something incapable of renewing its depleted spark without an external boost, without a kick-start, from outside. Like a human needing a shot from a defibrillator. You'd need a helluva lot of power to do the same kind of thing for a Decepticon or an Autobot." He looked expectantly at the leader of the Autobots. "Wouldn't you, Optimus?"

The big truck revved its engine loudly before offering a single-word reply.

"Megatron."

For a moment, silence returned to a particularly isolated corner of the Outback. It was broken by an intensely thoughtful Ironhide.

"Restoring a Spark by delivering a precisely focused burst of external power is theoretically possible. One way would be via a combined, simultaneous discharge from a number of heavily over-energized Decepticons. But I am not sure the kind of concentrated energy required could be derived from human-based resources. Only your Large Hadron Collider might generate sufficient power, and it is being carefully monitored by NEST. No matter how clever the camouflage it might adopt, not even a single Decepticon could get near it, especially when it is in operation.

"I suppose a concentrated burst of stored power *might* be capable of reactivating a spark. But I calculate that even in a best-case scenario the revived individual would not be fully responsive. The need to conserve the transferred energy would result in a revivification that was incomplete at most."

Lennox and Kaminari pondered the Autobot's assessment, but it was Optimus who commented. "We have been operating under a false assumption. We have proceeded from the incorrect belief that Starscream holds complete control over all the Decepticons here on Earth. Therefore we have been seeking connections where none exist. The dam was just a trap; this is something different.

"Starscream is de facto leader of the Decepticons, but only because of Megatron's death. He succeeded to the throne; he did not earn it. Due to the ambitious nature of the Decepticons as a whole, it will not be long before one or more rise to challenge him. His skills are formidable, but he would not be able to withstand a coup. It has happened before, as we Autobots well remember.

"He will need to prove his ability to hold that position. He needs to establish unquestionable primacy for the Decepticons to continue following him. He can only do this by destroying me and the remaining Autobots here on Earth. That would be sufficient to uphold his claim among most of his kind. But failing in that, and happily so far he has, he will be tested.

"We must now anticipate that there are potentially two Decepticon factions here on Earth. Those loyal to Starscream, such as we found at the dam in Africa, and a rogue element seeking some way, however tenuous, to restore their rightful leader. Given his arrogance, I doubt Starscream even realizes the plot that is unfolding beneath his feet. He has always felt that leadership was his birthright; he does not even conceive that others do not share this lofty view of his vaunted self. While we can, we must exploit this lack of enthusiasm for Starscream's new role.

"In the meantime, we must prevent the others from accessing the uranium deposits here, and we must then try to anticipate where they will seek it next."

⦿ 12 ⦿

While the need for some kind of road to accommodate Optimus restricted their searching somewhat, the big diesel proved adept at negotiating even the narrowest cattle-driving tracks. A surprising number of the latter crisscrossed the area they were exploring.

It was not until several days after learning of the ferocious confrontation in the Peruvian cloud forest led by Sergeant Epps that they came upon the excavation. While Autobot engines raced quietly as the three trucks pulled over onto the side of the road, Lennox and Kaminari climbed out to examine the odd dark splotch that marred the slope of the hill off to the west.

Lowering his binoculars, Lennox found himself unable to pronounce judgment. "What do you think, Kami?"

She let fall the monocular she was using. "I don't know what to say, Lennox. Previously I would have been all for charging in with weapons raised. Of course, that's what we did at the suspicious site we encountered two days ago and I'm still not certain the innocent rockhounds we found camped there have wholly forgiven us, despite the hush money you were authorized to pay out." She shook her head at the memory. "That one elderly gentleman would still be chasing you with his pickaxe had not Salvage intervened."

"I felt I had no choice," declared the pickup from behind them.

Lennox hastened to reassure the Autobot. "I don't think the old boy could have caught me, Salvage, but you did what you thought was best. Fortunately, since in your excitement you forgot to rez up a driver, he bought my explanation that you accidentally shifted out of neutral. And you barely bumped him. Thank goodness for NEST's discretionary field fund."

Kaminari nodded. "His anger level fell considerably when you handed him that money." Once again she raised the monocular to peer through its precision eyepiece.

"It was my fault." Ironhide's deep voice echoed across the open plain. "Sensing the presence of radioactives and seeing vehicles on the site, I jumped to conclusions."

"Any one of us could have made the same mistake," Optimus reminded him.

"That is so. But any one of you did *not* make the same mistake. I did."

"The important thing," insisted Lennox, "is that no one was hurt. And that none of the weekenders noticed there were no drivers in any of you until you realized they were harmless and rezzed some up."

"*Hai,*" agreed Kaminari. "Also that they did not notice that the 'drivers' in all three of you looked exactly alike."

"Salvage's creation appeared suitable." Optimus sounded nonplussed. "Given the need to generate an image of a human driver quickly, neither Ironhide nor I saw any harm in copying his projection."

Gazing across the spinifex-dotted terrain that separated the road from the oddly discolored hillside, Lennox shrugged. "If anyone questioned it further we could always have said that our drivers were triplets." With a nod, he indicated the new location that had piqued their curiosity. "I find myself standing here wondering if there's reason enough for us to announce ourselves to the operators of this site, or if we should continue on in the hopes of finding something more obvious."

"If the Decepticons are still operating in this region they will take pains to be anything but obvious." Trundling forward down the slight slope, Optimus paused long enough to allow the pair of humans to clamber up into his cab. "I perceive that the ore body here is especially rich, so much so that the residual radiation resulting from natural decay would make it an unhealthy place for humans to live. I think we should go ahead and investigate further."

"I suppose we must," Kaminari said as the diesel accelerated. "But if it's just another bunch of weekend prospectors they'll hit us with the same questions as the previous group."

"We can say that water is required for our cooling systems," Optimus ventured.

Lennox was doubtful. "They won't buy it. Whoever's working this site won't believe that anyone except a complete idiot would take a truck into this country without adequate supplies."

"Then confess that you are an idiot," Optimus suggested blithely. "Perhaps they will believe that. One way or another, we must get closer."

"Let's do it, then." Crossing his arms over his chest, Lennox made an effort to lean back and relax in his seat. Behind it, his launcher waited in readiness. Just as it had on the previous pointless occasion.

Seated beside him, Kaminari had primed her weapon. At first Lennox worried that its presence might stir awkward questions among the outlanders. He need not have worried. As eccentric a group of human beings as existed on the face of the Earth, the few people who made their homes in the Outback tended to favor the kind of individualistic attire that reflected a blissful indifference to sartorial norms. Confirmation had come from one of the part-time miners they had encountered earlier.

Seen up close the nascent mine was more impressive than it had appeared from a distance. In addition to the cut in the hillside that had initially drawn them to the spot, when they arrived at the site they found that surrounding brush concealed a deep, circular pit. Instead of being piled up in one place as was typical for such diggings, scree and tailings had been trucked away from the excavation and spread widely across a nearby dry lake. Though he was no miner, this action immediately aroused Lennox's suspicious. One thing freelancers and part-timers of any ilk were not inclined to do was spend any more time or effort than was absolutely necessary doing anything not specifically mandated by the local law.

Up against the hillside two big multiarmed excavators were removing soil and overburden while a huge bulldozer shoved the resultant rubble off to one side.

Concentrating on the work at hand, their drivers ignored the newcomers. Surely they couldn't actually be mining uranium ore here, Lennox felt. Uranium mining wasn't a small-time, family operation like digging for opals or sapphires. It required hundreds or thousands of workers and a full complement of heavy industrial gear. Then what were these people up to? He decided it was possible that they were working to expose an ore body in order to prove that they had a claim worthy of being purchased by some big multinational mining concern.

Descending from Optimus's cab, he walked over to the bulldozer, to speak with the middle-aged man who sat in its cab. The miner did not offer any welcome. Instead he focused his attention on the vehicles idling in place behind the captain.

"What do you lot want here, mate?" His tone was less than welcoming. "Something wrong?"

Lennox peered past the dozer, trying to get a better look at the diggings. "You fellas having any luck out here?"

"Would somebody in my position tell you if we were?" The miner glared back at him unblinkingly. "Your mob is a long ways from anywhere."

Lennox didn't flinch. "I could say the same for you."

The man jerked a thumb in the direction of the hillside. "This claim belongs to my mates and me. We work here. We live here. You don't do either." His expression narrowed. "You need to leave."

"Okay, okay." Lennox had heard enough. He turned to go. *Another useless detour,* he thought disappointedly. The belligerent miner hadn't even given him a chance to use his need-water-for-trucks excuse. "It's not like we were expecting Outback *hospitality* or anything."

The man raised and arm and pointed. "Plenty of hospitality about a hundred and ninety kilometers up the track. Rockhouse Station. Cold beer, too." The conversation was at an end.

"Good idea." Lennox offered thanks even though he and his companions had no intention of continuing along the main route—if the single-lane dirt-and-gravel track could be called that. Another forty kilometers and it would be time to take the first westward branching. If they could find it. Along with everything else, road signs were in short supply in this part of the world.

Kaminari had been waiting nearby for him to complete the interview. Standing off to one side, she amused herself by picking up small bits of debris. As he drew near, she opened her hand to show him her collection.

"See this dark, rounded mineral? Uraninite." When Lennox looked blank, she elucidated. "Pitchblende. There's uranium here, no question. Optimus was right about that. A really high-grade deposit, if most of it is like this." Dropping the bulk of her specimens, she saved the best chunk and tossed it to the watching miner. He reached out as if to catch it, then let it drop in front of him.

Lennox frowned. "I can understand being aloof, but that was—insulting." Bending over, he picked up one of the other stones Kaminari had dropped, turned, and chucked it directly at the bearded digger.

Not hard enough to hurt, but forcefully enough so that it wouldn't miss.

Catching sight of the oncoming projectile, the man tried to dodge. He wasn't quite fast enough. The golf-ball-sized specimen made contact with his chest.

It went right through him.

Eyes widening, Lennox let out a warning shout.

"Decepticon projection!"

As he and Kaminari whirled in the direction of the waiting Autobots, several things happened at once, and very quickly at that.

As Lennox's lob passed through the figure of the miner with whom he had been talking, the figure instantly derezzed. Their disguise blown, so did the images of the other three humans working the site. Turning away from their "work," the bulldozer and excavators came charging around the side of the pit in the direction of the waiting Autobots.

"Spread out!" Optimus was backing up as he spoke. "Be ready for anything."

Something about the looming confrontation didn't make sense, Lennox thought as he leaped up onto the diesel's running board, wrenched open the door, and reached in to grab both his launcher and the backpack full of sabot rounds. In Starscream's absence it was improbable that three Decepticons would attack three Autobots, especially if one of the latter happened to be Optimus Prime. They had to be overlooking something. But there was no sign of Starscream. Bracing themselves to meet the onslaught, humans and Autobots alike had no time for second thoughts.

"I'll take the big one," Optimus shouted. "Ironhide, you and Salvage the others!"

Muttering, the dually began to change shape and stance. "Optimus, why do you always leave it to me to look after 'the others'?" Nearby, Salvage had already transformed. The slightly smaller Autobot moved quickly to his left.

"He's not. *I'm* supposed to look out for *you*."

Rising to his full height, Ironhide stretched his weapons-laden arms wide. "As soon as we have dealt with these metal toys, we will discuss in depth exactly why that observation is so completely inapplicable."

Dropping down behind a pile of rocks, Lennox wrenched open the seal on the backpack, reached inside, and unlatched one of the self-propelled sabot shells. Setup would have gone faster with someone else to handle the loading, but he was alone and somehow he didn't think Kaminari would settle for serving as his assistant. A glance at the budding battlefield not only proved that to be the case, it had him yelling again.

"Kami, get back here! Get under cover!"

"Sorry—can't hear you!"

With her ready response contradicting her own words, she disappeared behind a small grove of scraggly red gum. It was a wonder, he decided as he hunkered back down behind his maroon-toned refuge, that when she ran her long hair didn't get tangled up in the gorse. He had to admit, she had some guts. Although she could grate on his nerves at times, he had come to rely on the scientist almost as much as he did on Epps.

Then something blew up in front of him, showering his place of concealment with earth and gravel, and he was too busy to worry about eccentric female

Japanese cyberneticists who saw themselves as a cross between Sailor Moon and Sarah Whiting. The three Decepticons had also changed shape. Reflecting their choice of terrestrial forms, they were massive examples of their kind.

Lennox was familiar enough with Transformers by now to realize that the two excavators appeared to be twins.

Optimus recognized the pair immediately. "Trample and Tread. I thought you had died on Cybertron."

The two excavators spoke in unison, giving their words an odd echoing resonance. "A lot of us did not die on Cybertron as you supposed, Prime. More of us have heeded the call than you know."

"It does not matter." Ironhide dropped into a fighting crouch as Salvage moved to try and get behind the nearest of the two identical Decepticons. "Scrap metal is scrap metal wherever it ends up."

"Have a care for your *own* components," Trample snarled.

Ironhide let out a battle cry as he charged. At the same time, Salvage came whirling in from the side. The four mechanicals shook the ground as they slammed together.

Closer to Lennox, the altered dozer boasted a formidable weapons array, and what had been its pushing blade appeared to now act as a shield.

"Surely you remember me also, Prime? You once called me a fool for following Megatron. But the universe is vast, and compared with some ancient powers, even Megatron is subservient. That power grows again, and against it none shall stand. We have here the means to revive our fallen leader, and when he sits again in power, he will remember those who were loyal to him, even in death." An arm terminating in a massive hammer rose high. "He will be pleased when I bring him your head."

Optimus readied himself. "My head stays where it is, Kickback. Whereas too many of you Decepticons seem to have lost yours."

"On the contrary," the huge Decepticon growled, "I have on this world of soon-to-be-slaves at last found a use for it. As I have for this!" He brought the hammer arm around in a sweeping arc. Still standing some distance away, Optimus held his ground—until the arm suddenly extended to twice its length, forcing him to flip backward to avoid the gleaming mace. Swinging through the air a couple of yards above the surface, it crushed several of the tough gum trees as if they were carrots.

It was only a feint. The weapon Kickback had been referring to was not his hammer, but the device that had replaced it. Hollow, cylindrical, and ominous, it erupted with a strangely muted puffing sound. The resultant recoil was strong enough to send Kickback's arm flying up and behind his back.

Looking on, Lennox saw nothing emerge from the gaping maw. No exhaust, no flame, no glow that might signify the discharge of an energy weapon. But several cubic yards of earth beneath Optimus's feet suddenly vanished and the leader of the Autobots was knocked a hundred feet backward. The concomitant sonic boom hit at the same time. Even though the shaped sonic charge Kickback had unleashed had not been aimed at Lennox, its subsidiary force was powerful enough to send him stumbling backward before he could take aim with the launcher.

As he fought to recover his balance, his gaze chanced again on the yawning open pit. Kickback had been working a bulldozer. From the first time he had set eyes on them, the sides of the pit had struck Lennox as unusually smooth. The Decepticon's mysterious weapon was some kind of sonic blaster. As he peered over the rim of his hiding place, Lennox saw that the unusual nature and force of the blow had taken Optimus by surprise. Lennox was shocked to see that the upper portion of the left side of the Autobot's chest now sported a conspicuous dent. Optimus's internal restoration mechanisms promptly reinforced the armor behind the concavity, but the big Autobot now eyed his approaching opponent with increased wariness.

"What's the matter, Prime?" Kickback chided his enemy as he strode confidently forward. "Getting old? Can't take a hit anymore?"

Missiles roared from both of Optimus's weapons launchers. One impacted harmlessly on the Decepticon's massive shield. Aimed lower, the other blasted only dirt and rocks as the Decepticon leaped high to avoid the strike. Spinning in midair, he fired his sonic weapon again. This time the invisible blow struck Optimus square in the lower part of his chest, not only knocking him off his stride but leaving him flat on his back and visibly dazed. Landing lightly on his feet, the uninjured and confident Kickback advanced to deliver a fatal blow.

"Even the greatest Autobots get old and slow," he sneered as he approached.

Fire erupted against his lower back and he let out a roar of pain and surprise.

On the move as soon as he pulled the trigger, Lennox was racing for the anonymity offered by a small, reed-fringed billabong. His flight was well timed. The chain of explosive slugs the enraged Kickback let loose tore up only the rocks where the captain had formerly been concealed.

"Insolent insect! How dare you! Where are you? Show yourself!"

Not this insect. Hunkered down in the murky, stagnant water, only Lennox's head and the business end of the waterproof launcher remained exposed.

Something skittered past his face. Experienced in the ways of forest camouflage, he ignored it. As the furious Kickback hunted through the now vacated rock pile in search of his diminutive foe, angrily tossing aside boulders the size of small cars, Lennox slowly swung the muzzle of the launcher around to bear on the lumbering Decepticon for a second time.

We bugs have to stick together, he reflected as he pulled the trigger. He was on the move again the instant the round left the mouth of the lightweight tube.

The shell detonated against the side of Kickback's head. Bellowing his outrage, the Decepticon forgot all about his tiny assailant as he flailed madly at the fiery burn on the side of his skull. When internal suppressors failed to immediately mute the searing chemical reaction, he resorted to a curative procedure that was as effective as it was primitive. Rushing to the billabong, he bent forward and ducked his head under the water. Steam exploded from the surface of the small lake.

As the sizzling faded, Kickback lifted his head. Ripples showed where a small portion of the metal on the side of his skull had melted and then cooled. As he straightened, his gaze happened to fall on a small, bipedal shape that was sprinting in the direction of the other ongoing conflict. His weapons-laden limb rose and took aim. Seeing this, Lennox frantically tried to reload.

"Goodbye, little insect," the Decepticon growled as he prepared to obliterate the sprinting scientist.

He never fired. Something massive and heavy landed hard on his back. Raising an arm transformed into his longsword, Optimus Prime brought it down sharply. A sound akin to an electronic moan issued from the prone Kickback as the point of the Autobot's blade penetrated Decepticon armor all the way through from front to back. Kickback lurched, bucked, and twisted, trying to throw his opponent off. The violent convulsive response was too little and too late. Holding the Decepticon down, Optimus struck twice more.

Kickback, severely injured, looked at Optimus Prime. "You cannot win this fight, Prime. Your small victory today is but a delaying action; nothing can stop the power that is rising. Decepticon rule shall be eternal, and the moment of your death will be celebrated for eons."

A last decisive blow, this time piercing the Spark chamber, and the exceptionally resilient Kickback finally stopped moving.

The red earth on the other side of the mine pit shook as Trample locked arms with Salvage and Ironhide lit into Tread. Lizards, insects, and birds fled the vicinity as the scene of battle was obscured by dust and flying grit. The twin Decepticons were giving a good account of themselves, Tread holding his own with the bigger Ironhide while Trample pressed his attack on Salvage. True to his name, the smaller Autobot was giving his Decepticon assailant a hard time by picking up and hurling at him everything he could find. Every time Trample prepared to leap or strike a blow he was hit by a rock, a small tree, or a car-sized clump of compacted earth.

"Stand and fight!" The Decepticon howled his frustration.

Salvage had no intention of doing any such thing. The Decepticon was bigger and stronger than he was, but Salvage was quick. Also more nimble. He wasn't Jazz, but memories of that late, lamented Autobot gave an added boost to his agility as he danced all around the stymied Decepticon. Flinging everything he could in Trample's direction distracted his opponent while the Autobot let loose with repeated bursts from his own weaponry. Dents and gashes began to appear in the Decepticon's armor as Salvage pressed the attack. He might not be as powerful as Optimus or as experienced as Ratchet, but he was nothing if not relentless.

Nearby, despite his strongest efforts Tread found himself weakening in the face of the pitiless punishment being doled out by the implacable Ironhide. The Decepticon had taken a calculated risk in separating from Trample. From a tactical standpoint it seemed to make sense. As Tread he would fight the old Autobot to a draw while Trample took out Salvage. The two would then attack Ironhide from both sides with enough strength to overwhelm the Autobot weapons master.

Unhappily, Salvage had proven a much worthier opponent than they had anticipated. With the other half of him not only still engaged but finding himself under serious assault, it was all Tread could do to fend off Ironhide's unrelenting attack.

"I've maintained this multiple missile launcher in excellent working condition, don't you think?" The big Autobot released a serial blast from the weapon in question that sent the increasingly apprehensive Decepticon reeling in retreat. "And this cannon—it's a personal favorite of mine." A heavy shell exploded against Tread's left side, nearly knocking him off his feet. "Then there is the two-thousand-round-per-minute minigun. I invite you to listen to its music." Hundreds of slugs pounded the Decepticon's body from head to foot, forcing him to throw up his arms to shield his vulnerable optics.

He would not be able to sustain this kind of mauling for much longer, he knew. Intimately linked to Trample, he could tell that his other half was also in desperate difficulty. Something had to be done, and done quickly.

Salvation presented itself in the form of an insect.

The human female was running directly toward him. Unable to believe his good fortune, Tread drew himself up and unleashed every weapon in his arsenal. The unexpectedly fierce barrage temporarily sent the oncoming Ironhide stumbling backward. The big Autobot was taken by surprise, but scarcely damaged.

By the time he recovered, Tread had reached out to

sweep up the oncoming human in one metal hand. He was careful not to crush it. Having been informed how foolishly, not to mention irrationally, the Autobots valued individual human lives, Tread fully intended to make use of the one that had fallen so fortuitously and literally into his hands. He held the small figure out in front of him. Seeing Kaminari trapped in the Decepticon's grasp, Ironhide immediately halted his advance and ceased firing.

"It's true, then." Relief swept through Tread. If not victory, then at least a standoff might yet be salvaged from this encounter. "You will not allow humans to be killed!"

Smoke rising from the muzzles of his multiple weapons, Ironhide glared across the red ground at his opponent. "There has been some discussion on this particular matter between myself and Optimus. From a strategic standpoint I find the admonition annoying." He continued to study his enemy intently, searching for but not finding a line of attack that would allow him to shoot without endangering the Decepticon's prisoner. "However, in the end I agree that we are morally obligated to always protect and defend those who have risked so much on our behalf."

"The more fools you, then." Holding the human close to him, Tread began to back away. If he could reunite with his sorely pressed other half, they could make use of the human prisoner to negotiate their safe retreat. Next time he and Ironhide met, he vowed silently, it would be with sufficient strength to take down the Autobot and dismember him piece by piece.

A sudden surge of pain shot through him. He staggered. It was the mutual awareness of another Decepticon's Spark going out: one that was more intimately linked to his own than any other. Trample was—dead. All the more imperative, then, that he make his escape to fight again another day. To enjoin his revenge. Humans had assisted in Trample's demise. Now it would be one of them who would enable Tread's flight.

"I will see you again, Ironhide. There will be a reckoning for the death dealt this day."

"Let the human go." The Autobot took a step forward. As he did so, Tread raised the hand holding the small creature.

"Keep your distance, or I will crush it until its internal lubricants leak out onto this ground!"

"Excuse me." The voice that spoke was calm and composed.

The preoccupied Decepticon barely glanced at his prisoner. "Silence! You are not a party to these negotiations, insect!"

"I beg to differ." Reaching over her right shoulder, in one single smooth motion Kaminari grabbed her EMP gun, brought it forward, and fired. The pulse made contact with Tread's left eye.

Letting out an electronic squeal, the Decepticon released her as he staggered backward and clutched at the affected optic. The effect was comparable to a human getting hit with pepper spray. Freed from his grasp, the tumbling Kaminari let out a grunt as she hit the ground, rolled, and sprang back onto her feet. She was preparing to attack again when something like a bipedal tank came pounding past her.

When the dust finally began to clear, Tread was on

the ground with Ironhide on top of him. The Autobot finished his work by firing a short-range missile point-blank into the Decepticon's chest while throwing up his other hand to ward off the effects of the explosion. At such close range the detonation was powerful enough to extinguish any Spark. Rising to his full height, he contemplated the now unresponsive foe lying on the ground beneath him. Then he turned wordlessly away. A glance showed that neither Optimus nor Salvage needed his help. Lowering his head, he gazed down at the human standing fearlessly beside him.

"You took a terrible chance, allowing Tread to pick you up like that."

Kaminari shrugged as she turned off and reslung her weapon. "I calculated the odds, reviewed what I have learned about the Decepticons, and came to the conclusion that it was a risk worth taking."

Ironhide crouched down beside her. "What if he had simply contracted his fingers?"

She shrugged again. " 'To win a war, one must be prepared to take chances.' Torawara, *The Art of Close-Quarter Fighting,* seventeenth century." Her expression was unsmiling. "My grandfather would understand."

The Autobot weapons master nodded comprehendingly. "As do I. Still, what if he had not let you go? What if after you had shot him he had retained sufficient strength and presence of mind to throw you against the rocks instead of simply releasing you?"

She looked away. "Then I might have died. Everyone dies, sooner or later."

"A truth well spoken. But the Sparks of your kind

flicker so briefly. I would think you would be more protective of them."

"Humans are brave. Nobody said we're sensible. The men in my family have been soldiers all the way back to the Meiji era. My grandfather wished for a grandson, to go into the army. Being a dutiful son in my culture, my father followed those wishes. But what he really wanted was to study physics. As I was an only child, my grandfather was terribly disappointed. Both in my father for only being able to sire a girl, and in me for having the temerity to be one. I studied traditional martial arts as hard as I could, but while I was doing so my father secretly encouraged me in my academic studies." Reaching back, she touched her weapon.

"So I can both fight *and* dispassionately analyze the physics of the action."

Looking around, she saw Lennox approaching. The captain slowed to a walk as he drew near. "I saw what you just did." His gaze shifted to the motionless Tread. "It was reckless. Why didn't you let Ironhide handle it by himself?"

Her expression tightened. "We are allies of the Autobots. Not their wards. As they fight to protect us, we are obligated to fight to defend them."

"Tempting death is a lousy means of defense."

"Look at me." Taking a wide stance, she put her hands on her hips. "Am I dead?"

He turned away. "Forget it. It's over and I already know there's nothing to be gained by arguing with you."

He stepped away, turning his attention from her and back to the recent battlefield. Optimus was striding toward them while Salvage had changed shape nearby and sat with his engine idling.

Lennox changed tack. "Right now we need to get in touch with NEST HQ and tell them what's happened here." Extending an arm, he indicated the torn-up ground in front of Ironhide. "This all has to be restored to something approaching its natural condition, the cut in the hillside and pit need to be filled in, and we need to get some heavy-lift choppers in here to carry off the deceased. Can't very well head back to Garcia and leave a bunch of dead Decepticons behind us."

"I'll let you handle the details, *Captain*," she told him. Pivoting on one heel, she walked off in the direction of the recumbent metal mass that had been Kickback, intent on inspecting the largest of the lifeless Decepticons. A thoroughly annoyed Lennox watched her go.

"Your rituals," Ironhide declared somberly, "are a never-ending source of fascination."

Lennox eyed him angrily. "She unnecessarily jeopardized her life, and therefore the special knowledge she can contribute to NEST."

Ironhide nodded in the direction of the dead Tread. "Unnecessarily maybe, but effectively."

An aggrieved Lennox shook his head in exasperation. "I might have guessed you would side with her. You're both weapons-crazy, like Epps." Turning, he watched as Kaminari Ishihara halted to inspect the motionless body of the deceased four-armed Decepticon. "I wish Epps was here."

"Ah," rumbled Ironhide. "You miss the company of your fellow warrior."

"Hell no." Lennox grimaced as he contemplated the long flight back to Diego Garcia that lay ahead of them. "I'd just like to borrow his iPod so I don't have to listen to you and that woman babble on about strategy and physics all the way back to the middle of the Indian Ocean."

🜲 13 🜲

Security at Diego Garcia was of a level unknown anywhere else on Earth. In addition to the normal radar, motion sensors, security cameras, and underwater listening stations, the base had highly advanced Cybertronian security measures. The early-warning net extended out into the Indian Ocean. The beaches were lined with seismic sensors capable of picking up the slightest tremor, or the vibrations of underground excavation. Infrared beams crisscrossed the island. In short, a bunny couldn't jump without the security staff knowing about it.

The indigenous life on the atoll was limited primarily to insects and crabs, with the odd colony of rats finding homes along the wharf. There were still domestic donkeys wandering about, leftovers from the old plantations that had existed here. But with the help of Ratchet, the security personnel had come to recognize the heat signature of these beasts, and that led to significantly fewer false alarms.

The most bizarre natural occurrence on the atoll was the general infestation of red crabs. These small creatures would show up anywhere, at any time: in showers, in the laundry, scuttling across the road. It took some getting used to. The creatures were so common that base personnel simply came to ignore their very existence, except in the case when physical intervention (such as removing a crab from one's bed at night) was necessary.

The ubiquitous nature of these crabs rendered them virtually invisible. So it was not surprising that no one noticed, and no security measure picked up, the solitary red crab crawl from the sea, up the beach, over the access road, and to the fence of the military compound.

There was no moon that night. It would take an exceptionally alert human to notice that this particular red crab moved with an intent of purpose rarely seen in these meandering creatures. That human, had he or she been present at this moment, might have paused to take a closer look, upon which he or she might have noticed a peculiar metallic sheen to this individual crab. And the observation of another minute would have removed all doubt. But there was no such human walking by at that moment, and the base rested easily at standard alert.

Unfolding a number of small but sensitive antennas, the crab spy was able to determine that several of the buildings on the other side of the fence housed electronic storage components that, while primitive, might provide the information he sought.

There were guards, of course. Their presence pleased the spy. Had there been no guards, he would have been forced to assume that there was nothing inside worth guarding.

Though he could easily have taken them down, he had no intention of revealing his presence by initiating a confrontation. Searching along the fence's perimeter, he eventually found a place where a quartet of large PVC pipes exited. The fence around them was sealed, of course, and the wire itself charged and monitored. Any breach in the barrier would doubtless set off alarms within the protected compound.

Folding down his tracking antennas, he transformed one arm into a gun. Having detected the presence of water within the second of the large conduits, the Decepticon employed the weapon's beam to cut a hole in the pipe large enough to admit him. Clambering inside, he headed up the pipe in the direction of the compound. At this time of night the gurgling rush of waste liquid was slight. The gentle current did not impede his progress, and he was indifferent to the smell.

Coming to a halt inside a building deep within the complex, he first scanned for indications of adjacent human presence. Determining that the area around his immediate location was clear, he forced an exit by popping a valve. Once outside the conduit he activated his weapon again and resealed the plastic surface behind him, marking its location for future use.

The hallway he entered was well lit but otherwise deserted. Unfolding his antennas again, he hurried in the direction indicated by his tracking signal. A secure metal door barred his path. Its coded lock quickly gave up its secrets to his ultrafast scan and admitted him into a room filled with storage servers and other primitive human computational facilities. It was at present empty of organic life, which suited the spy perfectly. Isolating the most likely console to be easily accessible, he proceeded to change shape.

Animated wires and connectors snaked outward

like slender tentacles from a body that was very much like Frenzy's, only smaller. Jacking into open ports or working their way past inadequate protective panels, they were soon sucking up reams of information and sending them back to the eager, energized intruder. The humans' prehistoric excuse for cybernetic geometry allowed him to initiate hacks that were simple and quick. In the silence of the room the spy continued to download a wealth of information. Whether any of it was valuable could be determined later. The important thing now was to acquire and depart. It was his job to amass, not analyze.

With the first successful hack, alarms went off in two different places on the base. One flared to life within the complex the spy had successfully infiltrated. The other lit up lights and sounded a warning deep inside an island on the opposite side of the lagoon.

Blinking away sleep, a graveyard shift tech for NEST put aside the magazine he had been perusing, sat up straight, and gaped at the impossible reading that was beginning to appear on the monitor in front of him. Still half asleep, the technician knew there were only a few suitable personnel with whom he could consult about such a reading. Together with the key NEST operatives Kaminari Ishihara and Captain Lennox, Optimus Prime, Ironhide, and Salvage were somewhere in far northwestern Australia, while Technical Sergeant Epps and the Russian scientist Petr Andronov were busy hunting Decepticons deep in eastern Peru in the company of Longarm and Knockout.

The tech weighed his remaining options. Among

Autobot allies only the injured Ratchet and a few recent arrivals were presently on station at Diego Garcia, and there were no humans on the base who'd had personal contact with Decepticons. He studied the readout on his screen more closely. There was nothing to indicate that this constituted an incursion by the Decepticons.

His initial anxiety gave way to curiosity and a calm professionalism. Every other alarm (and there were many) remained silent. There was only the single interrupt, and according to the alert it was occurring at the server station for the main military base across the lagoon. Though some unavoidable exchange of information took place between the base servers and NEST, the latter's essential information was isolated by the best firewalls humans and Autobots working together could devise. He allowed himself to relax.

Surely it wouldn't hurt to wait a couple of minutes. If the interrupt continued, then he would assume the responsibility of rousing his superiors and alerting them to its existence. If it went away, he could reasonably assume that the problem had been resolved by those charged with handling such matters: his counterparts across the lagoon. The cause of the alarm interrupt might be nothing more than a software failure or an electrical fault. Or they might be running a test over there. If he set off the technical equivalent of a fire alarm and it turned out that nothing was amiss, he would never live it down.

Sure enough, only a moment or so later the interrupt cleared and server integrity was fully restored. He smiled to himself and picked up his half-finished magazine. In a crisis the kudos are reserved for the one who doesn't panic. Maybe tomorrow he would get in touch with his opposite numbers across the lagoon and learn the details.

The service technician who burst into the server room was accompanied by two armed soldiers. Unlike his unperturbed colleague who was presently unwinding across the water, this tech specialist was anything but relaxed. Behind him, the two armed guards headed in opposite directions so that if necessary they could bathe the entire room in a withering crossfire. As they hurried into position the tech tentatively approached the console from which the distress call had been sent. That alarm was silent now, but moments earlier it had been very real.

Something had happened in this room. An incident had occurred. Though its duration had only been a couple of minutes, the tech was determined to learn what had caused it. Unable to satisfactorily resolve the inherent contradictions by using his own console in another part of the complex, he had commandeered the two soldiers on his personal authority.

Search scopes panned back and forth across the server chamber but found nothing. Neither did the tech as he approached the console whose integrity not one but two alarms had assured him had been violated.

He checked the panels, one after another. Telltales glowed according to programming; lights were dim, off, or flashing as required. Everything appeared to be in working order, nothing seemed to have been disturbed.

Was that a screw missing?

Peering closer, it was impossible to tell if the cover

above one particularly sensitive section had been disturbed. But if that was the case, then who had done the disturbing? Looking behind him, he checked the positions of the two soldiers. One gestured positively, then the other. The server room was clear. But the missing screw and the possibly dislodged security panel continued to unsettle the technician. He hesitated, ruminating on what he had not found.

Reaching a decision, he reached across to a panel of an entirely different nature and slapped his palm down on an oversized red button.

The spy was trapped.

Surprised by the ferocity of the alarms that were sounding and flashing all around him, he found himself caught in a corridor before he had managed to retrace his steps even halfway to the room where the water intake–discharge valve that he had employed to access the facility was located. The obscenely squishy sound of running human feet reached him and was growing rapidly louder.

He commenced on a speedy survey of the immediate vicinity. There was a room off to his left. Penetration scanning revealed a chamber full of consoles and chairs. Doubtless the chairs would soon be occupied and the room packed with sensitive equipment—it would be among the first to be checked. On his right was a much smaller chamber containing batch chemicals and manual devices of the most basic kind. The door on his left was secured and locked. The one on his right did not boast a lock of any kind. His decision was a simple one.

"Blue squad, deploy to the left," the running warrant officer barked. "Green squad, to the right. Yellow, secure the hallway!"

Several dozen grim-faced soldiers spread out. Locks were activated and doors wrenched open. Rifles and scopes swept room after room from ceiling to floor. The corridor itself was rapidly given the all-clear. While yellow squad moved on to the next building their comrades embarked on a more comprehensive security scan of the server complex.

Nothing was left to chance. Ventilation ducts were investigated, air-conditioning pipes checked, every piece of furniture moved, turned over, and closely examined. Not a space was overlooked in which a cockroach could hide.

Corporal Wallace stood back and raised his AR-15 while two privates advanced on the next door down the hallway. One grabbed the handle as his comrade prepared to fire on anything moving inside. At a nod from Wallace the soldier yanked the door open, stepped back, and raised his own gun. The muzzles of the three automatic weapons pointed at the interior of the room. As with the previous areas they had cleared, nothing stirred within this one.

Stepping forward, one of the privates began to shove brooms, mops, big buckets of detergent, and packages of dry cleaner aside. He was down to the last one when something in the utility sink caught his attention.

"Jeez, these things are everywhere. Did it crawl up the drain?"

Gripping his rifle firmly, Corporal Wallace stepped past him. The muzzle wavered. "What the hell?" He shook his head in disgust. "Nasty things. They're everywhere on this island. My wife found one in the toilet the other day. Damn thing wouldn't flush, either.

"All right, that's enough, this room is clear." Wallace shut the door to the janitorial closet. "Move on to the next!"

Left behind in the closet, the spy remained immobile lest another chattering organic unexpectedly open the door. The babble of calling voices and pounding feet soon faded into the distance. Taking no chances, he remained inert and in camouflage mode all the next day.

Late that afternoon a slow-moving unarmed man entered, removed some cleaning materials, and noticed the small red crab in the sink. Being a gentle soul, and not wanting to kill it, he scooped the crab up with his dustpan and dropped it outside.

That night, after conducting a thorough scan, the spy carefully but quickly made his way back to the fence. Once outside the compound perimeter he worked his way silently and unseen back to the edge of the lagoon. Wholly submerged in the water, a dark shape was waiting to collect him.

🛡 14 🛡

Greetings were heartfelt but kept to a minimum. The recent passing of Beachbreak had cast a pall over everyone at NEST. Conversation was low-key and formal—except between two of the soldiers, who hailed each other as effusively as soldiers who have recently survived combat always do. Their reunion was unreservedly informal despite the fact that one of them was an officer and the other a noncom. One of the two generals in the conference room frowned at the unbecoming fraternization but said nothing. As the men who had more experience than anyone else working with Autobots and fighting Decepticons, Lennox and Epps were immune from the typical petty annoyances that usually distinguished such protocol.

As for the massive figure of Optimus Prime, he sat patiently in the much larger Autobot assembly chamber on the far side of the conference room and waited for the humans to conclude their customary salutation ceremonies. It was not necessary for any of the other Autobots to be present, as Optimus supplied them with a simultaneous real-time broadcast of what was taking place. As he waited for the conference to commence he shifted his position slightly, his immense metal feet grating softly on the concrete floor. Humans were adept at many things, he knew. Unfortunately, from an Autobot standpoint wasting time was one of them.

"If you would all take your seats, please?"

By now the woman standing to one side of the wall screen was familiar to everyone present. For her part Ariella regarded each of them silently until the conversation finally subsided. Responding to her gesture, the screen came to life and the lights in the room dimmed. On the screen a series of images began to flash by in rapid succession. Lennox recognized those that had been recorded by Optimus and the other Autobots who had been with him in Australia. Some of the pictures that documented the ferocious confrontation that had taken place in southeastern Peru were new to him. As these appeared, Epps emphasized several of them by flashing his fellow soldier an appropriate hand gesture.

Stealing a glance at Kaminari, he saw that she was wholly intent on the information that was being displayed and commented upon by Ariella. In contrast with the Japanese scientist, Petr Andronov was looking down at his lap while he fiddled with a small but gaudy shell. Lennox shook his head in bemusement. He *knew* the Russian was hearing and absorbing everything Ariella was saying. It was well known by now among the staff at NEST that the Russian could effortlessly concentrate on more than one subject at the same time. But would it hurt the man to lift his head up and look up at the screen once in a while?

"Let me say," the woman with the steel spine was telling those who had assembled in the conference room, "that I and everyone else at NEST is relieved and delighted that all of you have returned safely, and that the Decepticon threat has been further diminished through your stalwart actions. But while the danger has been reduced, it has certainly not been eliminated."

"Indeed." Optimus's deep voice boomed from where he sat in the expansive chamber off to their left. "So long as Starscream remains at large neither Autobots nor humans can ever rest or be completely at peace. While we have dealt most satisfactorily with a number of his followers, there may be others here on Earth whose presence has yet to be revealed."

Ariella nodded and turned back to the wall screen. Employing supple hand gestures, she called up a new series of images. Lennox leaned forward intently. While the subject matter was immediately recognizable, all but a few locations were not. Ariella continued.

"Your recent encounters have led to the assumption that a rogue element of Decepticons, working independently of Starscream, have been trying to acquire extensive terrestrial sources of energy. In keeping with an understandable desire to carry out their activities outside the view of NEST, the locations of these sources have become more and more obscure. The Decepticons sought to make use of unexploited hydrocarbon power in the deep Amazon and potential nuclear energy in remote northwest Australia."

"That won't happen anymore." Kaminari sounded completely confident. "Now that we know what they're after, we can anticipate their next move." She looked over at Lennox, who nodded back politely.

"To a certain extent that is true," Ariella agreed.

"While our network of surveillance satellites keyed to detecting Decepticon transmissions continues to expand its coverage with each new launch, there are still gaps and interrupts in our coverage. There are many hiding places on the Earth's surface, and we cannot keep a satellite above every potential energy source." As she spoke, the screen behind her supplied images that underscored her words.

"But we *can* maintain a watch on the sites most likely to tempt them. Unlike Kariba–Cahorra Bassa, hydroelectric sources like Itaipu or Grand Coulee draw hundreds or thousands of onlookers daily. Those large dams that do not receive such large numbers of visitors are now under constant scrutiny. Oil and gas facilities such as those in the Middle East, Siberia, and even offshore Brazil are the focus of several of our satellites as well as on-site attention. Needless to say, every operating nuclear plant on the planet is already equipped with an extensive security system. In addition, undeveloped uranium deposits are now subject to regular checks." She looked around the room as the screen dimmed.

"This meeting has been called to discuss and evaluate the possibility that there might be other terrestrial energy sources we are overlooking that could be exploited by the Decepticons." The screen behind her dimmed but did not go out. "The floor is open for general discussion." Her gaze flicked to her left. "Your input is of course desired, Optimus."

The leader of the Autobots could not smile, but his eyes flickered. "Ironhide says that I do not speak as often or as forcefully as I should. If it seems so, it is only because as leader I am aware that my words carry added weight. Therefore I consider them carefully before I speak."

Leaning toward Lennox, Epps whispered. "Wonder if we could change the Constitution so that Autobots could run for president?"

The captain shook his head. "Wouldn't matter. He's not US-born."

As the two soldiers exchanged casual banter, the others seated around the conference table were doing their best to respond thoughtfully to Ariella's query.

"Solar," the senior general ventured straightaway.

The notion was immediately shot down by one of NEST's civilian specialists. "Even if they could manufacture and set up panels with a hundred percent conversion efficiency, they'd never be able to hide the facility. They would have to cover thousands of acres with such panels to come anywhere near generating the kind of power they seem to be looking for."

"That's right," agreed the civilian woman seated next to him. "To acquire that amount of energy before they were exposed they'd pretty much have to access a chunk of the sun directly." Turning in her chair, she looked over at Optimus Prime. "I'm assuming that neither you nor the Decepticons can do that."

"Not to my knowledge," the leader of the Autobots replied. "I should think that tapping stellar fusion directly would mean approaching a star far too close for safety."

Lennox nodded to himself. While he didn't know much about solar energy or fusion power, neither did he see Decepticons who could be injured by sabot rounds zooming through and around solar flares.

"Wave power." The remaining civilian specialist looked around the table. "Unlimited energy and plenty of open, uninhabited ocean to hide in. They could build a generating plant in the middle of the Pacific or the South Indian Ocean and our satellites would probably never pick it up."

This possibility provoked a brief burst of intense conversation among those present, until Petr finally looked up from his eReader. In the course of the preceding discussion no one had noticed that he had set aside his shell in favor of the device.

"I don't know amount of energy the Decepticons are after, but calculations say it is possible to acquire a quantity that has been speculated upon through the utilization of wave action." He tapped his reader.

"Then how the blazes are we going to look out for this?" The general who spoke was clearly perturbed at the prospect. "No matter how many satellites we put up we can't maintain a continuous watch on every square mile of every ocean."

"Not necessary to do so." Looking past the general, the Russian eyed the leader of the Autobots. "Optimus, to accumulate and store decent amount of energy, how long you think Decepticons would have to work at it? They would need to build many stations linked together to avoid detection."

Optimus had already considered the prospect. "Not too long."

The second general snapped at the Autobot behind him. "How long is 'not too long'?"

Optimus regarded the senior officer. "A thousand of your years, perhaps. Possibly two."

"Isn't it likely that by then we will have found and

dealt with the last of the Decepticons on Earth?" The other general struggled to mask his exasperation.

Optimus switched his attention to him. "Of course. But that is not the question that was asked."

Several muted groans echoed around the room. In front, Ariella licked her lips and asked firmly, "Any other thoughts on this matter?" She glanced in Optimus's direction. "Preferably those that do not involve such far-reaching, at least in human terms, time frames?"

"Just one."

All eyes turned to Kaminari. "I grew up in a country where a kind of energy the Decepticons are apparently trying to make use of is commonplace. Where people are exposed to it every day. They don't dwell on the forces that are represented by what they're seeing. They take pictures of its effects and try to avoid thinking about the enormous energies that are boiling beneath their feet." Her expression tightened. "That is, unless those forces are unleashed."

At the far end of the table, Andronov was nodding sagely. "Part of my country is also same. The part, interestingly, that faces yours: Kamchatka. But I doubt that the Decepticons would try to carry out such work on the peninsula. There have been big military bases there for many decades. So much so that satellite surveillance of area is not even necessary because so many locations on the ground already under close military watch."

Lennox leaned toward Epps and whispered. "What are they talking about?"

"Beats me." Straightening in his chair, the tech

sought an explanation with his usual subtlety. "Hey! What are you eggheads blabbering about?"

Taking no offense, Kaminari turned to him. "Volcanoes, Sergeant. We're talking about volcanoes."

Lennox knew as much about geology as he did about numerology, but in this case detailed knowledge was unnecessary. Everyone knew the power of volcanoes. Back home, even small kids could tell you about Hawaii or Mount St. Helens.

Andronov lent emphasis to the point Kaminari was making. "Is estimated that when the Indonesian volcanic island of Krakatoa blew itself up in 1883, the energy released was equivalent to about two hundred megatons." He glanced over at Optimus. "I am assuming that is kind of energy that would be adequate to satisfy even Decepticon needs."

"Your units of measurement are comparatively feeble when translated into Cybertronian terms," the leader of the Autobots responded, "but yes, that would be enough even when one is speaking in terms of hypothetically renewing a Spark. Again, finding a way to store such energy until it can be used presents a serious problem. But if such power could be accessed, stored, and then delivered elsewhere, it might be enough to revive an extinguished Spark. Or," he added ominously, "create a great deal of destruction."

"As did Krakatoa," Andronov concluded somberly.

Further discussion ensued. One of the generals demanded attention.

"We don't have to put a satellite over every active or dormant volcano on the planet. A lot of them, like Vesuvius or—what's that one in southern Italy?"

"Etna," Andronov supplied helpfully.

"Yes, Etna." The senior officer's attention switched to Kaminari. "Or Fuji. Or any volcano in Japan, or the US, or anyplace where there's a reasonable human population. They won't require satellite surveillance." He looked satisfied. "We just have to periodically check out those that lie in obscure places. Africa, I expect, and the Andes, and Siberia."

Andronov took immediate, if quiet, exception. "No part of my country is obscure. Well," he corrected himself, "maybe some parts. Is big place. But local watches can be put into effect on ground there also."

Ariella regarded the assembled. "Anyone else? Any other obvious terrestrial energy sources we're overlooking?"

"Probably," Andronov declared, "but if Decepticons could do something like clap hands and generate controlled fusion on a large scale, we would not be having this discussion."

She nodded. "That's it, then. In addition to the areas and sources of potential and existing energy we are already monitoring, NEST will coordinate surveillance of all active and dormant volcanoes across the planet." She looked a last time in Optimus's direction. "I see only one possible snag. If the Decepticons were inclined to try to make use of volcanic energy, could they do so at depth? Earth has many active volcanoes located in the deep ocean."

"Especially where continental plates are subducting," Andronov added as a dazed Lennox could only sit and wonder what the hell the scientists were talking about.

Optimus pondered before replying. "I think it unlikely. While our bodies are strong enough to survive the pressures encountered at considerable depths, even with the aid of artificial illumination perpetual darkness would make such complex work difficult. Not impossible, but difficult. What *would* inhibit development of such an energy source would be the constant presence of water, which would make welding and other industrial processes difficult. It could be done, but the time and resources required would tax the efforts of a considerable number of Cybertronians."

Ariella looked satisfied. "I'll see to it that some existing satellites are reprogrammed to check on the most likely oceanic locations first. And our patrolling submarines can monitor the most likely locations for evidence of unusual activity. Eventually we'll have every major active volcanic area checked for suspicious activity, including those in the sea."

Relief and confidence were evident among the conference participants as they exited the room. They felt reasonably sure that they had explored all obvious possibilities. Whether or not the theory of reviving Megatron had any merit, they simply could not allow it to be tested.

🛡 15 🛡

Having been built to accommodate large corporate aircraft, the hangar in the southern mountains admitted the sleek jet with ample room to spare. As its engines cooled, it taxied to a halt in the center of the building. Anyone familiar with landing procedures for advanced jet aircraft might have remarked on the complete absence of waiting mechanics, the nonpresence of a refueling tanker, the exceptional smoothness of the fighter's metal skin, which appeared to have been melted rather than riveted together, and the ease with which the newly arrived craft pivoted inside the hangar so that it was now facing the exit.

The fact that there was no pilot was also notable.

Several minutes passed in deepening silence. Then a small door opened in one side of the hangar and a man in his middle fifties appeared. He was alone, casually but elegantly dressed, white-haired, and with enough of a bulge in the vicinity of his stomach to mark him as an epicure rather than a glutton. His eyes were deep blue and hard, and missed nothing. His fingernails were as neatly manicured as a model's, and his shoes cost more than most of his fellow Italian citizens made in a year. In defiance of doctors and reason, he was smoking a cigarette that had been laced with several drops of liquid narcotic. This improved his mood without affecting his perception.

His name was Bruno Carerra, and while much of his wealth was inherited, he had acquired his personal obnoxiousness all by himself.

Taking his own good time he strolled completely around the parked aircraft before returning to the spot where he had started.

"Well, you are as striking in person as the secret reports insisted."

The fighter jet responded with a clash of virtually frictionless internal mechanisms. Twisting and turning like a ball of expanding aluminum foil, it contorted upward and outward until it had changed itself into a looming, menacing, bipedal shape.

"In order for flattery to have an effect, it must first originate from a source whose opinion is respected," the hulking figure growled.

"*Ciao* to you, too, Starscream." Carerra had not retreated, did not flinch. Instead he took a languorous puff on his artfully doped cigarette.

The Decepticon leader leaned closer. "You are not afraid?"

The industrialist shrugged. "What is the worst you can do? Kill me?"

"Humans die sooner than most. You are a conspicuously short-lived species."

"All the more reason then," Carerra replied, eyes glittering, "to make the most of what time is available to us."

This response appeared to satisfy Starscream—at least for the moment. "You have shown exceptional persistence and skill in managing to make contact with me. I was informed that you have offered to be of assistance in the task of cleansing this world of Autobots."

Carerra's head bobbed in a slight nod. "That is correct."

"You realize," rumbled Starscream, "that doing so would leave myself and my fellow Decepticons in full control of your planet."

Carerra let his gaze drift to the view outside the hangar. No casual hikers would find their way to this place. No lost travelers would be allowed to pass beyond the heavily guarded outer perimeter. Any who somehow did manage to find their way in would find it far more difficult to find their way out again.

"Someone has to control it. The present governments do not seem to be doing any better than their predecessors. Perhaps it is time to"—he smiled—"bring in outside consultants."

Starscream stood back. "You would submit willingly to Decepticon rule?"

"Why not? Much of our civilization is currently directed and controlled by machines, and they're not even intelligent."

"You might not care for the kind of rule we would impose."

Carerra's expression tightened, and he restrained himself with an effort. "I don't care for the rule the current governments impose. Most importantly, they don't include me."

"Ah. You do seek something for yourself. That kind of motivation I can understand."

Carerra reluctantly flicked the stub of his cigarette

aside. "Then despite our differences in origin and physical makeup, we have something in common."

Starscream pointedly ignored the industrialist's attempt to establish a bond. "You say that you can help us to eliminate the Autobots." The massive metal shape leaned forward again. "How? What possible assistance could you offer?"

As Carerra spoke he contemplated the forest that flanked the runway outside the hangar. It was a beautiful time of year in southern Italy.

"I have been studying you and your opponents ever since the first reports of your presence on our world reached me via my covert—and very expensive— contacts. This Optimus Prime individual is very powerful, but I believe that I have discovered his one weakness."

"Really?" Starscream did not try to keep the sarcasm from his voice. "And what might that be?"

The industrialist turned back to his alien visitor. "He is handicapped by an excess of morality. If he can prevent it, he will not allow humans to be killed by Decepticons, even if his intercession presents a risk to himself and his own colleagues. I propose to have you lure him to a city I know well. Know not just from border to border but, more importantly, from top to bottom. There is a place there I have unique access to because of a current municipal development in which several of my companies are participating. I have already set in motion a means and a method I believe is capable of trapping him, at least for a short time. With you and your own underlings positioned appropriately, that should be long enough to enable you to destroy him." He waved a hand grandiosely.

"With their leader eliminated, I would not think it would take long for you to deal with his disheartened followers."

Starscream was silent, but not for long. "You seem very sure of yourself, human."

"Please, call me Bruno. If I wasn't sure of myself would I risk standing here talking to you all by myself?"

"Humans are not known for good judgment of their actions. Yet I must admit I find your proposal intriguing. I would learn more." The Decepticon leader's voice darkened. "If you are wasting my time, you will join the other stains on this floor."

"I apologize for its appearance. It really needs a good scouring. Oil stains and all that, you know." Carerra was as unfazed as ever.

"Assuming I approve of your proposal and choose to participate, what reward would you seek?" Starscream was watching the human closely.

"Nothing much." Clearly Carerra had already thought everything through. "As masters of Earth, you'll need satraps to administer the different parts of your new domain. I'd like Europe. It's been overdue for an emperor ever since Napoleon."

Starscream could not help but find the human's presumption amusing. "You think very highly of yourself."

"Could I stand here making this offer if I did not?"

It took less than an hour for the Decepticon leader and the human industrialist to finalize Carerra's plan. When all had been agreed upon there was no shaking of hands, no farewell. Everything had been decided: time, date, modus operandi. The meeting concluded,

Starscream shifted back into his Raptor shape, fired up his engines, and blasted down the private runway to soar out of sight into the blue sky of southern Italy.

Flying higher than most human aircraft, but not so high as to draw attention to himself, Starscream pondered the details of what had just been decided. The human's proposal was certainly clever. Perhaps even clever enough to fool the Autobots. Now final preparations needed to be made. If it worked it would mean the end of Optimus and subsequently that of all Autobots on this world. Then it would be the Decepticons' to exploit at their leisure while they concentrated on the process of regaining full control of Cybertron. He growled with satisfaction.

Autobots were not the only ones capable of making use of human allies.

Starscream banked sharply toward the Adriatic. Megatron had referred to the local dominant species as insects. Based on the discussion he had just concluded with a powerful human who had proven himself willing to sell out his own species, he decided that such a comparison would be unfair to the tiny arthropods in question.

Simmons could not move everything at once. Not only the partial skull of the small Decepticon, but his entire setup with its monitors, tools, research materials, computer, and more took time to shift from the basement of his apartment. He did it a little bit at a time, unobtrusively moving a box or two after hours or on one of his days off. Almost as much time and effort again were required to unpack and laboriously reconstruct his research in its new location.

But when the last wire had been reconnected and the final switch thrown, he was convinced he had found an environment for his investigations that would draw no attention from the outside world. In its current location even the occasional electrical surge or outage could be attributed to other causes, for which he had already prepared a number of ready excuses.

It was a slow Saturday when he found himself sitting in front of one of the monitors and decided to ask a question that had been lingering in the back of his mind for nearly a year.

"This place you come from—what's it like? No people there, obviously. Just you mouthy toasters."

The incomplete head on the table crackled. After moving it from his apartment Simmons had not only bolted it more securely to its tabletop, but also screwed the table to the floor.

"Home . . . beautiful, once. Then war, dissension. Weak rule. Megatron deciding. Optimus objecting. Dissension. Fighting, war. Allspark lost. Searching, searching . . ." The voice sputtered out.

"Yeah, right. We're all searching. I can see why you tin toys wound up here. Trouble for you guys is, this dirt is already mortgaged. And we ain't movin' out."

One partial eye socket glimmered briefly. "Insects. Submit or die! Megatron will—!"

"Megatron sleeps with the fishes." Chewing on a strip of kosher beef jerky, Simmons tapped several keys. The partial skull on the table twitched. "Bunch of your other buddies are car parts now. But we still gotta worry about that Starscream. Nasty character, that one. It worries me what he might be up to. The new guys, this NEST bunch, think they can handle 'em." A flicker of undeniable brilliance flashed in the ex-agent's eyes. Or maybe it was just madness.

"But Starscream, I saw enough of him in action to know better. He's not just powerful. He's smart. He's tricky. And you don't eliminate smart and tricky with brute force. 'Course, you think they'd listen to me? Listen to Seymour Simmons, with all my years of experience? Nah. Office boys in Washington think they know everything. Wouldn't transfer me over to the new division." He subsided for a while. Then he looked up at the table. At his prize.

"That's all right. I'm still here. Plenty I can do on my own. Maybe it's better this way. No desk jockey looking over my shoulder asking what I'm working on. Nobody sending me off to Stockholm or Sheboygan to check out some jittery junk heap in an old farmer's garage." Turning away from the computer, he picked up a thick sheaf of papers and shook them at the skull on the table.

"It's all here, what's gonna happen! I know it is. I can feel it, I can sense it." Some of the papers slipped to the floor. He left them lying there as he sagged in his chair. "I just don't know *what* it is. That's why I need your help. And you're gonna help me, half head, whether you like it or not."

But the battered metal shape on the table did not respond, and certainly did not offer any answers.

The police gave chase even before the two cars headed the wrong way up the one-way street. Moving fast, barely missing startled pedestrians, they alternately slowed and sped up as the pursuit behind them gathered strength. It was almost as if the pair of street racers were daring the traffic cops, in their Fiats and on their bikes, to catch them.

How the pair managed to negotiate the narrow streets, byways, and heavily congested lanes of downtown Rome without smashing into other vehicles or overhanging structures was something to behold. When the police finally appeared to have them cornered, they eluded their pursuers by abandoning the narrow road they were on and careering wildly down the Spanish Steps, scattering panicked tourists and locals alike while nearly destroying the famous fountain at the bottom of the stairway. Speeding off, they continued with their own rivalry as seemingly half the traffic police in the city closed in around them.

They were finally cornered in the wide Piazza del Popolo. As police and hastily summoned *carabinieri* surrounded the square and cleared it of civilians, the two street racers zoomed around and around the obelisk in its center, their drivers acting for all the world as if it were their private racetrack and dozens of guns were not now pointed in their direction.

It was left to a captain of the *carabinieri* to step forward and shout at the speeding cars through an amplified megaphone.

"Drivers! You are both under arrest! Stop your racing, pull over, and exit your vehicles! I repeat, you are under arrest for endangering tourists, citizens, important national monuments, and yourselves! Kill your engines and pull over!" He did not add that between them the two competing drivers had broken every traffic law on the Italian books. There was not enough time to recite all their transgressions. That he would leave to the judges.

But despite his increasingly threatening entreaties, the two sleek, customized cars continued to speed around and around the square's famous central pillar. Occasionally one would lurch into the lead only to soon surrender it to the other. The captain knew he could wait until they ran out of gas, or . . .

He turned the volume on the megaphone all the way up. "You have exhausted the patience of citizens and police alike! Under the authority vested in me by the government of the city of Rome, I demand that you now pull over and cease this senseless activity or I will be forced to give the order to shoot at your vehicles. I repeat, pull over and stop or my men will shoot. While we will aim at your tires and engines, I cannot guarantee the accuracy of my sharpshooters. Your lives are in danger unless you pull over *now*!"

Finally, he thought as the two cars began to slow. A reaction. He did not like making threats, but it was his responsibility to ensure the safety of those few citizens who had persisted in remaining in the area to see how the confrontation played out—and possibly to applaud the antisocial boldness of the two racers. If it was up to him, he would have the applauders arrested as well.

At least, he thought as first one car came to a stop and then the other, no one had been injured in the course of their wild binge through the city. And the square had been cleared of nearly every gawking tourist and local. Given a decent, honest judge, both drivers would not only have their licenses permanently revoked but also spend enough time in jail to properly contemplate their transgressions. As he stepped forward, one hand holding the megaphone and the other resting on the butt of his service revolver, he was accompanied by a full squad of his men. Halfway across the wide square, a voice emerged from the nearest vehicle. It sounded—odd.

"Allow us to differ, human, but it is *your* lives that are in danger!"

As the eyes of the captain and his subordinates grew wide, the pair of street racers began to change shape before their eyes. Rising to heights that dwarfed the approaching officers, the two gleaming, boldly highlighted giants bellowed their defiance at the encircling police.

"*Fire.*" The captain found his voice and his pistol at the same time. "Open fire!"

The crackle of rifles and pistols discharging erupted around the square. Screams burst from those few citizens who had hung around to observe the outcome of the confrontation. Seeking cover, these isolated civilians scattered into the surrounding churches, restaurants, and shops.

The salvo of small-arms fire had no effect on the two lustrous machines. In contrast, their much more powerful weaponry began to take an immediate toll on the now rapidly retreating *carabinieri* as well as on the surrounding historic structures.

By the time heavier ordnance arrived in the form of Italian and American helicopters from bases outside the city, the two intruders had reverted to street racer form and vanished into the warren of ancient, narrow alleyways that honeycombed the ancient metropolis.

Behind them they left death, destruction, chaos—and more than a little bewilderment.

"It doesn't make any sense."

Standing at the table in the heavily secured hangar inside the US–Italian army base, Lennox studied the map of Rome that had been laid out before him. On it had been traced the route of the two Decepticons as accurately as the demoralized city police had been able to record it. Epps and Kaminari stood beside him while Petr was on the other side of the hangar deep in conversation with a tow truck. Ratchet was divesting himself of insights into Autobot metallurgy that the Russian found endlessly fascinating.

Two European NEST operatives, one American and the other Italian, stood on the other side of the table opposite Lennox and his companions. In the center of the hangar Ratchet and Ironhide relaxed in terrestrial guise and conversed quietly as a thoroughly bored Knockout zipped back and forth while popping an occasional wheelie. Nobody paid him the least attention.

"I agree, Captain." Leaning forward next to him, Kaminari let one finger trace a line on the city map. "What could the Decepticons possibly be seeking here in Rome? Certainly not some kind of power source. We are a long way from Etna, or even Vesuvius."

The Italian NEST officer did not try to hide his bewilderment. "There are large power plants here, but nothing exceptional. All the big hydroelectric dams lie far to the north, in the Alps, and there are far more nuclear facilities in France and Germany."

"We checked on Vesuvius first thing." The American operative looked assured. "Did a full aerial scan and ground search. If they're looking to tap volcanic power, they're not doing so here. Surveillance has been doubled down at Etna, too." He looked to his left. So did the others gathered around the table.

Unfortunately, the diesel truck parked nearby was unable to provide clarification. "I agree with Captain Lennox. This is Starscream's plan, and as such has nothing to do with the surrounding sources of potential energy. Once again, we are walking into a trap. This time we must see to it that it is Starscream who gets caught.

"From their descriptions I believe the intruders are—a moment, please, while I compile suitable human articulations—Deadend and Swindle. As they are remembered for their attitudes as well as their speed, it is not surprising that once on Earth they would assume such forms as have been described.

"Great," muttered Epps. "How many of you guys—or those guys—are there?"

"More than you can imagine," Optimus informed him. "Be thankful that so few have responded to Megatron's original signal and to Starscream's follow-up. It is yet another reason why we must deal with him as quickly as we can, lest he continue to gather strength by drawing additional reinforcements to him."

Lennox looked up again from the map. "I saw the bits and pieces of video. As Decepticons go these two don't strike me as particularly dangerous."

"It is true that Deadend and Swindle do not possess the capabilities of such as Starscream and Payload,"

Optimus agreed, "but human forces would not be able to defeat them without our help." The diesel's engine rumbled. "Ironhide and I could eliminate them, but their presence in such a heavily populated, densely crowded human city precludes the use of overwhelming force. Still, they must not be allowed to cause further harm, or to escape. That is why I insisted that Ratchet accompany us here as well, together with Ironhide and Knockout." He eyed the gravity-defying motorcycle that was racing around the hangar's interior.

"From the maps I have committed to memory, Knockout may prove especially useful in negotiating the constricted vehicular pathways of this city. If," he added, "he can keep his mind on the business at hand."

Epps had turned to admire the bike as it launched itself into the air and executed a complete flip. "Yeah, he's an agile one. How do we find these Decepticons, Optimus?"

"We have been scanning for their transmissions even before our transport landed here," the Autobot leader informed him. "Sooner or later they will communicate across distance utilizing Cybertronian mode. Then we will pinpoint their location." His words were confident. "With this many of us here, we should be able to deal with them with minimal collateral damage to human property—and hopefully without sacrificing any human lives."

Reaching back behind her, Kaminari tapped the sling that was holding her weapon and keeping it fully charged. "If it comes down to street fighting in tight quarters maybe we can lend a hand." She glanced to her left. "Even Captain Lennox might prove himself useful." At this Epps raised both hands and took an exaggerated step backward.

"It's all right, Sergeant." Lennox's voice was even, his attitude professional. "The lady and I have an understanding."

"Yeah." Turning, Epps headed off in the direction of the hangar's exit. "I understand that even Starscream wouldn't want to get caught between you. Excuse me. Somewhere at the local PX there's a pizza with my name on it."

"That's what we have, then." The Italian NEST operative began rolling up the map. "All we can do is wait for the Decepticons to reveal themselves." He looked toward the idling diesel. "Or for Optimus and his companions to detect their presence. As per follow-up operations at Mission City, the local authorities have been informed that there may be some dangerous spillover from secret and unavoidable NATO maneuvers in the vicinity. That's the excuse that has been propagated through the media and the Internet to explain the confrontation that occurred at the piazza. Fortunately the police had largely succeeded in clearing the area before the firing started."

Lennox nodded understandingly. "Are the people buying it?"

The operative shrugged eloquently. "This is Italy. Most people are too engrossed in their local problems to worry about what happens elsewhere. You can check the media for yourself. The garbage crisis in Naples got more national press."

"We'll try to keep the operation undercover as much as possible." Lennox looked longingly toward the door through which Epps had taken his leave. He was hungry, too. He took a step in the sergeant's wake, then hesitated and looked back.

"I don't suppose you'd like to share some good Italian food?"

Kaminari hesitated, then nodded her acceptance. "If this goes down the way I'm afraid it could, the Autobots aren't the only ones who are going to need all the energy they can muster."

They did not have to wait long for Deadend and Swindle to make their presence known again.

"They've been spotted back in the central city." Humans and vehicles alike gathered around the Italian NEST operative in the center of the hangar. Outside, the moonless night was pitch dark. Lennox rubbed at his eyes and checked his watch. It was a few minutes after three in the morning. What were the Decepticons up to at such an inhuman hour?

He smiled slightly to himself. The key word was "inhuman." Autobots and Decepticons could function just as well at night as in the bright light of day. Only human activity suffered from an absence of reassuring sunlight.

"Can you identify a possible target?" Optimus's voice emerged from behind the gleaming chrome grille of his terrestrial guise.

The operative shook his head. "If they have an objective in mind they're being very cagey about it. Right now they're doing a lot of circling in the area of the Pantheon. If I did not know better I would say that they are deliberately trying to draw attention to themselves, except that at this hour the city is largely asleep."

"Well, they have drawn *our* attention," Optimus observed gravely. As Lennox and his companions split up into different vehicles, Prime's call resounded through the length and breadth of the cavernous structure.

"Autobots—transform and roll out!"

It was a command easier given than followed. Originally laid out with chariots in mind, many of the eternal city's streets were narrow, twisting, marked by low overheads, and full of surprise dead ends. Provided with specific directions by NEST intelligence and in the fortuitous absence of traffic due to the lateness of the hour, the quintet of Autobots was able to locate and close in on the speeding Decepticons with comparative ease. Actually confronting the speeding targets proved far more difficult.

Seated in Optimus's cab, Lennox and Epps ran a last check on their launchers as the big diesel struggled to maintain contact with the speedy, evasive Decepticons. Forced to keep to the few wider avenues, the big truck was able to maneuver freely only thanks to the absence of traffic.

"This is frustrating." Optimus spoke to his passengers through the console radio. "The others will have to cut them off. I cannot negotiate these slender roadways without causing damage to buildings or becoming trapped."

"Hey, it's all right, big fella." Reaching out, Epps gave the dash a reassuring slap. "You can't do everything yourself."

"I know. Delegating responsibility is among the most difficult responsibilities of leadership. I trust the judgment and abilities of my companions implicitly, but I still feel as if I should contribute personally to the solution of every problem."

"You do contribute to the solution of every problem." Lennox checked the sight on his launcher. "You're contributing right now."

"How?" inquired the voice from the radio.

"By being Optimus Prime," Lennox reminded him.

A voice sounded over the cab's speakers: Ratchet. "I have them in sight! They are now racing away from the Pantheon area. I think they may be heading for the Via Fori Imperiali. If they reach it unchallenged they will be able to accelerate considerably on its multiple lanes."

The big diesel roared as Optimus shifted gears. "That is a wide road. I will be able to contribute there." His voice softened. "In addition to that which I already contribute, Captain Lennox, as per your thoughtful assessment."

"Ironhide and I are closing on them from the north," declared Ratchet.

Optimus picked up speed as his human passengers readied themselves for combat. "If Ratchet and Ironhide can cut them off while they are on the main boulevard, we can surround them and deal with them with minimal risk to humans."

The same realization must have struck the speeding Swindle and Deadend. "They're turning south again onto smaller roadways." Ratchet's disappointment was evident in his tone. "They're still heading in the same direction, south by southeast, but they're avoiding the Imperiali."

"Keeping to side streets." Lennox nodded knowingly. "They're not stupid. They know we're less likely to shoot when we're in among buildings. But they won't get away. We've got choppers in the air patrolling the circumference of the city and the NEST satellite that's over Italy positioned perfectly to cover the metropolitan area."

"Yeah," added Epps. "Maybe they'll oblige us by heading for the freeway." He tapped the launcher that was now resting in the storage area behind his seat. "Once they're out of town and in the absence of traffic at this hour of the morning we can take 'em out easy."

But it wasn't to be that simple. "They're slowing down," Ratchet reported. "As much as they can slow down. I think Deadend may already have sideswiped a couple of shops. They appear to be heading for— no, wait. They've changed direction again and are heading back toward the Fori Imperiali."

"Something about this is not right," Optimus concluded. "It isn't like Decepticons to pursue a goal, abruptly change course, and then pursue the same goal a second time. Perhaps we are seeking their true intentions in the wrong place."

"What d'you mean?" Lennox wondered.

"Myself, the others, the NEST aircraft—we are all looking on the ground. Excuse me a moment." Pulling over to a curb, the leader of the Autobots went silent. In the darkness, a lone wandering pedestrian paused to gawk at the unusual sight of a big rig parked in downtown Rome. As he was less than sober, it was doubtful the image would stay with him for long.

"Hi. Ciao." Leaning out the window, Epps smiled and waved. "How y'all doin'?" The man shouted something at the sergeant in Italian. On the Autobot's other side a pair of inquisitive cats showed signs of wanting to clamber up onto the polished running boards. Lennox did his best to shoo them away.

"I have it." With a rumble, Optimus started up again. The cats scattered as the big diesel moved forward. "Ironhide! Ratchet, Knockout! Sensors *up*."

Ironhide's familiar growl reached them a moment later. "I see them. It would appear that Deadend and Swindle's antics were intended to concentrate our attention on them. It nearly worked. Now," he rumbled, "we can deal with all of them at once."

"Deal with who?" A bemused Epps smacked the dash again. "Who are you all talking about?"

"Look out your window," Optimus advised him. "And look up."

Both men did so. It took a moment for Lennox to locate the spot of light that was moving fast overhead.

"Starscream," Optimus informed the two men. "I begin to perceive the outlines of this Decepticon plan. In the dead of night Deadend and Swindle reappear and make themselves known so that we will focus our attention on them. They speed through small side roadways where we cannot get a clear shot at them. Close to this large ancient structure humans call the Colosseum, the main road called the Imperiali is flanked by hills. Deadend and Swindle's aim is to use these side avenues to draw us out into the open at that place. There we will be exposed to strafing fire from Starscream. The surrounding hills will limit our mobility, and the need to avoid damage to one of humankind's most important historical monuments will restrict our ability to defend ourselves."

"Then we shouldn't let ourselves be trapped out in the open," Lennox contended.

Optimus was torn. "We may have no choice. I know Starscream. If we don't follow Deadend and Swindle out into the area they have chosen for their ambush, they will start wreaking general havoc and causing damage in order to force us to expose ourselves. Unless they can be stopped before they reach the location and have the chance to put their plan into action. But they are far more swift and agile than I, or Ratchet, or—"

"Knockout deploying!" yelled a voice over the speaker. Like the other Autobots, the smallest of the group had heard everything Optimus had said as soon as the Autobot leader had broadcast it.

On a small side street leading to a square that during the day was filled with vegetable and flower vendors, a brightly hued pickup truck skewed halfway around. As it did so, its back door flew open and an extendable ramp slid down. Sparks flew as the metal edge struck pavement. Seconds later the silent square echoed to the roar of a big bore motorcycle as it came blasting down out of the truck's bed. The bike went one way while the truck zoomed off down a different street. A few angry shouts came from local residents who had been rudely awakened, but all returned to bed as the noise rapidly receded from their immediate neighborhood.

After all, the sound of engines racing was far from unknown in Rome.

Deadend and Swindle were agile as lizards, but in

Rome's narrow byways nothing could handle the ancient twists, turns, and thoroughfares as well as a bike. With something to prove, Knockout blasted beneath ancient arches and tore past silent shops without so much as disturbing a rosebush. In minutes he had cut across sections of the central city too difficult even for a racing car to successfully negotiate.

Deadend nearly ran him over.

"Meddlesome Autobot!" the modified street racer shouted. "Your death will precede that of your betters!" Transforming a front fender into a rotating cannon, the Decepticon unleashed a burst in the motorcycle's direction.

Knockout dodged, and like much of the ancient city, the old apartment building the shells poured into was fortunately undergoing restoration. When they arrived in the morning, the local construction crew would find considerably more work awaiting them than they had left behind the previous evening.

"You jabber as fast as you juke, but that's all you two are," Knockout taunted them. "Nothing but talk!"

In response, Swindle accelerated and fired. Sections of pavement erupted skyward where his explosives hit home, but Knockout was already on the move down an abandoned alley barely wide enough to allow a human to pass.

"Where did the interfering machine go?" Cannon smoking, Deadend slowed as he and his partner searched the area. In the darkness their probing beams scanned crumbling stone and new brick. An urgent call clamored for their attention, but they were too preoccupied to acknowledge it. High overhead, a circling Starscream fumed impotently as his side-tracked underlings focused on the diversion.

"The task at hand!" The leader of the Decepticons transmitted furiously. "Attend to the task at hand!"

"Terminate this one first," the slightly larger street racer growled. "No midget Autobot mocks Swindle and keeps its Spark!"

As the cycle continued to circle the area, it, too, received a fretful call. "Knockout, this is Optimus! What are you doing?"

"Sticking some spokes in the Decepticons' plan," the Autobot replied. "And having a little fun at the same time."

"This is not a game." Optimus's tone was somber. "You are outnumbered and outgunned. If they catch you in a crossfire—"

"They're not going to catch me, period!" With that, Knockout's engine raced and he accelerated once more. "I won't let you down, Optimus. Not any of you."

In the big diesel's cab, Epps smiled and nodded to himself. "I always *did* have a thing for motorcycles."

The tactical concern that Optimus had voiced had also occurred to the maneuvering Decepticons.

"I will take this road to the left. You continue forward," Deadend muttered. "According to the roadway plans for this city, there is an ancient wall ahead. We will trap this insolent Autobot between us. At that point, even if he chooses to change his shape it will be too late. Ready your weapons."

As the smaller street racer peeled off, Swindle unlimbered artillery from both fenders and sped up. Yowling street cats and the occasional stray dog scrambled to get out of the way as the two determined Decepticons accelerated down different roadways.

Sooner than expected, the back end of a motorcycle suddenly appeared in Deadend's sights. Without hesitating or worrying about the surrounding structures or their sleeping occupants, the Decepticon opened fire. A part of him was aware that Starscream was yelling at him from somewhere up in the clouds, but Deadend kept to his course. One shell after another just missed his target, but the bursts were getting closer as he refined his targeting. One exploded just behind and to the right of the Autobot's rear wheel, sending Knockout into a wild skid from which no human rider could have recovered. The next shot, the increasingly animated Decepticon was certain, would cut the fleeing Autobot in half.

Trailing smoke, Knockout screeched around a corner. That last burst had to have wounded him, Deadend was sure, because though still moving fast his quarry was beginning to lose speed. One more corner and . . .

A Decepticon's eyes could not widen, even when in its natural shape, but the street racer's tracking high beams suddenly flashed red. In closing on Knockout, the eager Deadend had momentarily forgotten to maintain full awareness of his own companion's wildly shifting position.

A moment was enough.

As Knockout slid sideways beneath a parked delivery truck, the two Decepticons slammed into each other head-on. At the excessive speed at which they were traveling, far more than fenders were bent. Circuits were shorted and internal components shaken as unyielding metal met unyielding metal.

Quickly righting himself, Knockout cautiously eased out from the human vehicle beneath which he had taken momentary refuge. Neither Decepticon was moving very much. They would recover, of course. But being of equal strength, they had visited upon each other equal impact. Sure enough, as he looked on, crumpled metal began to unfold and renew shape. Bangs and creaks filled the small street. Those few humans in the immediate vicinity who had been awakened by the crash decided that in the absence of screams from any injured drivers the accident was now a matter for the police. Untroubled, they returned to their beds.

"Disrespecting . . . Autobot . . ." Methodically regenerating, a shaken Deadend stammered as he fought to regain his shape. "You . . . will . . . die slowly for . . . what you have . . . done."

"I don't think so," countered Knockout as a towering shape appeared behind him. At the same time, Swindle managed to restore a missile launcher. Rising slowly, he took aim at the front of the motorcycle.

Appearing behind Knockout, the just-arrived and fully transformed Ratchet fired once and blew off the Decepticon's reviving gun arm.

High overhead Starscream followed the fight as best he could. "Deadend, Swindle—get out of there! You forget yourselves! Move—*now*!"

The two Decepticons hesitated. Though both had been damaged by the collision, they were still fully capable of fighting. But Starscream's fury, if not his direct order, persuaded them to comply. As Ratchet tried to follow, the pair ducked down a side street that was barely wide enough for them to negotiate. Frustrated, the bigger Autobot could only retract his weapons as he and Knockout watched their quarry escape.

Bursting with hatred and frustration, the Decepticon leader's cry flared on all Cybertronian communications frequencies.

"Optimus Prime! You and your inferiors have put down your last Decepticon! I defy you, once and for all eternity, to make an end to this conflict. I challenge you to single combat between us, the winner to assume dominance over this planet and its swarming organic hordes!"

Slowing slightly on the still-almost-empty Via Fiori Imperiali, Optimus directed his response skyward. "I accept your challenge, Starscream, though we Autobots seek no dominance or control over any other sentient beings. Name the time and place."

"Here and now!" the thwarted leader of the Decepticons screamed. "Just ahead of you there is a large and primitive human structure in which, according to my records, human warriors once engaged in personal combat. It will prove a suitable venue for your termination! I await you there. You and you alone— lest you are too cowardly to meet me without the backing of your fellow Autobot renegades!"

A thunderous howl could be heard as the descending Starscream approached the Colosseum from the opposite side. Within the diesel's cab, Lennox found himself conflicted at the thought of the looming clash.

"I don't like it, Optimus. Starscream must know you can beat him."

"In a calm and reasoning moment he knows that," the Autobot leader replied via the truck's radio. "But at present he is neither calm nor reasoning. Yet again his intentions have been frustrated, and again by the smallest member of our company. At such times even the most calculating Decepticon may give in to uncontrolled rage. This is an opportunity to end the war once and for all. And as Starscream himself points out, the venue could not be more appropriate."

"Uh, you *can* beat him, can't you?" asked Epps guardedly.

"If I did not believe so then I would not take the risk. There is too much at stake."

Lennox shook his head doubtfully. "He's planning something. This is Starscream we're talking about. He may be daring, but he's not stupid."

Optimus's confidence filled the truck cab. "Ironhide, Ratchet, and Knockout are all present. They can position themselves outside the ancient structure Starscream has chosen for combat and be ready to counter any kind of surprise attack. And," he added, and both men were sure they could detect a touch of quiet satisfaction in Optimus's voice, "while I said that I would confront Starscream unsupported by any of my fellow Autobots, nothing was said with regard to humans."

"That's right." A smile crossed the captain's face.

"You, Sergeant Epps, Kaminari, and our rifle-carrying friend Petr can place yourselves to best advantage within this structure. Should another Decepticon or more choose to meddle in the forthcoming fight you will be in excellent position to intervene."

Epps was hesitant. "Our sabot rounds have an effect, but a couple of shells won't stop a Decepticon."

"You do not need to stop one if it intercedes: only to occupy its attention. Should that occur, then at that point Starscream will have abrogated the terms of our contest and my companions will be freed to engage. I would not want to be an intruding Decepticon should it find itself suddenly confronted by Ironhide, Ratchet, and Knockout all at once."

Lennox nodded slowly. "This will be the end of it, then—as long as you can beat Starscream."

"Have a little confidence, Captain." Appropriately reassuring martial music began to pour from the cab's speakers.

In the dark of predawn the outline of the ancient Colosseum loomed stark and uninviting, its pale limestone walls visible even in the absence of moonlight. Informed by local authorities who were in regular contact with Lennox and Epps that a secretive military exercise was about to take place in their immediate vicinity and ordered to seek shelter, the monument's bemused but responsive nighttime security personnel rushed to vacate the area. None of them could envision the kind of gladiatorial contest that was about to take place on ground where thousands of years earlier desperate individuals clad in considerably less armor had fought and died.

Starscream arrived first, converting spectacularly from F-22 to full-fledged Decepticon as wings became legs. He landed with both feet among the ruins of the ancient floor. Rolling in through a far portal that had been enlarged many years earlier to allow repair and restoration equipment to enter the center of the sta-

dium, Optimus shifted into his towering, gleaming
self. Outside, a quartet of seemingly mismatched vehicles spread out to keep watch. Within the stone
walls the four humans grouped themselves together
high up in the age-worn grandstands, taking cold
seats on the two-thousand-year-old equivalent of the
midfield stripe. As Lennox and Epps checked their
equipment and each loaded his launcher with a hot
round, Kaminari and Petr found themselves utterly
absorbed in the looming face-off below.

"They should use swords and shields," she murmured as she looked on in fascination.

"They might yet." For once, Petr Andronov did not
allow himself to be distracted by nearby arachnids, or
the weather, or a tiny flowering weed that was growing out of a crack in the ancient stone. "We are privi-
leged, I think, to be witness to a battle the likes of
which has never before been seen on our world. Or
even imagined."

The Colosseum's storied, much-bloodied original
floor of sand-covered wood had long since decayed
away, leaving the hypogeum, or underground, open
to the night sky. The exposed ranks of parallel, crumbling stone walls and arches would make footing difficult for the combatants. The complex network of
subterranean pathways, cage areas for wild animals,
and staging platforms meant that instead of clashing
on a level surface, the two armored fighters would
have to negotiate, bash their way through, or leap
over intervening barriers. Starscream was already
maneuvering for position. As if reading Kaminari's
thoughts, one arm had transformed into an enormous, glistening, studded metal club.

"It is to be hand weapons then?" Optimus spoke calmly as the two combatants circled each other, both looking for an opening. His right arm contorted. When it had re-formed, he was wielding the same immense battle sword with which he had terminated Bonecrusher. "For once you make a fitting decision, Starscream."

Starscream dropped slightly into a fighting crouch. "Yes. Just like old times on Cybertron. With one exception: now *I* am leader of the Decepticons."

Optimus stared stolidly across at his enemy. "I fear your leadership will be short-lived. Even if I do not defeat you here today, there are already those within your own faction who plot against you, and to raise their old master."

Starscream hesitated for a moment imperceptible to human thought. He remembered all too well his recent betrayal on Cybertron by the traitor Dreadwing. But surely those Decepticons who'd come to Earth had done so out of allegiance to him, Starscream? No matter. If there were more traitors among them, he would deal with them as he had Dreadwing. With extreme prejudice.

"Nice try, Prime. But you can't deceive a Decepticon."

Whereupon several simple mechanical latches gave way simultaneously and Optimus Prime plunged out of sight.

He had not detected the hinges because their workings utilized nothing of an electrical nature. No switches, no cables, nothing to which his electronically synced senses were attuned. Similarly, he had not thought to deep-scan the ground beneath his feet because it was already riddled with innumerable tunnels and corridors and storage areas from hundreds of years of ancient digging and excavation.

In contrast, the void into which he plummeted was of recent origin. Though it was not particularly deep, he did not have the opportunity to prepare for the shock of hitting bottom. Instead the bottom was boosted sharply to make contact with him. So were the sides of the cavity. Unlike the recently reconditioned surface over which the taunting Starscream had deftly maneuvered him and through which he had subsequently fallen, the material that now surrounded him was metal and not stone. Massive, unyielding, well-forged metal.

Taking the shape of a gigantic industrial vise, it enveloped him from beneath and on all four sides. Driven by huge pistons powered by unseen generators, it locked him in place and immobilized him far more securely than had the simple nets the now disbanded Sector Seven forces had once used to capture Bumblebee.

Joints straining, Optimus struggled to free himself from the trap. At any moment he expected a triumphant Starscream to drop down beside him and shove a cannon into his face. But strangely, the leader of the Decepticons was nowhere to be seen in the circle of starlit night that loomed overhead.

Quite unexpectedly, the unassuming figure of a single human appeared, emerging from a small side tunnel. He was stylishly dressed in the manner of his kind. A small cylinder of paper-wrapped weed protruded from his lips. It was on fire, but this did not seem to trouble the human. Casually, as if this were something he saw every day, the man contemplated the towering Autobot securely restrained before him.

"So you're Optimus Prime." The human's voice was soft yet somehow thick with menace. "I would have thought you would have been bigger."

The leader of the Autobots glared down at the human. "You are responsible for this? You have allied yourself with Starscream and the Decepticons against your own kind? What sort of human are you?"

"The self-interested sort. My name is Bruno Carerra. I build things." Removing the smoking cylinder from his mouth, he used it to gesture at the massive five-sided vise that pinned Optimus like a mouse in a trap. "My people built this." Turning, he indicated the access tunnel from which he had emerged. "Back in that direction is where we're building part of a new subway line. The city authorities won't allow it to run any closer to the Colosseum because they're afraid the vibrations from the trains might damage the foundations here and at the Forum. But the main tunnel is close enough to permit access via a clandestine subsidiary passageway to this part of the Colosseum's original sub-basement. We had to work very quickly, of course, but we had help. It's amazing how much dirt and rock a Decepticon can move when it is properly motivated." He took another puff on the smoking cylinder protruding from his mouth.

"It seems that the prospect of your ultimate demise constitutes more than sufficient motivation."

Throughout the entirety of the human's speech Optimus's servos continued to strain at the imprisoning vise. Already he could feel one corner of the mechanical snare beginning to weaken at its bottom hinge. They would not succeed in trapping him here. From above he could hear the distant sounds of heavy fighting. That was where Starscream had gone, he realized. To attack the other Autobots. He strained anew and another hinge started to give. In a few moments he would be free to aid his companions. Then they would finish Starscream and once and for all finally free this world from the threat posed by the Decepticons.

As for the individual quietly taunting him, Optimus would leave his fate to be decided by his fellow humans. He did not think it would be pretty.

The man turned to go. "I'll leave you now, Optimus Prime. I will soon have a great deal to do. There will be much to administer, many orders to give." He smiled at the thought. "Commands, really. Oh, and one more thing. There's someone else here who wants to talk to you. As it promises to be a noisy conversation, I'll leave the two of you to your privacy." With that he turned and disappeared back into the tunnel.

Once more alone in the trap, Optimus pushed and shoved against the metal slabs that continued to restrain him. He heard as well as felt the hinge on one corner of the enormous vise give way with an unmistakable metallic *snap*.

Hold on, Ironhide, and the rest of you. I will be at your side in a moment.

If Starscream believed that any kind of human construction could restrain him for very long, Optimus thought determinedly, then the Decepticon had miscalculated for the very last time.

As he resumed his struggle a high, vertical metal

panel that he had assumed had been put in place to hold back loose rock and earth revealed itself to be another doorway. One that was far larger than the portal through which the scornful human had departed. Optimus halted his struggling. A shape was becoming visible behind the opening door. It was massive, metallic, and intimidating. A pair of burning red eyes met Optimus's own. The voice that issued from the gleaming mouth was deep and foreboding.

"Greetings, Optimus. Greetings for the last time."

It was Barricade.

🛡 17 🛡

Even more clearly than the crash that had sounded from the interior of the Colosseum, the three Autobots standing watch outside had heard the troubled transmission from their leader. But before they could go to his aid, they had barely changed shape when they found themselves set upon by the leader of the Decepticons. With Starscream throwing himself at them in a fury the three Autobots had enough to do to keep from being overwhelmed. Had Ironhide not been present the battle would have ended quickly and badly for Ratchet and Knockout, staunch though they were.

Firing at the far more powerful Starscream with little effect, a worried Ratchet wondered at the Autobot leader's continued absence from the fight. Occasional fragments of transmission drifted through, but they were incomplete, as if Optimus's broadcasts were being blocked, intercepted, scrambled, or a combination of all three by some heavy metal or electronic barrier.

Something slammed hard into Ratchet's left side as the furious Starscream pressed his attack. For the time being the smaller Autobot was too busy to concern himself with Optimus's current condition. Besides, with Starscream fully occupied with the three of them, the leader of the Autobots was doubtless all right and would be arriving to join the battle as soon as he cleared away whatever minor impediment was delaying him.

"You are a devoted follower of Megatron." As he continued to exert every one of his servos to escape the imprisoning vise, Optimus worked to engage Barricade's full attention. "What are you doing groveling at the orders of a deceiver like Starscream?"

"Megatron is dead," the huge Decepticon rumbled. "I am a soldier. In his absence I follow the orders of Lord Starscream."

"How do you know Megatron is dead?"

"There are many images available of the final conflict in which his Spark was extinguished, and of his burial in this world's deepest ocean. Starscream is master of all Decepticons now. His orders are to kill you." A few errant sparks flew from the Decepticon warrior's activated armaments. "It is an order I did not need to be given."

He moved nearer, unafraid to match Optimus's stare photon for photon. "As I have often said, it is a large galaxy. Yet it is amazing how often the lives of two such as ourselves can cross." A heavily armed arm started to rise. "Your life ends here, Optimus Prime . . . ouch!"

Ouch? Optimus's perceptors scanned the blackness of the pit into which he had fallen. What he saw made him redouble his efforts yet again.

An angry Barricade whirled, searching the darkness. "Something *stung* me."

The voice that replied was small, but its volume was magnified by the enclosing walls. "That's what we insects do."

"What is thi—ow!" Letting out another yell Barricade reached up, started to slap himself on his right shoulder, just to remember that the weapons systems on that arm were activated, partially deactivated them in time to avoid blowing off his own arm, and struck himself forcefully.

But Kaminari Ishihara had already darted behind his head. As she did so, Petr Andronov took aim from the ground and fired at the back of the Decepticon's neck with his rifle. A burst of electricity shot through the startled metal giant, jolting his internal stabilizers and causing him to stagger briefly.

He staggered more when Lennox yelled "Fire!" and both he and Epps let loose with their launchers. Directed toward the same spot on the Decepticon's right leg, the two sabot rounds struck Barricade just a little too high above the critical joint to bring him down. But they did cause him to grab at his knee. Hopping violently on one foot, he shook off the human who had been clinging to the back of his neck. Tumbling toward the ground like a gymnast dismounting from the uneven parallel bars, Kaminari landed lithely on her feet and raced to rejoin her companions. The ropes they had appropriated from one of the Colosseum's renovation storage areas and had used to descend silently into the pit behind Barricade hung limp against the wall nearby.

Leave it to Kaminari, Lennox thought as he worked frantically to reload his launcher, to land on *top* of the seething Decepticon's shoulders while the rest of them had descended silently to the floor.

Regaining his footing, the enraged Barricade immediately located the fleeing human. "More of you meddling creatures! You swarm like bugs!" Raising an enormous foot, he started to bring it down as Kaminari and the others fled for the safety of the access tunnel.

The foot never reached the ground.

Making a supreme effort as he exerted himself to the utmost, Optimus Prime burst outward from the shattered vise and slammed into his old enemy. Locked together, Autobot and Decepticon crashed into the wall of the cavity, sending rock and crossbracing beams crashing to the floor.

Lennox grabbed Epps's shoulder. "Let's get out of here! Move, move!" With dislodged rock and earth crashing down around them as the two metal giants slammed back and forth against the enclosing walls, the soldiers joined the scientists in racing for the access tunnel.

The clash of the metal titans echoed behind them as they sprinted down the smooth floor of the covert passageway. Motion sensors mounted on the walls activated embedded battery-powered lights to illuminate their way: an addition on the part of the traitor Bruno Carerra's engineers that now benefited his enemies. At the end of the tunnel they encountered a heavy door that was locked from the outside.

"Everybody step back." A grim-faced Epps raised his launcher. "I just happen to have the key with me."

The single sabot round blew out the lock as well as a chunk of the door itself. Shoving aside the smoking remnants, they found themselves standing in a reinforced subway tunnel that was still plainly under construction. It was far too early for the morning work shift to have begun to arrive.

"Which way?" Kaminari was looking up and down the unfinished tunnel.

Petr was already gesturing. "Nearest station in service is this way. There will be access there to surface."

As they ran, Lennox caught up to the heavier Russian. "Let me guess. When we got here you memorized the public transport map for the entire city of Rome."

"No." Puffing as he ran, Andronov struggled to keep up with the others. "I memorize public transport maps and systems for hundred largest metropolitan areas when I first asked to join NEST. Thought it might come in handy one day." He nodded in the direction they were running. "Was not difficult. Moscow's metro is much bigger than this."

"So is New York's," Lennox countered, and the two spent the rest of the time it took them to reach the nearest functioning station arguing the merits of their countries' respective subway systems.

Crowded together in the lightless pit that Starscream had planned to be Optimus's tomb, the metal leviathans were unable to deploy swords and clubs, far less explosive weapons. The fight devolved into a contest of physical strength and determination that saw first one combatant slam his opponent into a wall only for him to be wrenched around and smashed in turn into the enclosing rock and metal.

"It's over, Optimus." One powerful arm jammed hard against the Autobot's throat, Barricade pressed

the attack, leaning all his weight against his opponent. But unlike a human, no life-giving air passed
through the Autobot's neck. For all the damage he
was causing, Barricade might as well have been press-
ing his arm against his foe's foot.

Reaching up and under with both hands, Optimus
lifted his massive assailant and threw him against the
far wall of the pit. "Indeed it is, Barricade. You are a
good soldier, but you've chosen the wrong side in this
war."

"More words," Barricade spat. Straightening, he
gestured for his enemy to come toward him. "Too
many words."

"I agree." Poising for another leap, Optimus prepared to engage his opponent afresh.

Instead, this time he jumped straight upward.

Barricade was an instant late in following. Halfway
through his leap he encountered a blizzard of cut
stone as Optimus proceeded to shove one ancient
chunk of rock after another into the pit. As soon as he
had shoveled enough on top of his fuming adversary,
the leader of the Autobots proceeded to activate one
of his more advanced weapons to melt the upper
layer of rock to as great a depth as possible. His aim
was not to imprison Barricade permanently—no simple entombment in molten stone would achieve
that—but to delay him.

The instant Optimus showed himself outside the
Colosseum, Starscream knew this was a battle he
could not win. He could inflict damage, yes, and
wreak collateral destruction. But he could not win.
Nor could he imagine what might have happened to
Barricade. Had Optimus actually managed to kill the

old warrior? One thing the leader of the Decepticons knew for certain: it would be unwise to wait until the truth made itself known.

"Deadend and Swindle: wherever you are, retreat!" he broadcast as widely as he could. "To the agreed-upon location!" Having issued the necessary order, he dodged another volley from the damnably persistent Ironhide, leaped upward, shape-shifted, and in his Raptor guise shot away to the south.

A frustrated Ironhide cast a volley of suitable Cybertronian curses after the fleeing Decepticon. Much relieved to see him alive and well, he then confronted Optimus.

"We can still pursue Deadend and Swindle."

"No." The leader of the Autobots was firm. "Spread out as they are, taking them out might well cause significant damage to the city. We have managed to avoid any human deaths. I would prefer to keep it that way. There will be another opportunity, later. And—Barricade is here."

Ratchet was visibly unsettled by this news. "Here—where?"

"At present he is safely immobilized. We will deal with him in a moment." Optimus paused as if listening. "I have just received a communication indicating that our four fellow human fighters are safe. Sam Witwicky may not be among them, but this is the second time I owe my life to humans."

As soon as the human soldiers and scientists had rejoined them, the Autobot leader explained what had happened in the interval since they had fled from Barricade and into the subway tunnel.

"Next time," he remarked gravely, "we must try to

see that such an encounter takes place in a location that will not endanger a large human population."

Petr looked doubtful. "Will be difficult. Starscream knows that your concern for our kind offers him protection. I think when he attacks again, it may be in a similarly crowded environment."

"Then we'll just have to find a way to kill him more quietly." Ratchet spoke while attending to Ironhide's slight wounds.

"Quiet killing is outside my area of expertise," the big Autobot grumbled.

As they returned to work that morning the machinists and drillers and excavators working to extend Rome's C line were surprised to encounter a previously unknown side tunnel that had seemingly materialized overnight. Running south from beneath the Colosseum, it intersected the existing line before disappearing at right angles to the proposed track. Following it, a pair of baffled engineers discovered that it curved sharply upward before finally breaking the surface in the center of a park.

Of whatever might have dug such an extensive tunnel in such a short time there was no sign, and the pit from which it originated was likewise empty.

Bruno Carerra sat in his luxurious villa north of Castrovillari and reflected on the week's events. Things had not gone according to plan, but he was accustomed to setbacks. They were part of life; it was only a matter of how one faced them, how one overcame them. Optimus Prime lived, Starscream had fled, and Bruno sat in his villa. There would be additional opportunities to set in motion his plans for personal power.

The roar of a jet startled him from his musings. Walking outside, he met Starscream standing on his expansive lawn. Pity about the crushed fountain, it would have to be replaced. He walked to Starscream, his arms wide, his expressions effusive. "Well, my formidable friend, the game has gone against us this time," ventured Bruno.

"Vile insect, you have failed me utterly. Prime lives. Your plan was worthless!"

"My part of the plan worked. It is not my fault you could not execute your end of the bargain. Come, let us forgive and forget. We have much to plan together."

Starscream chuckled a mirthless laugh. "Together? Oh insect, I will indeed forget, but I never forgive."

When the *carabinieri* finally traced some of the events at the Colosseum to Bruno's villa, they found only smoking ruins. It was as if the man had never even existed: wiped clean from the face of the Earth. Starscream had attended to every detail.

Some time later, back on Diego Garcia, Lennox and Epps were winding up a rare relaxing afternoon when they emerged from the water to find a revived, gleaming, and freshly customized motorcycle waiting for them just above the waterline. No rider was in evidence.

Flopping down on the hot sand and removing his sunglasses from their holder, Lennox extracted a cold brew from the nearby cooler, popped the top, took a long swallow, and addressed the bike like an old friend.

"Don't tell me, Knockout. You want to offer me a ride. Or else you're missing Kami and Petr." Following the encounter at Rome, both scientists had been called back home to render official reports on their recent encounters: Andronov to Uralmash's research facilities at Yekaterinburg and Ishihara to the university at Tsukuba.

"It isn't that," Knockout told the two men. "I think something significant may be about to happen."

Sitting on his towel, Epps let out a groan. "Oh man—didn't we just get finished with something 'happening'?"

Lennox sighed. "Just be glad we didn't end up in Antarctica. What is it, Knockout?"

The Autobot sounded uncertain. "There is some confusion as to specifics. I have researched the syntax, but I'm still confused.

"What does it mean to be 'shanghaied'?"

Lennox regarded the waiting Autobot. "It could mean one of two things, Knockout. Either someone's about to be taken somewhere or . . ." He looked over at the silent Epps. "First Rome, now . . . ?"

The technical sergeant looked grim. "Looks like it's time to practice my Mandarin . . ."